NOVELS BY THOMAS SAVAGE

The Pass
Lona Hanson
A Bargain with God
Trust in Chariots
The Power of the Dog
The Liar
Daddy's Girl
A Strange God
Midnight Line
I Heard My Sister Speak My Name

I Heard
My Sister Speak
My Name

I Heard My Sister Speak My Name

by Thomas Savage

Little, Brown and Company

BOSTON   TORONTO

COPYRIGHT © 1977 by Thomas Savage

ALL RIGHTS RESERVED. NO PART OF THIS BOOK MAY BE REPRODUCED IN ANY FORM OR BY ANY ELECTRONIC OR MECHANICAL MEANS IN-CLUDING INFORMATION STORAGE AND RETRIEVAL SYSTEMS WITHOUT PERMISSION IN WRITING FROM THE PUBLISHER, EXCEPT BY A REVIEWER WHO MAY QUOTE BRIEF PASSAGES IN A REVIEW.

Second Printing

Library of Congress Cataloging in Publication Data

Savage, Thomas.
   I heard my sister speak my name.

   I. Title.
PZ3.S2652Iah   [PS3569.A83]   813'.5'4   77-8473
ISBN 0-316-77139-2

Designed by Christine Benders

*Published simultaneously in Canada
by Little, Brown & Company (Canada) Limited*

PRINTED IN THE UNITED STATES OF AMERICA

For Hellie and Bill

One

1

SO I WILL call myself Tom Burton, or Thomas Burton, as the name would appear on the novels I write. I am too difficult for some readers and my sentences are sometimes more than statements. Many readers are comfortable only with the simple sentences, and prefer books that reward a belief in the happy ending and the pot at the end of the rainbow, even as the rainbow retreats and those who follow are footsore. There is no ending, happy or otherwise, only a pause.

I live with my wife, herself a novelist; together we make a decent living. Except for the children, we would make a better living. But we eat, pay the bills and see our way clear to having the leaks in the roof fixed — or at least located. We consider ourselves lucky to do what we want in the place where we want to do it. We have not seriously considered divorce, but sometimes after a few martinis we shout and pick at old scabs. My wife once hurled at me a plate of salt mackerel and boiled potatoes, a favorite meal until then. Months later we still discovered elusive bits of fish set in potato on the iron railing leading down into the dining room, on the rungs of chairs, and clinging to the spines of certain books, Peterson's *Field Guide to the Birds* and Pipes's *Russia Under the Old Regime*, each discovery a reminder of the fruitlessness of passion. Ordinarily we laugh and talk and worry about the children, like anybody else. In the past, our sons have troubled us. They didn't seem to fit into the world as it was, and we blamed ourselves for setting a poor example and not taking the business world seriously. There are so many people out there in that world it is better to know how to get along with them, to learn their ways and how to trick them as they know how to trick each other.

Our daughter gives surprisingly little trouble; she and her husband have so far kept their trouble to themselves. That may change tomorrow. Things have a way of changing, I find. That fact keeps us on our toes.

The children are all gone now, which means they all live somewhere else, but they come back with their children, eight of them and all beautiful — to me, anyway. The grandchildren rather like to sleep on the floor; they pretend this is an Indian camp. Everybody is here for the holidays because I was brought up to believe everybody should be with everybody else on holidays. They like Thanksgiving, Christmas and New Year's, which come so close together you can scarcely get your head up. My wife and I thought it might be easier this year, because of the small house and the new grandchildren, to have dinner out at Thanksgiving. The two youngest ones could sleep in those little trays you see now. We could get a big table in a good restaurant not far away that is built out over the ocean, as if we did not have the entire ocean right in front of our house, and we could sit there and watch gulls other than our own and have drinks and talk and order and everything would be brought and eaten and the remainders taken away, some in dog-

4

gie bags, and we would all go back to a clean house. However, there was such an outcry among the children that eating out was found to be an impossibility.

"Daddy, we've *never* done anything like that," my daughter said. "I'm surprised you'd even suggest such a thing."

"Well you see, it was only a suggestion," I said.

They said, the children said, that if now at our age we found it impossible to get together a simple Thanksgiving dinner of the things we'd been cooking all their lives and to clean up after it, well, they would be glad to get the dinner and clean up; one would bring the turkey, another the vegetables, another the pies. But a turkey is better cooked in the house where it is to be consumed; vegetables can't well be cooked ahead; they lose color and vitamins, the cream sauce for the creamed onions curdles, and neither my daughter nor the wives of my sons are much for pie crust, so that was that. The new Maytag dishwasher helped a good deal. My wife said she didn't know what we did without it, but I know what we did.

So we lived peacefully beside the sea on the coast of Maine on the rocks, and never a sun came up that we didn't thank God we lived where we lived. Each winter the storms shifted the rocks and each spring we found new ways down to the beach. A beach is a good place for grandchildren. (They never forget it.) Everybody likes picnics and when it got cold we built fires of driftwood and roasted frankfurters and our own childhood was close. We had enough frontage on the ocean so that later on my younger son could live in the house, my daughter and her husband could build on the next two lots and my older son on the next two lots and they could all see each other every day. My wife and I intended to be cremated, which is neater, and to have our ashes thrown off the rocks into the sea, although I understand that is now illegal, too many people doing it, people getting upset about it, afraid of having ashes cling to them. But it could be done where we lived because the place was isolated except in the summertime. In the summertime it could be done very quickly in the dark. I have read somewhere of a man who had his ashes put in under the bricks of the hearth and that seemed reasonable, but is it reasonable to wish to remind your son of you whenever he pokes up the fire? No. He will have his own problems. So my wife and I have decided to be pollutants.

Sometimes I felt I should be shipped out West where I came from, and have my ashes scattered over the sagebrush.

My aunts could not understand why I would want to leave the Rocky Mountains, which they called their mountains, and go and live on the coast of Maine. They said it was a lot nicer living where everybody knows who you are.

"Maine's sort of a crazy place to live," my Aunt Maude said. "Like living in Arkansas or Delaware. None of us ever came from there. I don't think Mama would have liked it."

Well, maybe Crow Point was a crazy place. In June the summer people came with their boats and their bathing caps and their ice buckets. The stomach muscles of the men were slack from abundant sitting, their skin pale from overexposure to fluorescent lights, and at sundown the wives pulled cashmere sweaters close and suggested a little fire. Some men had money, some advanced degrees; few had both. One pulled teeth. Another professed English.

Social status was based on how long one had been coming there summers. The first comers remarked that it was a shame the latecomers hadn't known the Point as it was, but latecomers, having established themselves with a sign bearing their names tacked to the birch tree at the fork in the road, were as suspicious of change and of strangers as the first comers. All sometimes trained their binoculars on those who clambered over the rocks with so little style, wearing shoes instead of sneakers. All stood against paving the road and the introduction of the telephone, but not against the power lines; after all, there are limits: people do need ice.

All objected to the removal of trees, even dead ones, except for those that cast confusing shadows over the tennis court and interfered with the view of the ocean.

Up the road, a couple conversed with spirits and had selected mediums down for the weekend. Down the road, an attorney had established contact with the mechanical world through the purchase of power tools, cranky in his hands. With them he cut off little pieces of himself, never enough to seriously cripple him or to threaten his happiness. He sometimes arrived, bleeding, to show me.

A congressman invited laughing friends down from Washington to drink and to eat native corn and lobsters. When he drank alone, he stripped down to his shorts and called to me from a rocky ledge.

"Tom!"

I sat in the early hours with a drink in my hand before his fireplace and watched him burn up old wills he had drawn up in favor of people he no longer favored.

There were parties. It was not uncommon to see an angry woman in fairly formal dress limping down the road with but a single shoe. Friendships blew up even before the tapers were set aflame. What had been said was unforgivable. Vows were taken never again to darken a certain door. Tow trucks came with flashing lights.

The day after Labor Day they all went away. The woods and the sea belonged to us and the birds and animals.

I believe I lived in Maine because Maine is about as far as I could get from the ranch in Montana where I grew up, and where my mother was unhappy, my beautiful, angel mother.

7

The morning in question — and it certainly was in question — was only a few years ago and began — for me — as I stood on the porch, which is so close to the sea you might call it a deck. The sea, that morning, was unusually calm; little ripples fled across the surface and caught the sun. Such a sun on similar waters had moved Aeschylus to write, "The many-twinkling smile of Ocean." He knew what he was talking about. It might have been a joyous day.

Then suddenly a seagull swept past — and so close I felt the draft and the glance of its beady eye.

Two kinds of gulls command our beach and the sky above. Herring gulls are common, protected by law because they are scavengers, and loved because they are graceful in flight and suggest freedom. Their likeness is painted on driftwood and carved in pine and sold along Route One as souvenirs of another Maine summer, the rocks and the eternal tides.

The black-backed gulls are not so common. They are bigger and stand apart from the herring gulls. They like the isolation of ledge or island; they steer clear of human beings. And well they might, for they are detested. They search out and eat the eggs and chicks and ducklings of other birds.

The gull whose draft I felt and whose glance I knew was a black-backed gull.

2

ACCORDING TO RECORDS kept locked up in Saint Luke's Hospital in Seattle, Washington, a female child was born to a young woman twenty-two years old named Elizabeth Owen. The nurse, whose name was Mrs. Alma Porter, wore her Waltham watch on a chain around her neck and she had looked at it. The time was exactly 2 A.M. The baby had no blemishes of any kind and had cried lustily after birth and then went right to sleep.

The year was 1912.

Mrs. Porter liked being a nurse. She felt that nursing was rewarding and she liked Dr. Gray because she did. He said she was a credit to the profession and had many times given her a lift in his Pierce-Arrow machine. She was a little too heavy and her feet were small. She liked the third shift. She liked being there when the little children were born into this strange, strange world. She herself had three grandchildren. Although her elder daughter had never before known a Norwegian, she had married one. They are clean and you can count on them. Her younger daughter married a policeman.

She was sorry to say that many young nurses were not so serious as they had been when she herself was young; they thought only of running around and so forth, so they didn't like the third shift. They wanted to be on hand to walk out with young men and so forth. The way everybody was acting now.

The young nurses were romantic and jumped to many conclusions. They thought if a girl had a ring on her finger she was married, but it is easy as pie for a girl to borrow a ring from a friend or even from her mother, painful as that would be for the mother, or a gold-plated ring from the five-and-dime, and sterling silver rings look like platinum or white gold but a sharp eye can tell silver rings from platinum rings because cheap silver leaves a smudge on the finger and you can tell when you are washing a patient. These rings you can buy at places are also worn by girls who check into hotels with men or as a protection from mashers who happen to be sitting and watching at nearby tables. And they are worn by plain girls who want people to think they are married. There is a good deal of deceit in this old world, some of it innocent enough. A lot of water runs under the bridge, a lot of it dirty.

You can't always tell what a person is or has got herself into by the suitcase she carries into the hospital because all those things can be borrowed, including the traveling clock that makes a good impression, and brushes and combs with silver handles. You can often tell by a toothbrush — that is, you'd be surprised how many people in the city of Seattle don't bring toothbrushes.

The thing to watch for is the underwear.

The small suitcase Elizabeth Owen carried into the hospital might have been borrowed, since it was made of genuine leather, and the photograph in the genuine silver frame of the young man could have been her brother, handsome as Francis X. Bushman in the movies that time. The stitches of Elizabeth

Owen's underwear were very, very small, like fairy stitching, and the garment was made of genuine silk, and it was not brand-new, as if she was maybe used to silk.

You do not so much expect people with silk underwear to get into trouble. Because they do not need to.

The baby was such a dear little creature. How could the young woman do it? How could she give the little child away? All her life the little girl would wonder who she was and if she had brothers and sisters, because somebody always tells.

The Reverend Doctor Matthews looked like a mad Lincoln; his eyes saw everything and he spoke with an angel's tongue. He was famous around Seattle for his sermons on hellfire and they were printed in the papers along with his photograph. His was the most important Presbyterian church in the city because most of those who worshipped there were blessed with money and large front yards. Down from his high pulpit he departed in his shiny black Jeffrey coupé, a gift from his flock, for Saint Luke's Hospital where he loped along the corridors and appeared at bedsides to encourage the sick and to quiet the dying. He urged those who yet possessed the strength to come down from their beds and to get on their knees with him. It may be that God looks with greater favor on those who grovel.

As the Reverend was himself unmarried it may be assumed he looked on sexual union as sinful and on children as the result of sin. He did however take a keen interest in the little girl born to Elizabeth Owen, for well-fixed parishioners of his had just a year before lost a little boy of seven. Lost meant that the little boy had been thrown from a presumably gentle horse and had had his neck broken.

"I know who would like to have that child," he told Doctor Gray, and then he and Dr. Gray and the well-fixed parishioners set things in motion. The result was that the baby born to

Elizabeth Owen was left on the doorstep of a Mr. and Mrs. McKinney in Seattle on Saint Patrick's Day, and for that reason Mr. and Mrs. McKinney saw to it that she celebrated Saint Patrick's Day as her birthday with green balloons, shamrocks and coiled serpents of green barley sugar, although the McKinneys had not an ounce of Irish blood between them. She was left on the doorstep as not so likely to cause neighborly comment as if she were publicly arranged for and taken either from the hospital or from an adoption agency. The McKinneys must have had a peculiar idea of what was most likely to cause comment, for in retrieving the infant from the doorstep they could have been hardly more conspicuous had they marched down the aisle of the church wearing lampshades and snowshoes. On the day the McKinneys took Amy — Amy after Mrs. McKinney — in, it happened that a young cousin of theirs who worked as a student nurse at Saint Luke's Hospital came to call.

"I know that baby," the young cousin said. She spoke of Elizabeth Owen as "a lovely young woman" who walked the corridors for exercise and she spoke of the photograph of the handsome young man. If the picture of the handsome young man existed, one wonders what the young man thought — doubtless that he was lucky that Elizabeth Owen was at least willing to abandon the baby, and that she did not hate him as evidenced by the photograph she kept and displayed. And what did Elizabeth Owen think as she walked the corridors? Certainly she considered the little child about to be abandoned in that hospital and tossed out like a weed. The young man might have been pleased at the young woman's sacrifice. Everybody is flattered by sacrifice.

Amy worked out well for the McKinneys. Her birthdays made it a pleasure to buy presents and to give again; Christmas once more had a point; there were cookies in the cookie jar. At five, when at last she was old enough to remember herself, she knew herself to be a quiet, orderly child who picked up and put away her things in their special places; she seldom forgot to wash her hands or to say her prayers in a clear voice. Already she was learning to save money awarded for the performance of little tasks suitable to her small hands; she dropped coppers into the china piggy bank provided, and although a small friend had demonstrated how these could be removed by sliding them out on a table knife, she let them remain in the pig until the pig was full, at which time another pig was provided and then another and another. She did not long for the day when each would be smashed with a hammer, for she knew and accepted the fact that then the money would disappear into a real bank. At five she had grown into the tricycle left behind by the little boy thrown from his horse, a machine that had been painful for the McKinneys to contemplate when they opened the closet door. They had been torn between the memories of it and their sense of thrift.

For a lawyer whose business was almost exclusively urban, Mr. McKinney was extraordinarily appreciative of nature and had years before acquired a nice piece of property on Puget Sound and there built a beach house of logs and a boathouse where he kept his dinghy. On long walks in fairly formal clothes, the McKinneys explained nature as they saw it to Amy, and she learned to be attentive to rocks, to seashells and hidden rookeries. She noted the indecisive flutter of butterflies' wings. A snapshot of the time shows her sitting on a high rock looking over the water; she wears a new pair of high boots of which she was most fond. It was perhaps the loneliness that surrounds this snapshot like a frame that moved the McKinneys to consider trying out a second child who would become a companion to Amy. They tried out first one and then another, both boys, but neither seemed to fit into the picture; possibly the McKinneys had a tendency to compare each child with the one they had lost and found each new one wanting. Neither child was with them for more than a week, so his leaving could not have made much more impression on them than his arriving. But the Mc-Kinneys believed in sticking to a thing—that is how one gets ahead—and they brought yet a third little boy into the big house in Seattle. He did not appear to be so abashed before the high ceilings and broad polished stairway as his predecessors—the McKinneys could not but wonder if his true parents had had some limited acquaintance with lofty ceilings, oak panel-ing and maroon draperies at the tall windows. But persistence like that of the McKinneys is sometimes a mistake.

The little boy of six was given the name Bobby; the name to which he had responded in the orphanage was not one the Mc-Kinneys could get used to, and he seemed more theirs with a name they had chosen. They saw him to be a manly little fel-low, not understanding then that the quality of manliness is not—at least in a child—entirely a blessing. He had been with the McKinneys almost a year when he and Amy and the Mc-Kinneys took the ferry, *The Virginia Five*, to the beach house one fine summer's day. Mr. McKinney was pleased to see how readily the little boy took to the oars of the dinghy. Later on they all gathered butter clams and Mrs. McKinney made a steaming pot of delicious chowder over which Mr. McKinney asked God's blessing. They were in bed in good time and fell asleep to the distant knell of a nun buoy.

Thick fog persisted the entire day following, but the fire in the big wood stove crackled away and while Mrs. McKinney baked her spice cake with Amy's help—"You children can lick the pan," Mrs. McKinney said—Mr. McKinney and Bobby got out the old Parcheesi board. Bobby caught on to the game very quickly and Mr. McKinney could not but be amazed at how gracefully and successfully he threw the dice. He allowed the little boy to beat him the first game; in the middle of the second game he realized he was going to have to look to it or be beaten and thus give the little boy a taste for gaming.

Amy had for so long been accustomed to the water and alerted to the dangers of going near it without a grown-up that the McKinneys saw no danger in her going down to play in the boathouse with Bobby, who caught on to things so quickly. They believed that the earlier human beings learn to be on their own, the better; that children, like anybody else, thrive on responsibility. So Bobby and Amy went hand in hand in the fog to the boathouse and the McKinneys touched each other as people will, who are of one mind. They murmured comfortably.

However, as Mr. McKinney liked to say, Mrs. McKinney was a great one to worry. She worried about matches and poisons, both of which were kept out of reach; she worried about heights and depths and the possibility of being caught in the elevator and therefore she used the stairs in Frederick & Nelson's and refused to get her feet into a streetcar until it had completely halted and the conductor had reached down his hand. It now seemed to her that an hour was a little too long for two children to enjoy a boathouse in which there was no other distraction than a dinghy, that and four cushions stuffed with a material that might keep the human body afloat until help came and a red flag they raised aloft on a pole beside the boathouse when they wished *The Virginia Five* to come take them away.

Mr. McKinney said they were perfectly all right down in the boathouse, not to worry, but Mrs. McKinney said, "Very well," and went on down through the fog anyway, and it was a good thing she did.

It was suspiciously quiet in the boathouse. She had expected to hear childish voices in the intervals between the spaced bawling of the foghorn, but no. She quickened her step, the first small seizures of fear, like fingers, stirring in her breast.

She hurried first to the edge of the water, but saw nothing

there. She turned to the boathouse; the door was closed. It opened in. And her hands flew to her breast. When she could speak, she did, crying, "Stop it! Stop it!"

It!

The little boy, who had dropped his pants, was kneeling beside Amy who lay on the floor; he was examining her private parts and she, alas, his. It was a sight Mrs. McKinney attempted to cast from her forever. When the little boy had sheepishly stepped back into his pants she drove both children before her to the beach house. They went silently.

"I'm not even going to speak about it," she told Mr. McKinney, "because it is unspeakable," but of course he knew what she had found because of the set of her mouth. Many people who have lived a long time together do not need to speak, and especially not of such things.

It was now late in the morning, and *The Virginia Five* for that day had passed the boathouse some hours before. It was therefore the following day when *The Virginia Five* came to take them back to Seattle where the little boy Bobby was given back to the place he had come from. Nothing was said to the people there of the incident in the boathouse, only that something intolerable had happened, so maybe later on he had another chance. He had certainly learned at an early age what havoc sex can wreak.

The Virginia Five keeps popping up.

The McKinneys took their Presbyterianism seriously and insofar as they could took Christ's precepts as their own. They believed Christ would look with favor on Mr. McKinney's teaching Sunday School, a group of fifteen- and sixteen-year-olds called the Youth League, and chiefly female. One cannot help but wonder why so many young men fall away so early from religion and so many young women remain steadfast in

Christ's service. It may be, as is sometimes said, that there is something more loyal in the female nature, that young men are so quick to feel their oats, are forever straying. Mr. McKinney did not feel put upon when once each summer he saw his Sunday School class safely on board *The Virginia Five* for a trip to the beach house and a nice day beside the water and in the woods. Young people from the city, even the city of Seattle, are not enough acquainted with nature. For the small voyage Mrs. McKinney prepared a lunch of fried chicken and potato salad kept cold in thermos jugs lest it become poisonous and kill everybody. There is nothing like the sea air to stir the appetite.

Among those enjoying the outing was a Miss Lovelace.

Amy, almost eight now, could scarcely keep her eyes off Miss Lovelace who appeared to be older than the other girls, some of whom still wore hair ribbons, but Amy sensed that she was not, that she perhaps ran roughshod over her parents, her father especially. Indeed, Miss Lovelace's footwear had special appeal. Already she wore the French heel, modified, it is true, but a heel and most certainly French. She did a thrilling thing with her hair, swept it up as if she were eighteen years old. It was an odd way to wear one's hair for an outing and strange to wear such an unsuitable heel. Amy longed to have Miss Lovelace speak to her and show her the picture she kept in her heart-shaped gold locket which she fingered and fingered after showing it to the other girls who made soft screams when they saw it. Sometimes Miss Lovelace paused in a grown-up way in the middle of a pretty gesture as if she expected the "click!" of a camera. She walked in a special light; the shadows of the pines touched her just so. Her future was assured; she would have many years to regard her profile in a complex of mirrors and whatever she wore would be transformed into a queen's raiment. Amy meant to own a heart-shaped locket should she live to be sixteen, and she would show little girls the picture in it. She would own similar shoes, for little girls are anxious to get into such shoes, at first their mothers', to be shod like an adult without a grown-up's responsibility. It was not because Mrs. McKinney was forty when Amy was adopted that she possessed no shoes to excite a little girl, but that she had always looked on shoes only as a cruel necessity in a society that frowned on the naked foot, and not as a means to increase her height or to tickle her fancy. Amy had once got inside satisfying grown-up shoes in a house down the block where there lived a little girl whose mother was very young. Mrs. McKinney knew her from church. There were all these shoes. The man was a salesman from over around Spokane on the wrong side of the mountains. Selling is a precarious occupation at best and success depends more on your selling yourself than on what you have to offer.

"I'm afraid they don't have very much," Mrs. McKinney told Amy. Amy was beginning to sense that people who don't have very much are likely to want some of what you have. The McKinneys were doubtful of people and had reason to be. Some allowed dogs to eat from their plates; others did not wash their hands before they left the bathroom; others treated the Sabbath as if it were but another day.

Now while the younger girls helped Mrs. McKinney tidy up the beach house and wash the cups in which there had been hot cocoa, and the two gangling boys played catch down near the boathouse, Miss Lovelace sat talking seriously to Mr. McKinney about her future. Amy stood within earshot against the wall, a dish towel in her hands. She was uncomfortable in formal gatherings, never knew whether to stand or sit or if to sit what chair to choose and then what to do with her feet.

Miss Lovelace clasped her pretty white hands together and spoke. "Oh, I just know my future will be bright because I love Jesus so!"

Mr. McKinney nodded gravely as if he shared the confidence

of Miss Lovelace, but Miss Lovelace must have realized at once how so cloying a statement must sound to an eavesdropper, and her eyes met Amy's and Amy felt drawn into an uncomfortable relationship whose exact nature was soon going to be resolved. Yes, before the hour was up and *The Virginia Five* took note of the raised red flag, Miss Lovelace would speak to her.

Pretty soon everybody began to move down to the boathouse. Everybody agreed that everything had been nice, that everybody had enjoyed the salt air and the smell of the pines, that it was a day of which memories are made. Amy moved to leave the beach house but in a curious way she was cut off by Miss Lovelace who passed before her and for the space of six seconds they were quite alone in the world, the voices of the others belonging to quite another age, quite another planet.

Miss Lovelace, smelling faintly of Florida Water, smiled. "Goodbye, little Amy," she murmured. "Oh, you are so lucky to live here in the summertime! Aren't you lucky not to be living in an orphans' home!"

3

"WHAT DID SHE MEAN? What did she mean?" cried Amy.

A prudent man far short of six feet tall, Mr. McKinney usually found opportunity to absent himself from scenes that might become emotional. As a lawyer, he refused to handle divorce cases not only because he disapproved of divorce but because the parties sometimes screamed at each other in court, nor would he take custody cases. A man of his temperament was correct in choosing to be a corporation lawyer where everything was cut and dried and the cogent facts did not prompt profanity or tears.

Amy was not old enough to realize that a female does not give rein to emotion while a man is yet in the house. He therefore picked up the felt hat he used near the water and put it on his silver-gray head and he departed.

Mrs. McKinney believed in the truth and honored it. At the University of Oregon long ago she had taken lessons in elocution and there learned to say, with appropriate gestures, "Oh what a tangled web we weave / When first we practice to deceive." She did not offer the truth gratuitously, for she knew that idly offering the truth shatters images, dashes hopes and blasts illusions and, carried too far, would not leave two people in the whole world on speaking terms. But if the truth was demanded of her, she felt bound to reveal it and to shoulder the responsibility. To conceal the truth was to place one's credibility in jeopardy. She might never be believed again. But after almost eight years, Mrs. McKinney dared hope she would never be called upon to tell this truth, that Amy would live out her life believing herself to be a true McKinney — and yet she knew that to have been a foolish hope. Doubtless many and many a member of the Presbyterian church knew the truth. It may well have been the Reverend Doctor Matthews himself who had exposed Amy as adopted, maybe as an example of the mysterious ways in which God works. The arcane fashion in which God worked in this instance was to cause to be born to a couple who did not want her a child who was thus available to a lonely couple who *did* want her. That, in a kinder way, is what Mrs. McKinney now told Amy almost as if the words for years had been ready on her lips.

"Darling, darling Amy. You just stop your crying now. You just stop it and listen to your mother." And when she had said what she said, she held the little girl and stroked her hair and felt the dear vulnerability of the back of her neck. "We chose you especially," Mrs. McKinney said. "So you see, dear, you are very, very special."

Mr. McKinney, as he knew he would, found everything calm and happy in the beach house. He hung up his funny old hat and that evening they sat down to a hearty clam chowder.

It is a pity that as the years passed Amy could not remain pleased that she was adopted and not simply born to the Mc-

Kinneys. It is a pity that the years alter the perspective just as they age the hands and face; and a pity that there exists such an occasion as Mother's Day whose founder died of a broken heart because the day was snatched from her hands by florists, candy companies and the printers of gaudy cards finished off with gilt and sleazy rayon ribbons. Perhaps no holiday, not even Christmas when the police testify they are most often called upon to quell family rows that sometimes end in flying bullets — perhaps no other holiday so contributes to feelings of guilt, loneliness and bereavement. Whereas once one simply wore a red carnation if one's mother was alive and kicking, and a white one if one's mother had passed on or over, now Mother had become so formidable, or was thought to be, that she must be appeased with concrete gifts. Sometimes cards, candy and flowers do not exactly suit. Sometimes a mother is pushed into being demanding simply because she is a mother, and no protestation that she wants nothing of her children but their love will alter their conviction that her feelings will fester if they do not come forward with appropriate and timely tribute. On the other hand, some mothers look on gifts and periodic recognition of their fecundity as their due, and cannot forgive children who are so engrossed in bettering themselves they forget a mother's many sacrifices, her frequent tears and all the nights she sat up with them when they were ill or apprehensive of monsters. No serpent's tooth, they say, has the sharpness of an ungrateful child, but no serpent's tooth has the sharpness of many an unappreciated mother.

Mrs. McKinney was neither unappreciated nor was she unappeased. On her knees each night beside the massive functional bed she shared with Mr. McKinney, she whispered formidable prayers of thanks and called on God to keep Amy well, to look after her progress in school, to render her chaste until that happy time when a good young man would step forward, take her in marriage and initiate her into those rites that women can do without and it seems that no man can. Mrs. McKinney had no reason to expect a sudden cloud on her horizon. Weekdays in the McKinney house were comfortably sterile. Meal followed meal with expected regularity and no menu was so altered that there was not something in some dish that was familiar. The tall clock at the bottom of the stairs was wound regularly by Mr. McKinney just before he retired at ten each Saturday night; he corrected its negligible irregularity after glancing at his watch which he had that day set by a chronometer kept in a jewelry store across the street from Frederick & Nelson's. An hour each week was set aside for Amy's piano lessons and an hour each afternoon for practice at the Steinway baby grand the McKinneys rented and meant to buy if Amy exhibited a true love of music. Amy mastered the once difficult "Tiger Lily Waltz" which used a black note, and she went on to a composition that required the crossing of her wrists. Appropriate books were pressed in upon her — Hurlbut's *Illustrated Bible; Wild Animals of the World* was a fine companion during many a rainy Seattle afternoon and containing a chilling series of pictures of a snake in the act of swallowing a white rat whole. The gentle McKinneys were perhaps not aware of this. Amy played with appropriate children who came in when they were called and did not track across a newly mopped kitchen floor.

If the weekdays were sterile, Sundays were antiseptic. The air was sharp with the matter-of-fact odor of Johnson's paste wax applied the previous day to every available wooden surface; the floors glistened and those in the hall reflected the morning sun that fell against the heavy oval plate glass in the front door. An almost life-sized steel engraving of Robert Burns had been chosen to compliment Mr. McKinney's own Scots ancestry. The poet stared across the living room at a sepia print of Rosa

Bonheur's *The Horse Fair*, a curious print to be hanging there since it was a horse that was instrumental in their natural child's death. It displayed such cumbersome activity it would have disturbed a less tranquil room. Mr. McKinney believed there was room for women in the arts and had himself marched in a parade organized by suffragettes, an occasion that was still murmured about in the Rainier Club where the poached salmon was so good and the waiters did not hover.

Now it was the Sunday of Mother's Day and Mrs. McKinney removed from the icebox, whose chilly interior kept them fresh, two carnations, perfect blooms, one white that she would wear to church in fond memory of her mother, and a red one for Amy to wear in deference to her. Both she and Amy wore new shoes of white kid, new dresses of white dotted swiss, and hats. She felt they both looked pretty perky and, thinking that, she smiled.

God knows what had gotten into Amy. One supposes she had been brooding, had overheard something at school. Possibly at nine she already felt the occasional human need to hurt somebody close.

Still smiling, Mrs. McKinney first pinned on her own carnation — a precious moment — and then she stepped forward with the red one.

Did a shadow fall across the new-waxed floor? Amy turned her face away, took a step back. "Maybe I ought to have a white one, too," she said. "Because maybe my real mother's dead."

Now it was Mrs. McKinney who stepped back, and in her eyes was an appeal that Amy take back, make unsaid what she had said. Mrs. McKinney covered her face with her hands and began to sob. Then Amy was in her arms and they both sobbed, and it was just so that Mr. McKinney found them, himself on edge because he had not ten minutes before nicked himself with the straightedged razor he preferred to the so-called safety razor, and the styptic pencil he counted on had been long in stopping the flow of blood. He spread his hands before him in despair, but it was the last time he was called upon to witness any such scene. Never again in his or in his wife's lifetime did Amy speak of her natural mother.

Now the former Kaiser chopped wood in exile at Dorn, in Holland. Certain women cut their hair short and wore lip rouge. President Harding died, some said after eating spoiled crabmeat from a faulty can, some said by his wife's hand. Amy had been warned about and then one day accepted the monstrous fact of the menstrual flow of blood. The "Tiger Lily Waltz" was but a memory, succeeded over the next few years by a hatred of Bach and a love of Mozart. In grammar school she had excelled in the new Palmer method which had replaced the elegant Spencerian script; it was a method that required everybody to write exactly like everybody else; anybody could sign your name to a check and you'd not be the wiser. She wrote the word "Lanning" over and over so perfectly and the phrase "This is a specimen of my handwriting" that she was awarded first the bronze and then the silver pin which she accepted just before eighth-grade diplomas were handed out in the happy presence of Mr. and Mrs. Mc-Kinney. They were on hand four years later for Amy's graduation from high school and all the special Girl Scout awards in between. There had been companionable fudge-making and taffy pulls with other girls who came over to spend the night, and giggling.

Now there was a motorboat in the boathouse instead of a dinghy, and camping in the woods; the world was indeed pleasant and the University of Washington was pleasant and certainly as fine as anything on the East Coast where, whatever else they have back there, they do not have Mount Rainier nor such wild flowers as grow on the flanks of Mount Olympus.

Amy no longer wore her Delta Gamma pin. She didn't feel like it. Later on when she began to collect gold charms to attach to her gold bracelet, she attached the Delta Gamma pin because most of it was gold. Throughout college she had preferred nature and economics to the *thé dansant*. Economics teaches the shrewd management of money and the handing out of the right things at the right time; thus she was quite prepared to take a position managing the women's dormitories at the university. She dealt easily with inventories, thousands of pounds of potatoes, sacks of sugar, tubs of butter, effective lighting and the installation of showers.

It was time now to be the comfort to her adoptive parents that they had been to her. They were both now over sixty and had no great record of longevity in either of their families. Mr. McKinney, never a tall man, was shrinking, growing shorter before Amy's eyes. The spaces between the vertebrae narrowed. Then the back begain to ache, and Mr. McKinney was in frequent pain. Both he and Mrs. McKinney became dependent on old photographs to recall the past, and it disturbed them when Christmas tree ornaments they remembered had somehow vanished. What had become of everything? Scarcely a week passed but some old acquaintance went, as they said, to his reward.

Since the house was right there in Seattle, no question arose of Amy's living at the university or having a place of her own, and besides they needed her at the end of their day. They saved up things to tell her. They met her late afternoons at the heavy front door; each wanted to be the first to greet her. They clamored, but quietly.

"Amy dear," Mr. McKinney would say, "I spent all morning hunting down slugs. I found more than twenty and destroyed them." So it was after he had retired from his law practice. He was having a hard time finding things to do; in the yard and around the house he walked slowly; sometimes he paused, as if listening.

Mrs. McKinney walked slowly, too, but did not complain about her right leg which hurt so much.

"Amy," she would say, "do you think maybe this evening we could get the hems of those dresses of mine let down?" She was disturbed at how short dresses were getting and perhaps thought that in letting her own hems down she could halt the trend. Amy let hems down and tried to keep the floors glistening as they had been, but her duties at the university were so demanding that Mrs. McKinney had a man come once a week to wax and polish and he did it so well that one of the small oriental rugs flew out from beneath her feet and she broke her hip for the first time. The following year she broke the other hip.

Women have a right to expect to live longer than their husbands. To begin with, they are younger. A woman is ready to marry earlier than a man is. If her husband is a good man, it is he who does the worrying, and worrying saps the strength and renders the aging body vulnerable to ailments and disease. A woman prepares herself to go on alone, and that she might go on alone as comfortably as possible, a good man arranges his affairs carefully, so that when he dies there is enough money and everybody knows where everything is and what not to sell. He will make the arrangements for his own funeral because his wife will be busy that day with people coming in and with getting out the china.

Mrs. McKinney had the right, too. She was often concerned that Amy had not married shortly after college, because that is what usually happens, and then that would be all settled and all the china and the silver and the rugs would have a more definite place in the future. But Amy appeared to feel it her duty to be with them rather than elsewhere when she had free time, so it was all quite complicated and thought-provoking. Both Mr. and Mrs. McKinney wished they were not so dependent on Amy for company, that as they'd grown older they'd made more friends, but the trouble was so many of their friends had died, and it is hard to make friends with younger people because they don't see much future in you. It is terrible how lonely you get when you get old and how you count on your children which may be the only immortality you have, however faithfully you have always professed to believe what the church teaches. If only one could be certain of an afterlife, there would not be all this dependence on children.

The Great Depression was felt by a great many people. Mr. McKinney was by no means a rich man, but he had not been a foolish man either. When he saw Auburn Motors go to 238, a company that manufactured an automobile — the Duesenberg — which nobody could afford and another — the Auburn — that nobody but young sports bought, he knew something was up. He sold what stocks he had and bought bonds. He couldn't understand why other men didn't know something was up, but you can't talk to your friends because nobody likes to talk about their financial affairs because they just don't, and they don't want to hear anything from an attorney, who is not even a businessman.

The McKinneys were not social people; they had few friends because they had never felt the need of them. Their life with Amy was quite enough, but it was now necessary to help what few friends they had because of the awful times. Mrs. McKinney said there must be some kind of sign on their house because so many people, some of them very young people, stopped around back for something to eat. She kept extra suppiles in the new, bigger Kelvinator. Without it, she said, she did not know what she would do.

And then as the Depression was ending because the War was coming and the factories were turning out guns and aircraft, Mrs. McKinney, who had always been so kind, had to have her right leg cut off and shortly after that she died.

So it was Mr. McKinney who wept. Everything he had arranged to be in order for her was now in order for him, and he wanted nothing of it without her. Amy hugged him and after the funeral they took the ferry to the beach house to get away, but of course they couldn't. The old wood stove was especially painful to see; for so many years he had fed it driftwood that his wife might make her chowders and her cornbread.

He had imagined that with him gone, Mrs. McKinney might like to travel, for she had sometimes mentioned Japan and China and on the rare occasions they went out, ate out, it was Chinese food and Japanese food they ordered. He had no wish to travel alone. He could not stand his own ocean without her, let alone another ocean which might have made sense to him with her by his side. Why, it had occurred to him that after his death she might meet a nice widower on the boat, someone with money equal to hers, so there wouldn't be any of that business; if this widower were traveling he was bound to have something himself, unless he was one of those other fellows. As for him, he did not care to meet any widow — there would have always been only one Mrs. McKinney, always, always. Tears sprang into his eyes when he remembered how she had once touched him and smiled at him.

Amy was doing well at the university and loved her work with the Girl Scouts; he could not be so selfish as to ask her to travel with him.

There was nothing much to do with his money; there isn't much to do with money so long as you own your house and have enough to eat. He already had his books. Maybe someday Amy could think of something to do with it. He realized that over the years they had been almost prodigal in their use of kindling for the fireplace that dispelled Seattle's damp. They had used Heaven knew how many sticks to start the fire. Now he saw it could be done perfectly with only two sticks, provided he rolled up into spills and knotted past issues of the *Post-Intelligencer*.

He had never before kept track of the variations in temperature; now he kept a log each morning and evening of the changes. He bought a device to measure the rainfall: it was no more than a beaker with graduated markings on the outside. Had he known what it was before he bought it — had he not got himself involved with the clerk, taken up the clerk's time — he could have made an adequate one himself.

He found a little later that there was no particular use in putting on his shoes in the morning, that slippers were more comfortable; he had come to dislike the sound of his own tread, and it was so much louder with shoes. The afternoons were hard.

"I was just sitting here waiting for you," he would tell Amy. "How about a little game," and after she had "freshened up" they would play double solitaire.

"You're such a good dad," Amy told him. "You ought to let me get you somebody to come in during the day."

"Don't want anybody," Mr. McKinney said. "Somebody who came in would put things in the wrong places, and I wouldn't have anything to do. Amy, it's terrible not having anything to do."

If he had had somebody in five years later, he would not perhaps have pitched down the stairs into the cellar. There Amy found him shortly after five in the afternoon.

He never regained consciousness; it is unlikely that on his deathbed he reviewed what his life had been or considered whether he got from it what he wanted. He had been given just seventy years, precisely the years the Bible he believed in had allotted him. He had been born, became a lawyer, married, grieved over a lost son, been kind to his wife and to Amy, grieved over his lost wife, and died. His life was as clean and two-dimensional as the steel engraving of Robert Burns, as immaculate as the regularly polished floors.

His funeral was solemn and decent. The right things were said. Those friends who attended — and those who did not were dead — were older than he, and Amy imagined that even as a child he had preferred older people who had put away childish things. Here in this decent church he had married his wife; here he had mourned his son who lay in a coffin hardly four feet long; here he had arranged with the Reverend Doctor Matthews for another child — she, Amy. Here he attended to the last thing required of him, the passing of the collection plate on the right side of the church. Where else? And here he ended — with someone not truly his own. She, Amy. As she would end, but with nobody.

What was missing, what had always been missing? Sparkle. Drive. Why did she feel that sparkle and drive counted? Joy? At the cemetery it rained and it rained; the undertaker had arranged for oversized black umbrellas.

She stood alone in the big house and her eyes moved to *The Horse Fair*. Maybe for a moment Mrs. McKinney had rebelled and had bought and hung that turbulent print of faunching, intractable beasts.

Amy stood there, weeping.

The economy straightened itself out; the country went to war again. Millions died, some quickly and some after exquisite suffering. More were maimed who would live out their damned years in institutions where they might sometimes be visited by those who could bear the sight of them. But the Depression was over.

Philip Nofzinger worked in a minor administrative position

for Boeing and ordinarily carried his lunch to work with him because he could count on it. He did not care much for business but rather for sailing and the violin; so much he confessed to Amy at a small party where everybody took drinks out into the garden and examined the flowers. It was declared that the hostess had a green thumb. Nofzinger shared Amy's enthusiasm for Mozart and asked if he might call on her and together they would play the duets? He was thirty-five and wary of young women who were not likely to have their heads on their shoulders. He had lived long with his mother and admired her settled ways, sane politics and ability to find things.

After their duet-playing, Nofzinger found himself troubled during the week by thoughts of Amy, and she of him. Marriage was decided upon within the month and "the knot was tied," as Nofzinger put it, at a civil ceremony which struck them both as more seemly for people of their years. Amy had not thought men any longer wore brown suits. She wore a dress of pale-blue crêpe de Chine and a small hat to match and high heels, an outfit not unbecoming but unnatural for her who preferred tweeds, heavy silver jewelry set with turquoise and shoes that made it less difficult to get from here to there.

She refused to move in with Mrs. Nofzinger, knowing that never works, and Nofzinger refused to move into the McKinney house as being somehow emasculating. So the McKinney house was put on the market.

Nofzinger and Amy moved into a small new house quite surrounded by a hedge of holly which does so well around Seattle and is so much appreciated at Christmastime by those who live elsewhere. They continued their duets in the evening and discovered they had in common an interest in wild mushrooms and knew which of the amanitas were not deadly. They both liked sailing. Each anted up half the price of a thirty-foot yawl which they moored off the boathouse on Puget Sound.

They named her *Sea Drift* after a musical composition by Delius. They were struck by the fact that they both knew Delius. Nofzinger was struck by the fact that Amy had a boathouse.

Nofzinger had early learned to be neat and did not want to talk about children. Children of friends of his had so little sense of value, so little knowledge of physics that cherished objects fell from the edges of tables and smashed. They did not close doors; they slammed them. He hated sudden, loud noises; he did not like to be surprised. He would not have one of those toasters that tick away and suddenly hurl the burned bread aloft. Children's noses ran.

So he worked and she worked; on weekends and for two weeks in the summer they walked in the woods. Nofzinger bought Amy a good microscope for looking closely at mushroom spores and she bought him a viola because he liked their darker timbre. They were both surprised at the other's generosity; they often went to bed at night quite pleased.

They both liked to drink, never to excess, and this went on for ten years until suddenly one rainy winter afternoon it all didn't seem to make much sense. They were, then, never more than good friends, and there wasn't anything wrong with that except that everything was wrong with it, but what, exactly? He wondered what secrets she was holding back — anyone her age has secrets. He had thought marriage was more a sharing of secrets. She wondered what he was holding back. Not quite knowing why, she had not told him she had been adopted and justified her silence in assuming he already knew. She wondered if he did not speak of it because he felt to do so would cause her pain, or whether he indeed did not know, and if he knew would it make any difference in the way he felt towards her? Maybe he did know, and that was why they were friends and not lovers, that part of what he felt for her was pity and nobody on

33

earth wants to be pitied, especially those who are deserving of pity. Good God, she thought. Is my having been adopted wrecking our marriage? Is that why he doesn't want children? — because I can name neither father nor mother, produce no grandparents for a child?

In ten years, Nofzinger had learned to play the viola so well he did some justice to a duet arrangement of Berlioz's *Harold in Italy*. It seemed to him that Amy was preoccupied with something more than the music. Sometimes he had to speak twice before she answered. She seemed far away.

Amy had read that if a woman is unfaithful, it is not wise to tell the husband; always deny it and he has a chance to believe what he thinks is true is not true. If you tell him the truth he will never forgive you. She had never been unfaithful, but she wondered if she owed it to him to share with him her knowledge of something she had found in her adoptive father's safety deposit box. That she did not share her knowledge seemed to her disloyal and distrustful. If he truly loved her, he would love her in spite of everything. Did she fear he did not love her? Or was there another reason she did not open an envelope she found in the box that said IF YOU WANT TO KNOW WHO YOUR REAL PARENTS ARE OPEN THIS ENVELOPE.

Oh yes. Her preoccupation had begun a long time ago.

A little voice said, "Who am I?"

Now, if she really loved Nofzinger, didn't need anyone else, then it didn't matter who was out there and belonged to her. Are we not told that a husband is enough for a wife — that they are to cleave the one to the other?

The little voice continued to nag.

The divorce was as unemotional as the marriage. She found she could look at the dress in which she had taken another's

34

name with but little sadness other than that anyone feels for the past. She believed he felt nothing at all in departing with his viola. In the main dining room of the Olympic Hotel — appropriate neutral ground — they had agreed that the ten years had been rather good, on the whole, that they had both grown and had had certain insights about life, and since Amy had enough money there was no trouble there, and he wanted nothing of her except maybe his share of the money from the sailboat, possibly as a loan? He would move back in with his mother who was now at the age when she needed somebody. She had reached the age when she would start breaking hips. As he said, it was all down hill, now.

So they toasted one another somewhat shyly in the dining room while a sedate combo of accordion and strings played "Nola," a sprightly little tune, a nice little background of insouciance. Then they both choked up a bit remembering good days, the smell of the pines in the fog, the spray on board the *Sea Drift,* and then it was all over because that evening Amy had to be with her Girl Scouts and Nofzinger's mother had a surprise in the oven.

Amy sat at her dressing table. She wished he had argued against divorce, just a little. Maybe if she had had more confidence the marriage would have worked. Maybe if she knew — had known — who she was, whose face this was in the glass, if she had had a picture of ancestors in bonnets and capes and an identity to pass on to a child. Something.

She remained haunted with embarrassment over her last words with Nofzinger.

"I should like," she began, "I should like to keep the name Nofzinger. Your name."

He looked puzzled. "Of course. You have a legal right to it."

35

"I know. That's the thing. I'd like to have you tell me it was all right with *you*."

"Amy dear, of course it is!"

Amy dear.

But even a husband you have once had is family, isn't he?

She had left the envelope in the safety deposit box in the bank; she hadn't wanted it around the house because something so dangerously charged must somehow set up a magnetic field that is bound to attract the curious. So now she went to the bank.

But first she sat at a counter across the street and drank a cup of coffee. She wore the good tweed suit and the Indian jewelry in which she was most comfortable — but still. If her adoptive father had truly wanted her to know who her real parents were, why hadn't he told her? To break the seal of the envelope was to deny in no small way the good, kind McKinneys who had sheltered her, put up with her childish tantrums, cared for her in her illnesses, turned the pages of her picture books, urged her to stay within the lines when she colored, sent her to college and left her comfortably well off. She brooded over the incident of the red and the white carnations. Never once had either Mother or Dad McKinney raised their voices in speaking to her. She recalled their smiles.

"They were so dear!" And so they were, in choosing for her the right foods, the right friends, the right clothing. It was for her that they — usually so prudent with money — had bought the *Britannica* that hulked behind glass doors in the hall. And for her the Packard, for Dad McKinney knew little of internal combustion engines and Mother nothing at all. They knew only that a sixteen-year-old girl is more comfortable when asked what make of automobile her parents drive (and they do ask) if she can say, "Packard." Yes, they were generous and they were dear, God knows.

But they were not hers.

Perhaps like many who wish to believe their motives unselfish, Amy deceived herself. She wanted to believe her wish to find her mother was unselfish — mother or father. She wanted to believe her true parents would want to know that she was "all right." All right? Clothed. Fed. Her first swing, the tricycle. Beach house. Packard. Had not been frightened at becoming a woman. Had an education, gloves for some occasions, handbags. Had learned to dance. Surprising how many young women married the wrong men simply because they couldn't dance. Able to cope with humiliation or was so assured that the question of humiliation never came up.

Well, she did want her true parents to know she was all right. So she paid for her coffee and left a tip as large as the price of the coffee, that the waitress, seeing her depart, might wish her well in whatever she was up to. She walked across the street to the bank whose Ionic pillars suggested the grandeur that was Greece and the religion that was money.

She went through the serious little ceremony that gave her access to the vault — smiles, words more whispers than speech, and then the little buzzer that warned that a small gate was about to be opened, and there she was with the safety deposit box in her hands. She carried it into a private stall set aside for people who wish to close the door and in private, away from envious eyes, examine things they own. Since some things people own are liable to make them nervous and in need of smoking, a clean ashtray and a book of matches bearing the bank's insignia waited on the table. Amy lighted a cigarette, held it between her lips and squinted against the smoke while she opened the box.

Now she held the sealed envelope that had been buried under stocks and bonds and deeds; when she had first come upon it, it had been on top as if Dad McKinney in placing it there would urge her to make a decision at once as the first thing she did in

37

her life alone. Earlier, in placing the sealed envelope at the bottom of the stack of papers, she felt she had made that decision, but she had not.

She broke the seal.

Nothing, nothing was ever the same again.

4

THE MANILA ENVELOPE contained somewhat more than the particular paper she was determined to face; it contained the whole dismal business of her adoption, not only the adoption papers themselves couched in legal jargon — the petitioner prays the Court, and so on, herself called "Baby Owen" and signed by a judge — but the required release of her by her mother. Her mother was described as a "spinster," a word long since out of fashion that prompted thoughts of hopelessness and discard. The papers had so unpleasant a texture she wished she had worn gloves. Here they were, the legal documents, the one giving her away and the other taking her up as if she were a piece of produce. Oh, she had been lucky, as a Miss Lovelace had said long ago, Miss Lovelace of the heart-shaped locket and the Florida Water. Lucky not to have ended in an institution rather than in the immaculate house of a Seattle attorney who was comfortable in the Rainier Club. And of what did her luck consist? That a little boy had been thrown from a horse and had broken his neck. That was luck for you.

Her mother's — her true mother's — last act as her mother was to sign that release with the name Owen. Elizabeth Owen, surely not her true name but a false one, for that poor woman must necessarily hide her true self even from herself at that moment she committed so unnatural an act. Yes, she wished she had worn gloves that either fabric or leather might insulate her from the haunting shame she felt for not having been wanted, for having been no more than an embarrassment to "Elizabeth Owen" and a fortuitous accommodation for the McKinneys who could not abide their loneliness. Yes, gloves.

For some moments she stared, fascinated, at the name Elizabeth Owen. The hand that had written that name had perhaps touched her? Somehow the handwriting was not what she might have expected. It was not a handwriting one expected to find on so squalid a document but rather on notepaper with a high rag content. Linen. However it was probable that the judgment of her eyes was tempered by her wish to believe something good about "Elizabeth Owen" who was certainly somebody else.

And somebody else she was.

For now Amy handled the last paper. This white sheet she drew out and unfolded. It was engraved at the top: ARTHUR H. GRAY, M.D., LUMBER EXCHANGE, SEATTLE. The few written words were set down in an elegant, old-fashioned hand. A perceptible trembling in that hand betrayed either age or emotion. That hand might be dangerous in surgery. The words were bald, the facts simple, as if nothing more could be had from Dr. Gray who really wanted nothing to do with this. You saw the brief confrontation in his office—of Dad McKinney the prominent Seattle attorney who so believed in human rights he insisted that an adopted child have the right to her true name (on the one hand) and a good old doctor hindered by the Oath of Hippocrates and his knowledge that in revealing names he was conspiring — he of all people — against the state and the authorities. The authorities insisted that no adopted child ever know his true parents. In making that impossible, the authorities relieved a child of the possible horror of what he might find. She might find. But at last Dr. Gray had revealed the names, for he, too, had a heart. One seemed to hear Mr. McKinney's formal thanks and Dr. Gray's formal acknowledgment of them. ". . . not at all."

Bracketed on the good white paper were the names Benjamin H. Burton and Elizabeth Birdseye Sweringen, and outside the bracket was the word "Parents." Under the name of Elizabeth was the name Thomas H. Sweringen and in parenthesis the word "Father," and under that, an address.

Lemhi, Idaho.

So she knew who she was. A Burton. What might they have called her? Elizabeth after her mother? But they had not named her. The state called her Baby Owen, who was no one at all. But it is the last name that counts. Now she had identity. She could now imagine herself a relative of any Burton she met anywhere in the world. In a bookshop. In a telephone book. She had a *name*.

BURTON, she wrote on a blank sheet of paper. And again. BURTON. How often must you write a name before it's yours? But alas, it's not the name alone that counts. It's knowing who your parents are that counts, and your parent's parents and your parent's parent's parents, for the more heritage we can produce the more secure we feel, the more and older the snapshots and portraits and silhouettes, objects, candle molds, wooden churns, brass tea kettles, locks of hair, faded letters coming apart at the folds, valentines and pressed flowers. A name without a knowledge of those who gave it to us, the tilt of noses, the ring of voices, is hollow, and this Amy knew well when at first she told herself she wanted only to know her name. But in pursuing her ancestors she was afraid of what frightened or closed faces she might see, what living conditions, what doors sagging at the hinges, what empty shelves. And much as she might wish to know them, it was doubtful they would wish to know her. For better or worse they had made their lives without her, kept their own hours, managed the holidays. They would not wish their lives disturbed by one who had first disturbed them.

She thought she had better leave things alone.

She found no Benjamin H. Burton in the telephone book.

As an attorney, Dad McKinney had arranged his affairs perfectly, and Amy had no need of a lawyer until her divorce; amicable as that divorce had been, the fabric of American life is so poorly woven that a lawyer must have a hand in it to keep it from fraying. To lend her divorce a casual touch, she had chosen a lawyer at random from the yellow pages. She had found him, a young man, most pleasant and understanding; they had lunched together and it transpired that he, like her, often drove to the coast and walked solitary beside the sea. Now she wrote to inquire if he would meet her for lunch at the Olympic Hotel, pleased that she could write "Olympic Hotel" without too much regretting Nofzinger's companionship. She wrote that she wanted to speak about personal things.

She gathered up her adoption papers, which she believed pertinent, the release signed by Elizabeth Owen, Dr. Gray's terse words, and drove into Seattle. Neither the freeway with its swift, impersonal traffic nor Mount Rainier, which had appeared a few minutes before when the clouds parted, looked as they had ever looked before.

She left her station wagon with the doorman at the hotel and entered the lobby which, unlike good eastern hotels, is fitted out with many comfortable chairs and settees where those who wish to be seen can sit and be seen; in Seattle, it is assumed that nobody who does not belong there will be there, and that assumption is usually correct.

Mr. Keith Compton, the attorney, was waiting with a good briefcase into which he might slip valuable papers entrusted to him. He arose smiling from a chair, and both he and she remarked that it was good to see each other again, and that time had passed. When they had touched hands they moved into the grill. She had her papers in the battered briefcase Dad McKinney had thought to be good luck, but she was so used to the Olympic Hotel she didn't care what she carried there. She thought she might show Compton the papers, or she might not.

Yes, she said, she would have a martini. So, then, would he, and a new little bond was established. "I shouldn't be surprised," she said, "if what I have to say sounds strange. But then, lawyers must be used to strange things."

"Very strange," Compton said, and smiled as one who knows a thing or two.

"All right, then. I was adopted as a very small child, and couldn't have had better adoptive parents." She felt tears about to spring to her eyes, for their faces, framed by the years, were before her. Reaching for a cigarette in the leather case beside her, her hand touched and tipped over the poorly footed martini glass. A waiter was at once on hand to do the small mopping up. He covered the damp so deftly with a napkin it was clear that spilled martinis were usual. However, she had never before overturned a glass in public.

"You were lucky to have found such a family," Compton said.

43

By so many people, she thought, I have been described as lucky.

"I know," she said. "But naturally, out of curiosity, it has sometimes crossed my mind to try to find my real parents. Maybe it's a woman's curiosity, or is that foolish, to believe that a woman's curiosity is any greater than a man's?"

"I think not," Compton said.

"I think anybody would be curious," she went on. The ease of her words, the control of them, was meant to convey to Compton that her wish to know of her real parents was hardly more than a velleity, a thought that would come to one while watering a plant or peeling an orange. She wished she had not spilled that martini.

"I understand your feelings," Compton said. "But to find out is next to impossible. The laws of this state prohibit the Bureau of Vital Statistics from giving out that information."

"I know that. My adoptive father knew that. He was an attorney. He once told me he felt a child had the right to know. He left papers. I have thought about all this."

"I hope you have thought about it a great deal," Compton said.

"And I decided that because of what I might find, it was better not to pursue the matter. I suppose what I want from you is a professional opinion. But maybe it's a personal opinion I want. Someone's opinion who can be — someone who can be both objective and subjective."

"All right," Compton raised a hand to summon the waiter to bring lunch. "I wouldn't pursue the matter further."

As they parted, Compton said he hoped soon to get to the coast with his family, all of whom loved the out-of-doors. But the moment before he turned from her, she felt he was about to say something else. His mouth had that look.

44

She was grateful that now the spring was so far advanced she could put her mind to her garden, especially her rhododendrons which sometimes had won prizes. She was serious about gardening, enchanted with the power and beauty that hides inside a tiny seed. Serious about camping, collecting driftwood which she prepared and polished. It took little imagination to see in driftwood some fanciful creature, to feel, looking at it, a tender emotion. She was serious about her duties as a Girl Scout counsellor — knowing well enough that the girls were her substitute for a family. Oh, she was lucky, and in a sense the girls were lucky, for an encumbered woman would not have had the time for them, time to show them how to kindle fires, to tell them what berries not to eat, what is the best way to survive.

To survive.

She was grateful for those girls who, as they grew older and now knew that life was not what they had thought it, sometimes wrote her and recalled the past when things had seemed otherwise.

"Keep in touch," she had told them. "Keep in touch."

Her Christmas card list was long, but it became harder and harder to put a name to a face.

She had been not more than ten when she realized that certain objects in the McKinney house were looked on with special regard. These objects were more carefully and more often dusted, more often polished, were more carefully placed and lodged and spoken of with a quiet reverence, as if they were true relics. Among these objects were some that had belonged to the Crowells, her adoptive mother's family, and among these were a dozen antique English tablespoons that appeared only at Christmastime. For the remainder of the year these haughty spoons, each in its private chamois pouch, were put out of sight in a tooled leather box. Mothballs are said to retard tarnishing.

These old utensils were under discussion by the two Crowell cousins when once again they arrived by Buick automobile for Christmas dinner. Having already entered the university, they had begun to put foolish things behind them and to look on property because you never can tell. Amy, not yet twelve, had stood in the kitchen where a woman who had come to help out basted the goose which the McKinneys preferred to turkey. The woman said the trouble was, she couldn't find anything. The Crowell cousins were in the pantry where the dishes were kept and the silver was polished beside a small soapstone sink. Surely the conversation in there was not meant for Amy's ears — unless it was, and they wanted to make clear to her what was made clear.

"Those spoons," one cousin said, "shouldn't go to Amy, but to some of the Crowells."

They had looked on her as no Crowell. She was quite lucky enough to have been a sort of McKinney. How could they have looked on her as a Crowell? And had the spoons belonged to the McKinneys, they would have looked on her as no McKinney, no matter what the adoption papers said. Blood will tell. But the selected McKinney objects she years later brought with her to the house she and Nofzinger had bought — the tall clock, the captain's desk of teak and brass, the carvings of jade and ivory and alabaster, the silver tea urn — all these continued to give her a sense of identity, at least with a past, and were doubtless looked on by friends and acquaintances as rightfully hers because she had possession of them. It was only when the Crowell cousins, somewhat faded now, for their faces had not held up, stopped to see her that she once again felt herself a ghost, drifting without a voice of her own. But aging had not diminished the Crowell cousins' resentment of her lease on the Crowell spoons. She had erred in displaying them. Flaunting them, they

46

might have said. So at last, to appease them, possibly to test their acceptance of her as a real member of the family who might reasonably expect to lie at last in the family plot, she offered them the Crowell spoons.

"Why, Amy!" Their faces were bright with astonishment. Oh, they accepted the spoons. How quickly the one cousin swept them into her big bag! And how their spirits lifted, and how suddenly warm they were, as to an old acquaintance who had been presumed lost or dead.

"Do you know what, Amy? I think it would be nice if we had another drink!"

. . . having been warned by Mr. Keith Compton that it would be unwise to hunt for her natural parents, she was glad of her rhododendrons.

But Compton could not possibly know the insistence of the small voice that asked and asked, "Who am I?" Compton knew who he was. He wore no mask, was no fraud, would not understand her frequent feelings of inferiority when addressed by people who assumed she looked back on a real family. He was not troubled when he heard the words "Father" and "Mother" so easily dropped by friends.

"Mother's been sneezing lately. She puts it down to pollen."

"My father gets these restless streaks. Now he wants to look at something west of here."

She supposed that Compton had based his advice to her on his conception of morality — that parents who abandon a child aren't worth finding, are condemned because they shirked responsibility, thought first of themselves, did not love. Compton had given his advice so promptly that she was certain he had had much experience looking into his clients' pasts and that he knew the chances were that she would find poverty, madness, adultery or promiscuity, and with such facts before them, clients must abandon any fragile illusion that might have brightened an hour — that there may have been some special circumstances that led to their being abandoned and adopted.

Could there have been a special circumstance? And what was it Compton had been about to say that day?

She'd spent a lifetime adding up figures in a firm, clear hand — somewhat angular — making out budgets for the Girl Scouts, arranging hours. She was adept as well at arranging her emotions. It was not likely she would tip over another glass. She had been one who could face the truth — had she not faced it with Nofzinger and the Crowell cousins? — and she had been more comfortable with facts than with possibilities.

Who was she, this controlled woman? She was the adopted daughter of the McKinneys, those good people who had given her every possible thing. She was familiar with the interior fragrance of Packards and heavy station wagons whose doors closed with authority. She was five feet eight inches tall and maybe that's why she married Nofzinger. He was tall. Nine tenths of available males are out of reach of the tall woman except on tiptoe. She had been the wife of Nofzinger and now she was adrift, independent, not wealthy but comfortable with such stocks and bonds as Presbyterians chose, stocks that seldom moved up or down but always paid a dividend, and bonds whose names suggested vaults under Fort Knox. She was still, however, at the mercy of a small voice who asked, "Whom am I?"

Of course she could face who she was!

She picked up the telephone and called Mr. Keith Compton.

He wrote her promptly. She filed away the letter, for she had been taught to file things away and to keep canceled checks and to make carbons of everything.

Compton wrote from his lofty office far up in the IBM Build-

48

ing in Seattle that he had decided the best thing was to start searching on the paternal side. "Namely, to look for a Ben Burton," which was the same as looking for both of them because, although he had found no recent leads, he had found in the Seattle directory for 1912 Ben and Elizabeth Burton living together as man and wife. After that, they vanished.

"I've written the Bureau of Vital Statistics in Olympia," he wrote. "We may find something there."

Amy scarcely read that line. The words that rose up were "man and wife."

"They were living together as man and wife."

In 1912 that meant they were married and not *said* to be married or pretending to be married, for cohabitation was punishable in those days. Living in a furnished apartment. Heavy, cheap mission oak. Morris chair, seat of worn corduroy. Lamp with wooden base, lampshade of leaded green and white glass. Folding Murphy bed. One window looked down on the street, milk bottle on the sill when the ice ran out. Other window faced the airshaft where the homely odor of frying fat drifted up. But they were young, they were young. They could dream of dozens of windows, half of them opening on the sea. After her birth they had married. She had been born illegitimate, but had they kept her she would not long have been illegitimate, for the days and the months and the years recede. People forget. Once long ago, before the First World War when the seventh Edward sat on the throne and the ship's band played "Autumn" even as the Titanic slipped under the waves, Ben Burton and Elizabeth Sweringen Burton glanced at one another when a knock came on the door.

"I'll get it."

Census taker.

Oh, they had loved each other. But not her; they had not married until they had given her away. In the face of things, it's a wonder Amy did not say, "Well, to hell with them, both of them." But it's not easy to say the hell with your parents. And you see, there might be some funny circumstance.

However, a family is more than a mother and a father. How she had loved Mann's *Buddenbrooks* and the Jalna series with that wonderful old grandmother and the uncles and cousins and brothers, all those families in *Little Women* and *Little Men*, the close ties, the pride of the head of the family; the love of the young for the old has a place, really has a place, in a good family. But while she waited for word from the Bureau of Vital Statistics, she clung once again to the McKinneys, summoned up their voices, the odor of the foods they fancied, roasting pork and applesauce, the starched linen and the china, the opening and closing of familiar doors, the striking of the clock. Oh, the protective ghosts of the McKinneys would stand beside her if the Bureau knew nothing. Bureaus are glacial in their drift because of the piles of paper everywhere and because bureaus are staffed by stout, elderly women whose children's marriages have not worked out, and elderly men who, as they grow even older, come to look more and more like their wives. These are civil servants and somehow accountable only to the state, and you can't put your finger on the state; there is no one to hear your complaints about the many coffee breaks and the good-natured bantering that takes place in the corridors.

The Bureau of Vital Statistics was glacial even for a bureaucracy, for there were all those millions and millions of names drifting in, many of them misspelled, papers signed on the wrong lines and people being born and dying and moving away leaving no word and suing for divorce and hailing each other into court.

Three times in the days that followed, Amy took up the telephone to call Compton and three times she replaced it to silence the impatient dial tone. She must let the truth unfold as it would; to force it might be to alter it.

Suppose she herself called the Bureau? But now the Bureau had become a threat; it had become a Presence that must be approached with caution. She might hear what she did not wish to hear.

And when at last she heard from Compton, she did hear what she did not wish to hear.

Ben Burton, Mr. Compton wrote, had lived for some years at the Gould Hotel on Third Street. "He died last year of cirrhosis of the liver."

She held the letter as if weighing it. It was a fine example of a good attorney's reticence and tact, for "Gould Hotel" and "Third Street" and "cirrhosis of the liver" were all euphemisms. Gould Hotel meant flophouse; Third Street meant skid row; cirrhosis of the liver meant Ben Burton died an alcoholic. But because the letter contained the first and probably last news of her true father, she felt an obligation. Her father's life, the end of it anyway, had been a tragedy. As his natural daughter she felt she was bound to know the place where he had spent his last hours, to share with him who was now dead the peculiar shadows of his humiliation and his failure. That's what a daughter must do. That's what family means.

She dressed simply in old clothes. She would pass as the slightly more fortunate friend or relative of one of the old men living in the Gould Hotel.

The Gould Hotel was a three-story firetrap. The brick foundation was zigzagged with cracks as the earth beneath it gave way and sank towards the Pacific Ocean. At the entrance she stepped over an empty pint wine bottle; a stage manager couldn't have arranged a more dismal scene.

Attached to the thick, dog-eared register on a stout length of string was a pencil, not a pen; those who signed themselves in to the Gould Hotel need not expect the permanence of ink. That the Gould Hotel might have seen better days was suggested by the mounted head of an antlered mule deer, the glass eyes glazed with dust and smoke, a souvenir of a long-ago encounter between predatory man and timid beast in the woods to the north. Under the head sat four old men playing rummy, the chips beside them a reminder that once they had owned and even understood money; they had not lost, even now, the will to be a winner. At the feet of one old man was a brass cuspidor, for he was of a generation when, in some circles, it was acceptable to spit. At a second table two old men played solitaire. What did the end of the game mean to them? Another chance? Yes, here she was at home with those who, like her, had rejected their past and sought in the cards a future. Her signature as Amy McKinney or as Amy Nofzinger was as temporary and as easily erased as their signatures in lead pencil. Coming here dressed as a woman she was not, she was a ghost as they were ghosts.

How could she, without embarrassment to them or to her, speak of her father, how say, "Did you know Ben Burton? How did he look? What did he want?"

She sat on a wicker chair hard against the wall, such a chair as was seen on verandahs in the summertime and taken in when it rained, if anyone remembered. Tossed into the seat of a neighboring slatted folding chair like those in public halls and in the basements of churches were a copy of *Reader's Digest* of another year, the *Elk's Magazine* of another month, and a fresh copy of the *War Cry*, that journal of the Salvation Army that promises failures a friend in Jesus. It had been but little disturbed.

Amy opened her handbag, carefully chosen because it was worn, and drew out a Zippo lighter, a small leather cigarette case and a holder that entrapped some irritants and was her answer to stopping smoking; but even as she fitted the cigarette into the holder, she noticed that the younger of the two solitaire players glanced at her in a certain way. She realized that Third

Street was not Queen Anne Hill, and that her elaborate prepara-
tions to smoke were taken as the provocative gestures of a cruis-
ing whore, that the clothes she wore were regarded as the best
she had, rather than the worst. Whatever question she now
asked in the Gould Hotel would be misconstrued; an inquiry
about Ben Burton would mark him as one who kept low company. She closed her bag on the offending articles and rose and
left the place, believing that the man who had smiled and risen
to follow her was a man who might have been her father, no
different from her father, who had been a drunken derelict and
knew that mule deer and that shabby register with its roster of
the damned.

What she found could have been worse. For Compton in his
letter to her had revealed a shocking little story. He said he was
relieved that she had now resolved to drop her search. Clients of
his, he said, who were bent on adopting a little boy had insisted
on knowing who the natural father was.

"The father," Compton wrote, "turned out to be the last man
executed in the state of Washington before capital punishment
was outlawed."

They did not adopt the little boy. Where was he now, do you
suppose, and where was Bobby who had lasted for so short a
time and kept his face turned away from them that day on *The
Virginia Five?*

As far as she was concerned, the book was closed.

5

FRIENDS EXCHANGE GLANCES when one has been unlike oneself.

"You're more like yourself, now," her friends said.

Although her parents were living when she was handed over to the McKinneys, Amy was as vulnerable as a true orphan to the uncertainties, vicissitudes and humiliations. Like a true orphan, she learned early to show gratitude in order to survive. Gratitude is the price you pay. From the moment Miss Lovelace in modified French heels had suggested she was lucky not to have landed in an orphans' home, Amy was grateful to the McKinneys for having spared her that dismal fate — the long halls, the iron cots, the sour smell of mops. The fear of orphans' homes is congenital, the stuff of nightmares in which no father or mother exists to explain away the shadows. Even children with proper parents have such dreams. At seven she knew what an orphans' home was, a place where a child was an object, an object to be clothed and fed as cheaply as possible and taught homely skills to make her at last independent of a society that had stepped in when parents or God failed. But at sixteen, released from such a home, an orphan finds no hiding place, has no sheltering name but one set on her like a hat by the authorities — as once the wandering Jews were assigned names by the German government, and slaves assumed the names of their masters.

And Amy now realized that Miss Lovelace, whose real parents possessed no beach house, must wait to be brought to one as a lucky member of a certain Sunday School class. Miss Lovelace felt bound to humiliate a little girl who quite by accident had access to a beach house, had an intimacy with the drifting fog forbidden to Miss Lovelace — legitimate and flanked by parents though she be.

The ewe tells her own lamb by its smell and rejects the stranger. When you want the ewe whose lamb has died to take an orphan lamb, you dress it in the warm skin of her own dead lamb. Except for the death of their little boy, the McKinneys would not have taken Amy. She was lucky. And it had been easy to be grateful to the McKinneys, to be kind to them as they grew old and forgot things, repeated themselves. She had vowed she would make them proud of her, and she had. They were good, gentle people. But hadn't they, in fact, dressed her in the memory of their own little boy? Hadn't she "grown into" the tricycle and the dinghy?

Amy had learned how shaky the underpinnings, how uncertain the foundations of many a legitimate family. Fathers reject sons. Mothers reject daughters. Or a mother dies, is replaced by a new woman. The children of the dead mother are first outraged, then estranged from the new woman and then from their own father. The new woman takes down pictures, hangs new draperies, puts dear things away in drawers out of sight. From the drawers into the ash can. She invites her own friends to parties.

55

Or, a young woman's son steps out from behind a parked truck and is instantly killed by a speeding car. After the hurried funeral the young woman's family goes its way. Life must go on. For them, anyway. Indeed, the tragedy might even strengthen the grieving young mother, make her strong for future tragedies. Future tragedies there will be. It was Amy who comforted the young mother, sat with her, who put away the little boy's toys, his clothes, the tennis shoes he had worn the day before. Oh, those shoes. She stayed in the house until one day she saw the young woman smile.

Well, then! The family she had dreamed of did not exist, that big, loving, loyal turbulent family who cared more for each other than for anybody else.

What a family that would have been. "Amy must have the heavy silver spoons," that family would have said. "Get them out before we forget."

Dreams. Everybody deals with insecurity. If her own was in not knowing who she was, at least she was financially secure, she had lost no child, had never feared for her job, felt little awkwardness in a roomful of people, had friends, was healthy.

And anyway, *the book was closed.* That was a relief. Hope is a painful emotion and stands between what one is and what one should be. Gratifying to know that now she need no longer think about all that. She understood now why the authorities made it impossible for the adopted child to find her parents. She would have been better off if Dad McKinney had not left that paper behind. She had learned her lesson. She had found her father, found a part of her past. It could have been worse.

Those good McKinneys!

"You're so much more your old self," friends said. "You seemed troubled."

Felt so much better, too. Her life became normal as she shopped with shrewd eyes at the supermarket and had the station wagon tuned up for a trip to the coast. She took a jacket to the tailor's to have rewoven a hole she had burned in it with a cigarette sometime during the days when she had been dreaming away.

She resumed an active correspondence with old friends all over the United States. She wrote on her adoptive father's old L. C. Smith typewriter. His fingers knew those keys. Friends in Texas. Everywhere. Many friends she had not seen in twenty years, nor had their families seen them. Family roots had dried up as the leaves scattered. Distance is destructive to families. A parent scarcely recognizes the child he meets at the airport — beard, mustache, glasses or a new way of doing the hair. The parent remembers one thing and the child another; they had been strangers from the beginning. Why, those with similar lives have more in common than those with a common blood. It is just as well if a child is independent of his family; he learns self-reliance. For each of us is born alone, lives largely within the confines of his own skull, and dies alone.

But then she did an odd thing. She wrote to Compton on notepaper engraved AMY McKINNEY. She had put that paper away on the top shelf of a closet soon after her marriage to Nofzinger and came across it again quite by accident — well, almost quite. She did feel she owed Compton a letter because he had warned her of what she might find. She owed him a description of the Gould Hotel, must tell him that she now realized that inordinate curiosity about the past is bound to lead into dark and twisting paths.

"Dear Mr. Compton . . ."

She had no reason to expect a reply. *The book was closed.*

Then why, in the next few days, did her mind wander to the mailbox and why did it occur to her to drop in at his office? Well, because he was the only link she had with her real family. He must see her as others did not. Compton was the only one on earth who knew her name was Burton.

And wasn't it kind of him to write her — to keep in touch. In him she had possibly found a real friend. She would have him and his wife to dinner and they would all be quite comfortable sitting together at her table sharing a common knowledge, that she who basted the roast and poured out the wine was Amy Burton.

But the brief letter from Compton was hardly what she expected. She stood in the middle of the room. It was early but she poured herself a drink.

"As a friend," he wrote, "maybe I should keep this knowledge to myself. I hate stirring things up. But as a professional man, I must speak out. As your friend again, I've got to let you know. . . ."

The old alcoholic in the Gould Hotel was not her father. The Bureau of Vital Statistics had erred. The Ben Burton whose records they had was a Benson Burton, not Benjamin Burton.

"I believe this matter is extremely sensitive," Compton wrote. "But of course if you wish we can now search on the maternal side."

On the coffee table before her she laid out the cards for solitaire, a habit of hers when she looked for guidance, a habit the sensible McKinneys would have questioned, like a belief in spirits.

Ten minutes later she picked up the telephone.

Two

6

SOME SAID the stranger rode into Jeff Davis Gulch on a sorrel horse. Some said a bay. That high-stepping horse could have been either — a bay horse might look sorrel in the first light, for the sun is already high when it soars up over the Rocky Mountains. But when the sun slides down over the other side, a sorrel horse might look bay. The light fades fast. What does it matter what color the horse was? It matters because a man, looking back, might one day want to start a story with the color of the horse the man rode who brought in news that changed a man's life.

"This fellow rode in on a bay horse . . ."

The man got him a room in the nearly empty Placer House and ate his supper there. Later on he was seen talking and laughing with one of the whores.

It was the three whores who left town first. For some time they had been quarreling among themselves, raising their voices, abusing one another with such words as they used. One said there wasn't enough gold in the whole damned Gulch to make it worth rolling over. She was the good-looker. The two plain ones sat beside their windows over the boardwalk and tapped on the glass with their fake diamond rings. Gold was so scarce some men wondered if sex was worth the price of a sack of spuds.

The stage rattled in not two hours after the stranger rode away next morning on that horse. When it pulled out, all three whores were on it with whatever duds they had and such little things as they'd picked up here and there.

"Leesburg," the man on the horse was said to have said. "Up around Leesburg."

Leesburg was seventy miles over the mountains.

Next to pull up stakes were the newcomers who hadn't tied themselves down with a cabin. They just picked up their tools, folded their tents and lit out with a packhorse. Didn't even look back.

Then first one and then another cabin was left empty. The packrats moved in from outside and turned their heads this way and that, suspicious of the silence. By and by they began to search for shiny trinkets, a bit of tin, a coin, a thimble, for glitter dazzled their tiny brains.

Chip Hartley, the saloonkeeper, loaded what remained of his booze into his spring wagon and picked up his carbine to protect it from needy whites and Indians. After that it wasn't a week before the store closed down — there wasn't trade enough within fifty miles to support it. Eggs had dropped from a dollar to two bits apiece, and Fred Meany, the storekeeper, was tearassed because the bastards had hightailed it so fast they hadn't paid their tabs. He had their worthless paper on hand because he, like them, had believed in the Gulch, but shit. When you got right down to it, the Gulch right from the start promised more than it delivered, always just enough pay dirt to keep a man a-hoping. Hope was more powerful medicine than booze, and left a wicked hangover.

Fred Meany knew damned well that what cheese he had on hand would spoil on the way out, that damned sun around noon, so he'd a left it to the rats except for a fellow name of Sweringen, tall, quiet fellow, looked something like your late Mr. Lincoln, full beard and eyes not like other people's, slanted like a Chinaman's, but the opposite of a Chinaman's, slanted not down but up, you see. Meany knew eyes. Sweringen had kind eyes, kind when he looked at his wife and the two young ones, the boy maybe ten, the girl maybe eight? Meany had eyes, himself. The young ones would be sashaying around in the sagebrush looking for flints and agates and arrowheads as young ones will sometimes. Damnedest thing — the gophers and rabbits and sage hens, even the killdeer down by the creek weren't afraid of those young ones. Sometimes you hear of that. These kids walked hand in hand up the side of the hill where their paw hacked away in the tall sagebrush with pick and shovel. They'd be picking Indian paintbrushes and shooting stars. Bluebells in the spring. Another father would have seen to it that a boy that age helped out with pick and shovel, but it appeared that Sweringen believed the boy would have long enough later on to be a man with a man's worries and a man's work and had a right then to look back on a time when life was hunting pretty things. Flowers pretty up a cabin and it was nice to think that later on, whatever happened, that little girl would love her brother and by and by when the boy had a little girl of his own, he would love her and she would love him. Meany understood a thing or two.

Mrs. Sweringen, the woman, the wife, had a real pretty voice and she'd be singing those old hymns, and him, too, and he'd read out of the Bible because of course no regular church there. Oh, time to time a preacher'd ride in on a swaybacked nag and shout up hell's fire in the saloon for an hour; sky pilot, they called him. Chip Hartley'd open up to him, close down the bar, open up to the preacher and the Lord, kind of a fire insurance for Hartley, say, because Hartley said about the Life Beyond, you never can tell. But more like a regular entertainment than church, preacher telling about going to hell, as if they didn't know that, except maybe George Sweringen. So Meany carried the cheese over to the Sweringens and he got Sweringen aside.

"Call me a liar if you want, George," Hartley said, "but I figure you're making a mistake hanging on here."

"There's room in life for mistakes," George Sweringen said.

"Excuse me, George, but not much room when a man gets our age." It's a harsh thing to remind a man he's getting on, but Meany felt he had to speak. He'd a said the same to his own brother. And he spoke coldly, now, as a man will. "You're a good man, George, and I wish the best for your lady and the young ones."

"I won't soon forget your words," Sweringen said.

Oh, the rest of them, the half a thousand, had all been young, twenty, thirty. Hadn't any responsibilities, not yet even to their own hearts. For most of them it was the chasing after the gold that counted, not the finding. But Sweringen must have been forty-five, and old for that age. Meany had him sized up as a man who had consulted his stars, the lines in his hands and his God and had accepted his death not many years off and was often lost in thought about how to best use his few remaining years. He'd watch those kids of his with those blue, blue eyes. A man forty-five, taking the long chance of striking it. If he didn't strike it, he'd be an old man who looked back with sadness on his days. A man shouldn't get married so late.

"Then, so long, George," Meany said and held out his hand.

Meany didn't look back as he drove out of the Gulch. He didn't want to see George Sweringen standing in that lonesome place where everybody had failed. The hot August wind began to whisper in the sagebrush. Son of a *bitch!*

Looked like Meany was right.

The little girl, Nora, was sick that winter. A diet of spuds and root vegetables and not much venison and the awful, awful cold. You could hear it, smell it. The little girl needed milk. George Sweringen rode a hundred miles across the mountains. He hired a man to haul in hay. He bought a milk cow and led her back, stopping at this place and that to let her feed. By and by the little girl got all right. Now again she made fine progress in the Second McGuffey Reader. The boy Thomas was finishing the Fourth and was into the Eclectic Spelling Book with hard words like, say, eclectic, and what it meant — to pick out, to choose the best. That book taught truths as well, truths that lead men and women along paths of goodness; the truth that impatience is a costly vice; that physical beauty isn't to be proud of, and can be downright dangerous to him who has it and to him who sees it; that nothing lasts but Love and God.

George Sweringen taught them to write a good, firm hand, and to sign their names with pride. He taught them their sums. Already Thomas had learned some algebra. A boy must know later on that the product of the means is equal to the product of the extremes — he must know how to solve the single Unknown. George Sweringen looked on his wife and children with a full heart. He wanted much for them, but no more, he thought, than any man wants. He knew that Lizzie wanted nothing but to be with him and the children, although one time she said how she admired a Paisley shawl a woman wore, came into a room wearing it, and he wanted for her a watch of solid gold to pin at her breast. The children would want things beyond his craziest dreams, so was the world changing. Nora, so pretty she could be excused for a little vanity, wanted a looking glass and comb and brush all matching. Later on she was bound to learn it is not the face but the heart that matters.

Thomas wished for something equally disturbing. He wanted a violin, a fiddle. George Sweringen hoped that didn't foretell that kind of future. Thomas had stood near the saloon to hear the music inside, the man playing the fiddle, and one of the women at the piano. It is best not to judge. Lizzie did not cross the street when one of them was about to pass. Lizzie said, "Good morning." Lizzie made people feel better.

Thomas might have wished for a set of tools, for a saddle, or a rifle.

When the water ran in the creek again, when the bluebells pushed up close to the tall sagebrush, George Sweringen went to work again. He turned the water back into the sluice box; day after day he hauled down earth from the hillside in the wheelbarrow and shoveled it in, and what was heaviest lodged against the riffles in the box. What was heaviest was almost always only sand, only sand. And it was not sand that bought fertile land along the river down in the valley, that land always behind his eyes, the land he dreamed of when he stepped out of doors some starry nights. On windy nights if the wind was right, he could smell the clover down there, brought in on the mist. The smell of that clover was heartbreaking, and mocking like the impalpable end of the rainbow.

Twice again the bluebells pushed up under the sheltering sagebrush. Seven hundred suns rose and set, seven hundred moons drifted.

One morning Lizzie Sweringen looked out the window and saw her husband walking down the hill without his wheelbarrow, without his tools. She knew he had made a decision; she knew that when a man, or a woman, is near fifty it is harder to make decisions: when you are younger it doesn't much matter what you do, but the time comes when you are in the middle of things, you see this before you and that behind you in a kind of balance and it cripples you. You weigh this against that, the past against the future.

When you love a man, you know by how he touches you, and where, that he has made a decision, but first you know because of how a man walks, how he wears his shoulders.

Now, what can a woman do but foresee disappointment and failure, and declare when the time comes that "all things pass," as indeed they do. But the time comes when at last there are no more things to pass. However, Lizzie drew up in her mind a list of disappointments endured — for none of them was a failure, none attributable to a lack in her husband, but simply acts of God. She believed that eventually God looks smiling on a good man who tries so hard.

In touching her husband she would remind him of their first son, stillborn, of the fire in Illinois that had destroyed the tin shop; he had taken that for a sign they should move on west. Except for his careful savings, they'd never have made this try at the diggings. Well, it hadn't worked out.

She could not suppress a lump in her throat, lodged there partly because those four walls had been home, but mostly because of George. She turned her thoughts to practical matters. She must now decide what was worth taking away with them. Her husband's set of razors, one for each day of the week, and tidy in their leather-covered box. Her mother's chamberstick of brass and the candle molds George himself had made. His buckskin-covered Bible. Nora's doll with the china head. Thomas's fiddle he had last summer made from a cigar box, the bow an arch of willow strung with combings from the saddle horse. And the horse itself. George would turn it loose, and the cow, poor bossy. But in the late spring both might survive and fall into the hands of strangers, kind people, she hoped. But now George must go down into the valley and hire the stage. It no longer called at the Gulch.

Some disappointments are easier over a pot of coffee; she had

67

come to look with affection on that old pot. She touched her cheek where she knew he would touch it, and drew the old blue pot back over the heat. With the little gold he'd found he could set up shop elsewhere. People need pots and pans.

He must see that what he had had, what he had done without, had made him a good man.

She laid out the two tin cups.

He stood framed in the low doorway, so low he had to stoop to enter. "George," she said, "I've been thinking."

"But I never got beyond those words," she told again and again later on when there were those around to call her Grandmother and, when her old legs began to fail, to help her down into the garden when she wanted to smell her sweet peas. "Those tin cups never got filled that time. He spoke so quietly I hardly heard him! But in a moment I knew he had said, 'Lizzie, I found it.' "

7

QUITE A LONG TIME ago a determined young woman named Emma Russell said goodbye to her determined father at a railroad station in Illinois. She would never again walk in that lazy town, never again smell the Mississippi River. Her father, a Civil War captain with a fine record for discipline, was the warden of the prison. He had only to look at you. Emma had a look, too.

She had a normal school education, excelled in elocution, English and mathematics; she was dependent on nobody.

Some in the world can't imagine their own failure. Yours, yes, but not theirs. She would teach school in Idaho Territory, Idaho, Gem of the Mountains. That had a ring to it! If the German woman her father was bound to marry meant more to him than his daughter and the memory of his dead wife, she must go. She was surprised at him. Thought he had more common sense. Remarriage was an indulgence. He was no longer young. But that was a man for you.

His beard was trimmed. He saw no reason why he must go a widower into old age, have no one to warm his bed.

He coughed. She was a strong young woman.

Then the tracks hummed with the magnificence of the approaching train.

"Goodbye, Paw," she said.

"Goodbye, Emma," he said. They touched cheeks. Neither flinched. "You'll do well," he said.

"Indeed I will," she said. "Write, and I'll write."

He moved his hand to touch her. He couldn't believe she would leave, but he did believe.

She boarded the train with her sturdy leather luggage. When the train pulled away, she took a copy of the *Atlantic Monthly* from the Gladstone bag.

"Sometime during the middle of the second night out," she later told her grandson, "the train stopped out there on the prairie. Nobody knew why. So I stepped down off the train and smelled the sagebrush. You know how it smells after a little rain. I looked up at the millions of stars. You can't look up at the western stars and be much concerned with your own death. We're all a part of things, dead or alive. And then for the first time in my life, I heard a nighthawk dive. It was as if Someone had cast a cord across the heavens and tightened it like a fiddle string, and plucked it."

Her grandson, Thomas Burton, never forgot that.

For two years she taught in a one-room school, sod roof, sturdy black wood stove with a kettle of water on it that simmered away and moistened the dry winter air. At noon she brewed herself a cup of tea. Slate blackboard. Colored map so old more than half the country consisted of territories, not states. Fruit jar on her desk for the wild flowers the girls brought her. Privies for boys and girls, well separated, out back and a shed for saddle horses. She rode, too. Bought a chunky black gelding from the man in the family in whose house she boarded and roomed, half Percheron, half Standardbred. So many women out there rode astride with their divided skirts, but she preferred a sidesaddle. Looked better for a woman. Women and men are not alike. Each has powers.

She was strict. They said she had eyes in the back of her head, that she saw around corners. She seemed to sit at her desk long after she left her chair. Before her the guilty stammered the truth; and the innocent recalled with icy clarity earlier transgressions. Her rectitude was chilling, but she played lively tunes on the piano for dances in one ranch house or another.

The young man who played the fiddle was the son of a man who had discovered gold, who had had the gumption to put his money in land instead of kiting off when the gold failed. She had no use for rolling stones.

She wondered that a young man should play the fiddle and so well, as if it mattered; but he had a thousand head of Durham cattle and he laughed when she spoke of her interest in sheep because everybody in the Lemhi Valley knew you couldn't run sheep and cattle on the same range — sheep grazed the land so close they destroyed the roots. She thought about his laughter.

He paid her little attention apart from asking her to sound her A. A dozen young women were after him, rolling their eyes this way and that, cinching in their middles and pretending to be helpless, and all the time seeing themselves riding about the Lemhi Valley in a Studebaker surrey behind high-stepping Hambletonians. Didn't he see through them?

Men see what they want to see. They were all prettier than she, who was never pretty. Years later her own children remarked that Mama was never pretty, but they meant it as a compliment: she didn't have to depend on looks.

No, Thomas Sweringen had no need to make a hasty choice; it was pleasanter for him, when he laid down his fiddle, to dance with this one and that one of those scheming girls while she thumped out the tunes he danced to. It made her blood boil. The pretense, the flattery.

She refused to think of it. Some are born pretty; some with brains. She would not think of it.

He was tall and lean, with a way of putting on his hat as if it didn't matter; he had three hats that she knew of. His fingers arched and stretched on the neck of that fool fiddle, as if he loved it. His eyes had a strange shape; his high cheekbones were a Slav's or an Indian's.

School began again. By the river the willows turned a rusty red; smoke from far forest fires trailed over the mountains. But excitement was in the air: Idaho had just become a state. President Harrison journeyed out to Boise for the signing of the constitution and he was said to have been very pleased with how everything looked. The Glee Club was on hand from the university and sang the state song, the words yet unknown to anybody else, but they recognized the tune, "Maryland, My Maryland," a good choice because everybody already knew it and "Idaho, My Idaho" fits right in.

Governor Shoup himself urged those who believed themselves artistic to submit designs for a State Seal.

Even school children were included in the rites of Statehood and it was they, district by district, who chose the syringa as the State Flower — or it was said they chose it. Her own pupils had chosen the bluebell for the very good reason that the bluebell was the first up in the spring; and she doubted that any child, anywhere, would choose a flower with so ugly a name as "syringa," even if he could spell it.

Why, the excitement filtered right on down to the man next door. You might have thought that Statehood had some mystical significance. People seemed to think they were in for a sobering change, that they stood on the threshold of a world so altered that in years to come they must sometimes pause, perhaps looking into a mirror at an older face, trying to recall the structure and the meaning of those earlier days.

Statehood appeared to be an excuse for many parties that fall.

One evening she sat in a house she had never before entered. She had been bidden to have dinner, and later on to play bezique. She didn't think much of social card playing — not because it was immoral, Lord knows, and anyway people's morals are their own blamed business — but because cards were a sad waste of time. A game of solitaire was a different matter: you played it to settle something in your mind, and you played it against yourself — your other self, your only significant adversary. The poet Walter Savage Landor put it very well indeed:

I strove with none, for none was worth my strife . . .

It meant little to test yourself against another. It was only one's own self who could settle one's own hash.

She had learned to play bezique because the nice old couple with whom she boarded were restless on winter evenings. They were not of a thoughtful turn of mind, nor did they read or play an instrument. They pined for their card-playing daughter who, having married, had elected to desert them, since the new husband's business was in the state of California.

And ah-ha! She was pretty good at bezique! She had a good memory and could sense in an opponent's discard what he was holding back.

It was a pleasant party in that house — crisp chicken and plenty of good rich gravy for the biscuits.

And there she met the mother of Thomas Sweringen, who sat across the card table. The lady — and lady she was — was a widow, and about her shoulders was the handsomest Paisley shawl you ever laid eyes on. Her hands were narrow, long-fingered like her son's.

"I believe you know my son," the lady said.

73

"I do indeed. He plays the fiddle well."

"He loves his fiddle. Would you be so kind, and come to supper with us?"

That evening Emma Russell looked long at herself in a mirror, perhaps for the last time. Ever afterwards she believed there was a plot against her, that she was part of a plan, that Thomas's mother had detected something in her that Thomas needed, that his dead father would have wanted her for his son, that his mother had said, "She is what your father would have wanted for you." Certain families are liable to make such plans, and certain others are likely to take advantage of them.

But to tell the truth, she did love Thomas, and he had a great deal she wanted. *He* was the beginning of *her* plans.

And so they were married and one night everybody came with food and drink and a banging on pots and pans and charivaried them.

As a joke — because he did remember — he gave her two sheep for her birthday. He remembered birthdays and everybody remembered his. And by that time their first child was born, Elizabeth. Beth. By the time their fifth child was born, a boy, Tom-Dick, she owned seven thousand head of sheep and it didn't seem to her that a house with a sod roof and muslin under the ceiling to keep the dirt from drifting down was the place to rear children, so she caused to be built a house of sandstone with six bedrooms. Downstairs was a library, for she had long since had all her books shipped out from Illinois, all now behind glass in sectional cases and not read again because there was never time to read. There were electric lights; sconces with fluted globes sprouted from the walls; chandeliers hung from the high ceilings. For some years the electric lights worked, and from up and down the Lemhi Valley the curious arrived on horseback and in buggies to see the sixteen-volt bulbs glowing.

The house was piped for water, but the tub, the toilet, the handbasin and the sink in the kitchen remained dry. A water pump was never installed. Anyway, to abandon the hand pump out front was a radical break with a past that had been kind. Water or not, the *Recorder Herald*, published in Salmon, the county seat thirty miles down the river, described the house as "palatial," and everybody came to a party.

Two years later, in 1909, the railroad came in over the Continental Divide from Montana, and down in the town of Salmon they celebrated.

"The Salmon City Band came," said the *Recorder Herald*, "with a soulful blow of voluptuous music, and the thousand people present felt like the Fourth of July."

It was assumed that the Gilmore & Pittsburgh railroad — the G&P — would do great things. It would open up the world to the Lemhi Valley; the price of land would shoot up. Freight rates would go down. Friends could be visited. Only scoffers repeated the story that a traveling salesman had once asked Andy Burnham, the conductor, if he couldn't go any faster and Andy said yes, but he had orders to stay with the train. And suppose it *was* slow — wasn't it pleasant to take a box lunch along and look out the windows and sit and visit with strangers and to share an orange? You could go into the toilet and by the time you were through in there you might have covered several miles. Suppose the train did get stuck in the snow on this or that side of the tunnel at the summit? Wasn't that an experience to savor — eight thousand feet in the air and the night coming down and lamps to light?

Emma Russell Sweringen now had ten thousand head of sheep; a journalist dubbed her the Sheep Queen of Idaho. Printed in the *Salt Lake Tribune* was a picture of her riding in the baggage car of the G&P. She sat on a coffin. There was no place else to sit. She is quite heavy now. In her hand and in the hands of those around her are tin cups, for Andy Burnham kept a pot of coffee on the stove for people he knew. Strange how Fate returns us to the same stage and the same director but hands us a different script. On that train a few years later the Sheep Queen held a dying child in her arms.

Thomas Sweringen was not troubled that he sat at his wife's right at the table, that her foreman sat opposite her. He disliked routine and was often late for meals; his absence was not so conspicuous if he was not sitting at the head of the table; he could slip in and out. He might have been out riding or walking; when he walked he carried one or another of several walking sticks he had fashioned from carefully chosen cottonwood or aspen. So his children and grandchildren and then even his great-grandchildren remembered him as he walked with them to their cars, their Appersons and then their Franklins and finally their Chryslers and their Cadillacs, and forever they saw him in their mind's eye as they had seen him in their rear-view mirrors, one of those old sticks raised in a benediction of farewell. At least one of his grandchildren began to carry a walking stick early on, and he carried it when he walked with his children and then his grandchildren out to the garage and he hoped they would remember him as he remembered his grandfather, in the rear-view mirror.

Thomas Sweringen might have been out hunting arrowheads with eyes that could spot and identify an animal on the side of a hill a mile away. He might have been out fishing or visiting the Indians at the agency. In him, the Indians saw something of themselves, a stoicism. He was not so much close to nature as a part of it, of the water in the streams and of the trout that waited just under the lip of the bank for the unsuspecting dragonfly. His affection for the Indians he passed on to Beth, his eldest daughter. As a child she raced with them on her own

76

cayuse; from them she learned which berries to eat and which not, how to smoke salmon, and where the Indians buried their dead.

Nor did it trouble him that the world looked on the ranch as his wife's, not his. She made the hard decisions and dickered with the wool buyers. His mother had told his bride long ago, "Thomas isn't like other men. He needs more sleep." The Sheep Queen had thought first by example and then by insistence she could get him out of bed when other men got out of bed, but he was fluid, slipped between her fingers, and at last she laughed and gave up and their life was pleasant together. They did a lot of quiet laughing. They liked to get their hands on their children and grandchildren. They got their hands on the great-grandchildren.

He wanted his children to be happy. She wanted them to be a success.

The mother of a beautiful daughter has the right to expect she will marry well, marry a man who is certain who his great-grandfather was, who is stable and adoring, will provide flat sterling service for twelve, jewelry to excite envy, and money for the proper shoes because if the shoes aren't right the whole costume is awry. He will provide a house as a proper display case and will bring his wife home for Christmas. He will be liked by the family who will consider him one of them. He will sit a horse well.

If the daughter is a truly great beauty, the mother's expectations are boundless, especially if that daughter has been educated at a private Episcopal school where she has learned to be not unfamiliar with the stylish French tongue, can paint a still life of bread and fruit, has a stunning handwriting, walks in a special light and sits a saddle like a princess. Such a girl was Beth Sweringen.

When the railroad came through, it was preceded by young surveyors, college men who had read Owen Wister's *Virginian* and like Wister had long thoughts of big skies, tall timber and rolling prairies. Out there beyond the Mississippi, beyond even the Red River, they could test their manhood; if the test proved unfair, there was Tuxedo Park or the Berkshires.

Among these young men were several who did not expect to meet out there the Girl of the Golden West, whose family was quite as important in the state of Idaho as theirs back East where their father's grounds might be reckoned in acres, while the Sweringen Ranch was reckoned in sections of six hundred and forty acres each.

One of these young men was ardent; his sister was sent out West to investigate, and investigate she did. The Sheep Queen's daughter was pronounced more than suitable. She was not only a great beauty; she had been presented at Court in Ottawa.

As for the Sheep Queen, she had long since decided her wedding gift to her daughter would be a sum of money and a Steinway piano, since the Chickering on which Beth had learned to play Schumann and Chopin was some years old and anyway should remain on the ranch because Beth would be back Christmases. The young man had made his proposal and had been accepted by the Sheep Queen, if not so warmly by Thomas, and by Beth. All was well.

The young man left the valley on the now-completed railroad to go East to have a house designed and built and to staff it with servants.

In the Lemhi Valley was a round of parties, young ladies and young men coming in from around the state, some of them by motorcar and some by train. The train was still a novelty and the Sheep Queen preferred it to the Model T Ford that Thomas had bought to see if there was anything to this automobile craze, and it was the train she and Beth took down to Salmon for a shower to be given by a Mrs. Melvin who published the *Recorder Herald* after her second husband, an unpleasant man, had been gored to death by a Jersey bull.

The G&P had published an unreasonably strict schedule and did not follow it; the train would stop anywhere to pick up passengers if the engineer or the conductor knew them, and therefore it was wise to call neighbors up or down the valley to ask if they had seen the train pass and how fast it was going.

On the day of the Melvin shower the train was comfortably far off and would arrive at two instead of noon so there was plenty of time to dress and then walk across the field where the train would stop because the Sheep Queen wanted it to.

"Mama, have you your gloves?"

"Gloves, Beth? What do I want with gloves this time of year?"

"The ladies will be wearing them."

"Let them. I have no reason to hide my hands. Anyway, you can't make a silk purse out of a sow's ear."

"Mama."

"Beth, I have no gloves."

"Mama, I gave you gloves at Christmas."

"Why so you did."

The Sheep Queen routinely misplaced objects that did not appeal to her, a way of saying she stored them in the library where all the books were that she no longer read. Over the years the library had become so cluttered and piled with foreign bodies that it was almost impossible to reach the telephone on the wall: saddles that had come to rest there instead of in the barn, a brace of pheasant skins somebody had meant to stuff and mount, Indian saddlebags of thick buckskin embroidered with dyed porcupine quills of red, yellow and green; a broad-brimmed Mexican sombrero once worn by Thomas Sweringen to a masked costume ball, but he was recognized by the way he danced; boxes of dried fruit and soda crackers, ailing furniture on the last stop before the dump on the side of the hill where there were so many rattlesnakes; branding irons, canned milk and cases of the slick, flinty peaches preferred by the Sheep Queen's sheepherders; boxes of tallow candles and drums of kerosene for the lamps that had replaced the electric lights that no longer worked. In the library she was likely to get side-tracked; she paused to read old letters, to wonder again if anybody on earth could do anything about her old beaver coat, to consider old snapshots; she shuffled through Christmas cards and wondered what had become of time.

"Mama, we're going to miss the train."

"The train will wait. I told Andy last week I wanted it today."

"You've found your gloves?"

"I was about to look."

"Mama."

"Beth, you Sweringens are so impatient about things that don't matter and so tolerant of things that do." Thomas was tolerant and his sister Nora was tolerant and so were the girls. She didn't know but for her what would happen to any of them. Alone among them, her son had something of steel about him.

But at last she walked with her beautiful Beth across the horse pasture with their purses and their gloves; the wild roses were a-bloom along the barbwire fence; the alfalfa in the next field was getting a good start — and yes, that was a rattlesnake, all right. Behind her was the big stone house and the handsome new barn which was even bigger. In it, protected by the best of lightning rods, was her husband, checking over the harness for the coming haying season. Everything but the wild roses and the rattlesnake was her creation.

"Beth," she said, "I don't see how you walk in shoes like that," and felt a queer pleasure that Beth could walk in them. At

St. Margaret's School Beth had been taught to walk correctly in various shoes because for some women there are various shoes for various occasions. Of her own shoes little could be said, only that they were wide but not wide enough. Not even comfortable. At forty her feet troubled her. She was too heavy; she must get around to doing something; why could she not be trim like the rest of them? But it was lovely to have such a daughter who understood shoes and was about to marry well.

Far up the track the train whistled and then in a little while the rails began to hum.

The train slowed and stopped. Many curious eyes looked down. Andy the conductor stepped down with a metal stool.

"How are you there, Mrs. Sweringen? And here's my little Beth!" Small civilities passed. How many antelope had Andy seen on the trip over the hill? And elk? Yes, there were still deep drifts on the Montana side piled against the snow fences but the grass was greening. Good to see Old Sol climbing higher and higher. Going to a party in Salmon, were they? Yes, Andy had heard of the engagement. You hear everything quick enough in this valley, don't you? "My goodness, Beth," Andy said. "You know you have my good wishes."

"Andy, you're a dear."

The Sheep Queen admired her daughter's ability to please simple people without allowing them to come too close. They, on their part, took no liberties with her. You can't beat money and education and knowing about shoes and gloves.

"Two months before Beth leaves," the Sheep Queen said. "They'll marry at the church in Salmon. I'm having his people out."

His people. She had done her own checking. The president of the G&P had come from Pittsburgh and now lived in Salmon.

He was a close friend and knew a thing or two about who was who in Pittsburgh.

"I hear tell of a honeymoon in New York City," Andy said. "East side, west side, all around the town. That about it, Beth?"

"That's about it, Andy."

"Always wanted to go up in the Statue of Liberty," Andy said. "Hear you can go up and look out through the eyes."

Up ahead the engine sighed.

The passenger coach was crowded. Few even among those who could afford motorcars drove over the Divide; in places the road was so steep that the stagecoach, while it still ran, dragged logs behind it to keep it from running over the horses; mere brakes would not hold.

There was, in fact, but one vacant seat, but already a dozen men were on their feet, for this was the Sheep Queen of Idaho and her fabled daughter.

A face caught her eye; she stood suddenly amazed, alert as a beast to danger from some yet unknown quarter. She could smell it. Yes, the young man who rose beside the one empty seat was handsome beyond belief. The Arrow Collar Man whose likeness appeared with tiresome regularity each week in the *Saturday Evening Post* faded before this stranger. Except for Thomas, she did not care for even ordinarily handsome men; they have an air about them even as children on a playground. They are likely to trade on their looks, to accept favors without deserving or asking for them. Plain people courted them, made fools of themselves. It is a different thing with women; except for women like her who had been given brains instead, looks are a woman's stock in trade.

She darted a glance at Beth and then back to the impossible stranger. For a moment she was confused, partly by the apparition of male beauty which spoke to something in her she thought she had shed long ago and partly because the car lurched and she feared losing her footing. She would have died before she would have let him help her up. As she was standing so close to him, it would have been pointedly rude to reject his offer of his seat, and to reject it would in a sense show him that for a moment he had a power over the woman in her. He might even interpret it as coyness. No doubt he had often exercised that power over women. Certainly he was the male counterpart of Beth, his profile as startling, features as compelling, so you might say once and for all, "Well, there you are."

He wore no wedding band.

"Madam?" he said. "Won't you please?"

She had been called Ma'am many times. Her sheepherders Ma'amed her, storekeepers Ma'amed her, pupils had Ma'amed her. Never before Madam. Never in that voice. She couldn't place his accent, but his voice was tuned like an instrument.

And she allowed herself to be bowed into the seat beside the window. She and then Beth sat down. Now, had the young man the manners he pretended to, he would have moved on down the car and sat on the narrow bench beside the stove. For heaven's sake, there was no fire in the stove. But he did not. He thought his presence wanted. Smiling a smile she could feel touch her skin, he spoke again. "What a beautiful part of the world this is," he said. "Nature has been lavish. You would be the Sweringens."

"Not only would be," she said, "but are." So he wanted to play games with the subjunctive.

He shook his head, the smile intact, painted. "We hadn't got through the tunnel on top before they all began a little betting. Some bet you'd be waiting here and some wondered if we'd get to see you walking across the fields. My name is Burton."

His grandfather, he said, his grandfather the judge, had been a friend of Benjamin Harrison's, and that's why he was Benjamin Harrison Burton. He himself had been born the year Harrison took office. He removed from his pocket that tinkled with loose silver a gold coin, probably gold-filled only, that bore in bas-relief the bearded profile of Benjamin Harrison, a coin struck, he said, at the time of Harrison's inaugural.

He was now sitting on the arm of the red plush seat; the fabric of his stylish clothing at one point touched the blue velvet of Beth's suit. Why on earth, the Sheep Queen wondered, had she allowed herself to be shown the seat beside the window. She didn't give a hang if his clothes touched *her* garments.

He understood from talk roundabout that Miss Sweringen had gone away to school? "There's nothing," he said, "like seeing different parts of the world." Had she, in school, been interested in dramatics?

"She was in several plays there, yes," the Sheep Queen said.

"Just little parts, I'm afraid," Beth said.

"It's precisely the little parts," Burton said, "that are the hardest to play. You know — make them memorable?"

Precisely!

He might have been an actor. Perhaps he was.

"I'm afraid I wasn't awfully good," Beth said.

Now Burton turned to the Sheep Queen; he smiled as if he had accepted her as his confidante. "What is it," he asked, "that is so appealing in modesty?"

"I'm quite certain neither you nor I would know," the Sheep Queen said.

He hardly listened. She felt his brief attention to her move like a draft to Beth. "I should have loved to have seen you onstage," he said. "I truly would have, Miss Sweringen." He spoke the words "Miss Sweringen" as if he tasted them. He himself had been interested in amateur theatricals. Shakespeare, chiefly. Some Congreve, some Dekker. "You would have been charming as Portia. When you turn — your profile, you know?" He turned a moment. "I take great stock in profiles,

84

Mrs. Sweringen," he said. "And I take great stock in hands. Mrs. Sweringen, do you believe in the lines in the palm of the hand?"

"I believe in hands," the Sheep Queen said. "Yes, I believe in hands. I do not believe that the lines in the hands foretell what a person will be. I believe in what hands can do. I believe that with your hands you can make whatever you like of yourself."

Burton inclined his head in a certain way and nodded. "Well put," he said as if he had received a correct answer. "All too often we judge by the wrong facts."

The train had long since passed the mud and timber fort where old George Sweringen had once defended his family against the Nez Percé Indians. Then carelessly young Burton proceeded to destroy his image — as Beth might see it, anyway. It was an image that might fool some fool woman who thought she could change a man.

At sixteen, he said, he had shipped as a cabin boy to Siberia. This ring he wore, this stone in this ring had come from there. He held out his hand for them to see. "Vladivostok," he said. Further, he had been for some time in the circus. God alone knew what he had done there — cleaning up after the animals? And now? Now he was with a fine company selling a fine line of merchandise. "You know, Mrs. Sweringen, how hard it is to keep food? From spoiling? My company has solved the spoilage problem. We draw out the moisture from both fruits and vegetables. Without moisture, you see, they can't spoil. It's the water, you see. You know that already — raisins and dried apricots and so on. Prunes. We apply this process to all fruits and vegetables, including berries. You have only to soak the product in water — and there you are. My firm is Everfresh Products."

Everybody in the car was listening; he had charmed the car to silence, rambling on about dried turnips in that Shakespeare voice of his, that circus voice. She knew about circus people,

85

the lives they led, the looseness and the tinsel. In such a voice he might have introduced sideshow freaks. A young drummer now on the prowl and thank God there was the railroad station on the outskirts of Salmon. Never had she been so glad to see a building.

She was first on her feet, her purse in her hands. She had not removed her gloves, neither knowing nor caring whether you removed them when traveling on a train. She glanced at Beth. Beth was wearing only one glove. What significance had that?

"Beth, where is your other glove?"

"My other glove? Oh!" Beth cried out in an artificial voice most unlike her own, and there was a pretty confusion, an unnecessary confusion that cries out for the help of a man.

The three of them now stood. And then young Burton stooped and retrieved the white kid glove from the floor of the car. He seemed not so much to have stooped as to have bowed; he might have worn and removed a plumed hat as he swept towards the floor. Now he began to hand over the glove, his head bowed, and when he thought the Sheep Queen's head was turned, he brushed it with his lips.

Many had expected Mrs. Melvin to have changed in looks or attitude — at least for a little while — after her husband had been gored by the bull, but she had not; at the core of her personality was a gentle acceptance. She knew that sooner or later something happens to husbands and that a woman prepares herself unconsciously for a husband's passing. By what means he passes is of no great significance. She had been forward-looking as well, had trained herself in the newspaper business even before he had gone into the pasture that morning — it almost seemed she had expected something untoward in the near future. Forward-looking, too, in her clever gathering of dormant forsythia from the big yard behind her house in Salmon. Now it

86

bloomed many weeks too early and in precocious golden splendor in her house for Beth Sweringen's shower like thousands of perfect butterflies posed for flight.

"How lovely!" and "What an idea!" were on many lips, and now it was understood why for some weeks Mrs. Melvin had not entertained, not wishing to expose her secret flowers. All the ladies were there, the brooding Rocky Mountains beyond the windows a strange, somehow disapproving background for the pretty frivolous clothes and the dainty talk. All the ladies, not just the ladies from the old landed families who had once been frightened by the Nez Percé uprising and remembered the first discovery of gold. There would not have been enough of them to make a good showing at a shower. The new ladies were there, too, whose husbands were in business, but although times were changing rapidly the new ladies understood and accepted their position. When two ladies of about the same age, one of an old family and another of the new, approached an open door at about the same time, the new lady slowed down a bit and allowed the other to pass through first. For it was understood that however successful a husband's business might be, Salmon Feed and Seed, the Red Cross Pharmacy, the Ford Automobile Agency or even the State Bank and Trust, business was but the fantasy of some man's imagination and might vanish like a puff of smoke. The land, on the other hand, was eternal.

Nora, the Sheep Queen's sister-in-law, was there, looking the twin of her brother, the same high cheekbones, the deliberate movements, the lean figure. Nora ate whatever she cared to without gaining a pound; she had an annoying habit of pausing in the middle of a meal, putting aside her utensils and sitting there with her hands folded. Resting, she said. Like Thomas, she was tolerant of everything and everybody and had indeed married a Southerner, a doctor who admitted of having once fought a duel. As the daughter of a Civil War captain, the Sheep Queen was suspicious of Southerners; their voices alone set them apart; they talked like darkies. She could not imagine why they would wish to talk so and why they allowed themselves to react to such primitive feelings as revenge. She would have preferred that her husband had no sister. It is easier without in-laws. Nora called her brother "Brother" in a gentle, possessive voice that underlined their relationship, their closeness as children, making it clear that Thomas was not the Sheep Queen's alone but was part of a tribe that had existed and flourished long before she had set foot in the state of Idaho. It pained her that Nora and Beth were close, that Beth was quite a different person with Nora. You might have said they were girls together with their silly secrets.

"What were you telling Nora over there?" she asked Beth. "I saw you just talking away."

"Nothing really, Mama. She was saying how Marcia and Laura wanted to come today but they are too young, and how interested they are now in boys. Marcia wants to start sweeping her hair up."

"I don't doubt it." Nora was left-handed and had a special pair of scissors to accommodate that handicap. The Sheep Queen believed that if a child is left-handed he should be trained to be right-handed, like the rest of the world, and not encouraged with special left-handed scissors. "Nora seemed interested in what you were saying."

"She wondered if she ought to let Marcia sweep her hair up. I was simply saying that at St. Margaret's some girls sixteen were beginning to sweep their hair up in the afternoons."

"You seemed to be going on at some length."

"Yes, and she asked if we won't stay the night with her and Uncle Doctor."

"Where else would we stay?" How like Nora to extend an invitation where one wasn't needed and to extend it to a young woman barely out of boarding school while her mother stood in the room.

"Mama, you're on edge again."

"I don't like parties and my feet hurt."

Mrs. Melvin moved smiling among the guests, dropping words. She served coffee and tea and little sandwiches, some containing nothing but butter and lettuce brought in by train from warmer climates.

She admired Beth's ease, how she could charm with small talk. You might have thought she meant to spend the rest of her life among these people, so attentive she was to them, so sure to ask them of their children and their little ailments and accomplishments. In her own house, if she found her audience worthwhile, the Sheep Queen was a notable storyteller; she read well aloud, had regularly read aloud to her daughters and still read aloud to Tom-Dick.

But now the last cup had made a last contact with the saucer, here were the gifts, and exactly what was expected, articles each lady would have wished for as a bride: tea towels hand-embroidered with such flowers and songbirds as easily come to mind, a corn popper, an orange squeezer — something of a joke since fresh fruits other than apples and cherries and wild berries were seldom seen in Lemhi County except in the toe of a Christmas stocking. Here were all the homely tools, knives to apportion, bowls to contain that spoke not of the drudgery of homemaking but of the first years of marriage and the good wishes of friends, precious objects to look back on as the harbingers of home and family.

But the shower for Elizabeth Birdseye Sweringen was no more than a ritual, and the homely offerings simply a part of it. Beth would herself never have need of tea towels. Her dishes would be wiped for her, her oranges squeezed. The ladies knew this and they knew that except for brief encounters over the years they would see little of her. They would never even know her. Pittsburgh was a long way off.

As for young Burton, his grandfather may have been a judge, or not. But if he had meant to lie he would not have revealed that he had shipped to Siberia as a cabin boy and had got mixed up with circus people. Sold Everfresh Products, did he? Imagine — dried turnips that swell up!

8

OUT IN THE WEST you still come across rusted metal signs tacked to fence posts like the crosspiece on the letter T, the paint flaked off in sun and blizzard, the words hardly legible: AR-BUCKLE'S COFFEE. And SLOAN'S LINIMENT.

Sloan's Liniment was thought as effective for the kick of a horse as for old joints swollen with rheumatism. HORSE-SHOE PLUG might be deciphered long after the chewing of tobacco and the casual — sometimes expert — expectoration of its juices was considered acceptable in the front room. They were a wandering breed who tacked the signs there, akin to the zealous ghosts who later painted JESUS SAVES on overpasses and across the bodies of abandoned cars.

The ranchers were tolerant. Some even thought the signs improved the lonely landscape, brought in something of the promise of civilization, were a link with the cities to the east and west where people ate fine foods and dressed in stylish clothes. Signs might conveniently identify a spot:

"Ed here claims there's ten head of strays about halfway between the Gold Medal sign and Trail Creek."

But the beckoning billboards in those days before the First World War were the broad sides of barns. Arrangements had to be made, money must change hands or tickets for the circus whose agents wished to paint elephants and tigers up there and shapely ladies in tights who flew through the air.

There was no advertising on the white Sweringen barn, though its size and location in the valley was so tempting. Many an eager salesman, first in buggy and then in automobile, had stopped at the ranch to inquire and had been sent packing. The Sheep Queen had no need for a few bills. As for tickets, she would buy her own. Word got around. The salesmen no longer stopped.

She took pride in her barn. It was half again as big as the sandstone house, and long. Down its length a trolly ran overhead and on that ran a gondola that could be halted behind each stall and the manure shoveled in. At one end was a tack room for saddles and harness, big enough for the harness maker to come with his tools each year and make repairs — who, like a wandering minstrel, came with stories of other ranches in other valleys. Overhead under the vast hip roof was stored hay enough to fill the mangers below for an entire year; there were bins for grain — of metal to foil the rats and mice, and a machine to separate grain from chaff. It was a place for her children to play on rainy days, protected from the lightning by the most advanced of rods. When at last the barn was completed, the neighbors came and danced up there to the music of Ed Cronie and His Foot Warmers. Even more than the sandstone house, the white barn dominated the Lemhi Valley.

She had said nothing to Thomas about the young man Burton, and after a few days she wondered if maybe she'd only imagined he had brushed Beth's glove with his lips. The mind plays funny tricks. Beth herself had not mentioned him. That was either a good sign, or it was not.

She was now ready with plans to take the G&P over the hill to Montana to catch the Union Pacific for Salt Lake, where she did her banking. Some thought it odd and disloyal that she didn't bank in Salmon, but she had preferred sounder resources behind her and had not been surprised when the Salmon bank failed in the panic of 1907, brought on by the costly Russo-Japanese War and the rebuilding of San Francisco. That the bank reopened did not inspire her confidence. She knew old White down in Salt Lake, and he knew her.

Nobody touched the newspapers until she had read them; each evening after supper she retired with them to the bedroom upstairs where she had her rolltop desk and safe for more sensitive papers. The library downstairs was now too crowded a room for thought, contained too many distracting objects that called out to be touched or considered. The telephone might ring, somebody might want something.

She read her papers not casually for idle gossip but closely, for on them she based her strategy. She believed the march of events reveals a pattern on which to fashion the future. She noted business trends, changing habits, the shift of factories from North to South. As early as 1905 she looked closely at the international scene so often buried in the back pages as of no more than passing interest — it was difficult for some to look out on the awesome Rocky Mountains and consider the prosaic fact of Europe. But she saw a Russia humiliated after the war with Japan; she noted a France eager for revenge after Versailles, an England concerned with the new German navy, a sick and crumbling Ottoman empire and a corrupt Austria anxious to gobble up the remains. Then she noted the visit of the Czar of Russia to France; the visit of King Edward to the Czar in the port of Reval, and finally the Kaiser's visit to old Franz Josef in

93

Vienna. These were far more than social events, dancing and cakes and ices. For then came Austria's annexation of Bosnia.

"Bosnia *who?*" Thomas had said, laughing. He had never heard of Herzegovina.

"Thomas," she said. "There's going to be a war."

He was looking out at the mountains as he so often did. He kept looking at them. "Emma, you must be crazy."

He was too gentle a man to imagine such a thing. She could. She knew that each generation of men is bound to test its contempt for death and to exercise its bloodlust. Taking twenty years as a generation, a war was somewhat overdue in both France and Germany. A generation had grown up that had not yet moved to kill. And to kill each other, young men first, like children, dressed up in uniforms to mark this side from that side.

Whether for Jean or Fritz or Tommy, uniforms are made of wool.

They would need her wool. Why here in America in 1911 — Lord how the years fly by! — it had been thirteen years since the Spanish War. Oh, she thanked God she had but one son and that he was but ten years old. If this country went to war he would be too young to fight and the next war would find him too old.

"Where're you going, Tom-Dick?" she had asked that morning in 1911. She was about to leave for Salt Lake to borrow money to buy more sheep to grow more wool. She was certain war was coming. At the sight of Tom-Dick her mouth, as usual, softened. She felt quite a different woman in his presence, afraid she would touch him and speak in such a way she would reveal a weakness he must never know, a dangerous capacity for sentiment.

"Going fishing, Mama."

"Watch out for snakes," she said. He would watch out for

94

snakes. Knew how to kill them, too. "Now God bless you, my boy." She had to bend but slightly to touch his cheek with her lips, he had grown so tall.

She took his words with her to Salt Lake. "Going fishing, Mama," and her lips moved as she silently repeated his simple words.

She had always avoided mirrors, and used them only as practical instruments to help remove a cinder from her eye or to see that her hat sat fairly straight on her head. As the years passed, as her acres and her sheep multiplied and the ranch prospered, she might have forgotten that she was not a pretty woman had it not been for Beth. The presence of Beth, the very fact of Beth was a reminder that beauty is an end in itself, perhaps even the most desirable end.

As for herself, she had once heard another woman say of her that she looked a deal like pictures of Madame Schumann-Heink. Alas, she hadn't Schumann-Heink's voice, only a recording of it on the Edison; she had only enough voice to sing little songs to Tom-Dick about the frog who would a-wooing go.

Mirrors had once told her she was going to be an old maid, and maybe the truth was that she had left Illinois because she was afraid of that, and that back there where everybody knew her they would pity her father for having an unmarried daughter, that maybe in the West where there were fewer women she might have a chance. Maybe it wasn't the German stepmother at all.

And then, as she saw it, Thomas's mother had stepped in. Thank God for that. Thomas appeared to be as uncritical of her appearance as Tom-Dick was of her voice.

"Going fishing, Mama." Oh, it was all worth it.

It was hard to avoid mirrors in the Hotel Utah; there were many of them in the lobby; they reflected the stylish women who stopped there on their way north or south or east or west. Salt Lake City was to the Rocky Mountain States what Chicago was to the Midwest, what New York was to the East, what Paris was to the world, a crossroads of elegance and fashion, a city of shops and theaters — Maude Adams had come from Salt Lake City. She wondered how other women did it, how they learned to dress so, to carry themselves with grace instead of purpose. Was it a gift granted along with beauty? Suppose she had been a pretty woman?

Something had happened that morning at the bank where the tellers greeted her with the usual cordiality; they knew her name and bank account and her old friendship with old White.

She loved the smell of the bank. "Mr. White is waiting for you. Go right on in."

Old White stood in his black suit such as an undertaker might wear; money and banking are as serious as death. He stood in his polished black Congress gaiters; he had reached an age and position where he might coddle his feet. His gold watch chain glowed against his dark vest; it proved him to be a Mason. Only his figured red-and-white cravat suggested that in rare circumstances he was prepared to take a chance.

"Ah, there, Mrs. Sweringen," he said, and stepped forward and took her hand. "You're looking fit."

"It's good to see you, Mr. White. You're looking top-drawer yourself." They both smiled because they both meant it and the good old bond was reestablished, two people who understood each other.

But a much younger man had risen, too. She judged he was about her age, but men look younger — their faces are not so early damaged by the force of gravity. They have more muscle. A pity they don't live so long as women.

"Mrs. Sweringen," old White said, "may I present Mr Wil-

96

liam Cutter? I have brought him here from San Francisco." Old White smiled. "We can't last forever, you know."

Mr. Cutter's hair was red. She could not recall having seen redder hair on a man; it surprised her that old White would consider so redheaded a man as his successor. Red hair hints at caprice and violence.

"Be assured it's my pleasure," Mr. Cutter said. He took her hand but he did not shake it. He touched it, and he inclined his head as perhaps they did in San Francisco where the ships come in bringing in Lord knew what manners and customs.

"Thank you, Mr. Cutter," she said. "My pleasure, too." The morning light out the window on Temple Square fell on the red hair on the back of Cutter's hands.

There came a tap on the door; a uniformed waiter from the hotel across the street entered carrying a tray, a large, silver insulated pot, and cups and saucers. She wondered how he must have looked crossing the busy street. Behind him a second waiter came, bearing a folding table. After smiles and a mild confusion and the waiters had gone, old White spoke.

"I remember Mrs. Sweringen likes a cup of coffee and at about this time."

"I do, and you are very kind."

He turned to Cutter. "As a Mormon, of course, I should eschew coffee. But as you see, Mrs. Sweringen has taught me bad habits. I now like a cup of coffee too, about this time."

"It won't go any further," Cutter said, laughing. "Will it, Mrs. Sweringen?"

It was comfortable, but strange.

"Now then," old White said. "Mrs. Sweringen, do you mind if Mr. Cutter sits in with us? I've been telling him about you. I'd like to have him hear first hand what you've got to say."

She was surprised that old White had brought in a third party to talk about money. Ordinarily, she would have minded. "Not

97

at all," she said, and old White continued to stand while Cutter bowed her into the customer's chair, then turned, poured coffee and came forward with it. Cutter wore no wedding band, but nowadays some married men didn't. Thus they are not so easily identified as a married woman. They prefer it that way. They are, can be more mobile. "I'm here," she said, "for money to buy another band of sheep."

"Yes, yes," old White said. "No problem there. But here — I should like Mr. Cutter to hear your reason for wanting more sheep *at this time*." Old White's eyes twinkled, but he spoke in measured, didactic tones as if he had rehearsed the speech, talking like a schoolmaster, drawing her out so Cutter could learn a thing or two about those who have good reasons to do what they do. She placed her bag which served as both purse and briefcase on the heavy carpet beside her. She took a sip of coffee, set the cup down.

"Mr. Cutter, there's going to be a war."

Mr. Cutter lifted his red eyebrows. "A war?" People with red hair sunburn easily. About her age, he was now too old to go to war. He might have a son old enough. They would have to stay out of the sun.

"I believe so," she said, and went on to speak of the Balkan problem and of Turkey and Russia which seemed so remote when one looked out the window at the magnificent Wasatch Mountains at eleven in the morning. "There appear to be two armed camps," and then in carefully measured words she said, "two armed camps *not yet clearly defined*."

Mr. Cutter smiled. "You refer to Italy," he said. "You don't believe Italy will side with the Teutonic Powers."

She was pleased with him. He might have been a star pupil who reflected her good teaching. "I do not," she said. "It's not in Italy's interest."

Old White laughed his growly laugh. "Nor in our interest,"

98

he said. "I told Cutter I would wager a good cigar that I knew what your reasons would be, but I didn't tell him what they were."

"Nothing but common sense," she said. "I'll wager that Mr. Cutter knows the Italian position quite as well as I do." She smiled on Cutter.

"Common sense is the most valuable commodity in the world," Cutter said.

"I'm not yet prepared to say this country's going to get into it, but if Europe goes to war, they're going to need our wool."

"I take my hat off to you, Mrs. Sweringen," Cutter said.

She laughed. "Keep your hat on for now. Let's wait and see."

Cutter chuckled and then was suddenly serious. "And speaking of cigars, do you mind if I smoke?"

She was alert to the faintly old-fashioned request and could not recall another man who had asked her permission to smoke. Old White did not smoke in her presence, not because she was a woman but because he was a Mormon. He might risk a cup of coffee with Gentile friends, but a cigar, never. Her sheepherders and irrigators and hayhands took it for granted that she knew men smoked and chewed and spit and Lord knew what else.

"I wish you would," she said. "I like the smell of a good cigar, Mr. Cutter."

They talked of the international situation and of things they did and did not like the looks of.

"When were you last in Europe, Mrs. Sweringen?" Cutter asked.

"I have never been to Europe, Mr. Cutter. I have never been anywhere. Someday I hope to be." Yes, she deeply hoped she would be. His cravat was of dark green. Maybe he had chosen it himself.

"Mrs. Sweringen doesn't have to be anywhere to know what goes on," old White said. "So I shall now deposit thirty-five thousand to your account, Mrs. Sweringen."

"Will you be much longer in Salt Lake?" Mr. Cutter asked.

She liked to take gifts to the children, nothing expensive, just some little thing from the ZCMI, the big department store that smelled so good of leather and cloth and talcum powder where everything can be bought and is owned by Mormons who own everything in Salt Lake City. Mormons were shrewd businessmen. Coming from San Francisco, Cutter was probably not a Mormon. Mormons were loyal to each other. Cutter must be a good man of business indeed if old White would bring him in over the head of some Mormon. Spoke well of old White, too, not letting his religion interfere with his business.

For Tom-Dick she bought a dozen dry flies for his fishing, all of them Royal Coachmen. There are far prettier flies than the Royal Coachman. There is the Silver Doctor, for example, but there is no fly the fish rise to as to the Royal Coachman, drab though it be. It is not what appeals to you but what appeals to the trout.

For Roberta she bought a graceful little chocolate pot of white china because Roberta had reached that age; half a dozen pretty hair ribbons for Maude and Polly because they were still that age. And then a few minutes later she was wandering — it was wandering because there she was so out of place — in the women's lingerie department.

"May I be of help?"

You could hardly have told this saleswoman from the women who swept in and out of the Hotel Utah, their hats so enormous this year you could hardly see their faces. This woman stood beautifully corseted and straight, smiling with the assurance that comes of knowing the feel of silk against the skin, how to manage scarves and folds.

"It *is* lovely, isn't it," the woman said, and smiled at the garment as if it lived.

And indeed it might have had a life of its own if by life you mean the ability to move and to charm. The garment was long, a full robe of satin brocade fit for a queen, the color of rich cream. It was picked out with nosegays of violets, each petal and leaf so distinct you might pluck them, each little bunch a gift in itself, a quite useless garment to be worn in the hour before dressing or at the hour after disrobing when some woman might wish to be for a little while other than what she was on the street, or managing a household, or writing checks. Emma Russell Sweringen was acquainted with no room where that exquisite robe would be appropriate, not even in her room in the Utah.

"It's possible I have it in your size."

She laughed. "Oh, Lord no," she said. "I was thinking of my daughter. She's being married."

The woman's voice softened. She must have had a daughter too. "How lovely, about to be married. Wouldn't this be a perfect gift?"

Yes, for Beth. So she bought the thing. The younger girls would have to forgive her and realize that for the time being Beth was a special person.

Now, suppose Cutter had called her at the hotel, suggested supper? But he would not. The mirrors told her so. And if he did, she would refuse, plead another engagement, for she knew long ago what her life would be, how she would manage it.

When he inquired, she had told him she would be another two days in Salt Lake, and therefore she telephoned friends, the director of the Union Pacific whose daughter had been at St. Margaret's with Beth and several times as a guest on the ranch.

They urged her to have dinner with them, as they called supper. She called the wife of a United States congressman and lunched there at a great house entirely hidden by trees. They talked of Taft and the tariff.

"And do give our dearest love to dear little Beth," they all said.

What Cutter had said was, "Will you be much longer in Salt Lake?" In his words was an implication that if he could finish whatever he had already committed himself to, why then — why else would he want to know "how much longer?" How, otherwise, would it have mattered to him?

On neither day was there a message at the desk. She could not rid herself of a sense of humiliation, nor could she put her finger on what had caused it. But the attraction she had felt had surely been reciprocated: for the magnet is no less necessary than the iron filings. Why had he touched her hand just so?

But of course it was impossible for him to have approached her since she was who she was. Old White would never have brought in a man with other than impeccable manners. Impossible for him to have approached her.

But it might have been. And had it been, she'd have refused. All that was contained for a moment in the embrace of past and present in Salt Lake City. She would never consider it again, nor Cutter's hands and the sound of his voice, the aroma of his good cigar.

All that was remote when she boarded the Union Pacific that evening. Settled in her compartment she rang for the porter to set up the folding table and to bring a deck of playing cards. As the train pulled out, she was laying out a game of solitaire; not long after, she looked up from a jack of diamonds.

"Common sense," Cutter had said, "is the most valuable of all commodities." Suppose he had forgot that for a moment; suppose the mirrors had told her other than they did. And suppose that mirrors could reflect the mind.

The train was passing along the edge of the sterile lake, its leaden surface reflecting the arching, empty sky. A line of Byron came to mind:

> *Like to the apples on the Dead Sea's shore,*
> *All ashes to the taste.*

Dusk washed down over the Wasatch Mountains. By and by it was night.

9

WE SAY and we say again that we do not love one child more
than another, for to say so would make another child suffer and
advertise that our capacity to love is so wanting it can embrace
but one. We say it, and we lie, for we love most the child who
needs us most or who needs us least, the wastrel or him who
keeps his nose to the grindstone. We love most the child who
looks like us or has our voice or the mole on the cheek, who has
overlooked our failure or has comforted us in our humiliation.

Thomas Sweringen loved Beth above his other children because she was his firstborn; he could almost taste the love that
consumed him when he first saw her in Emma's arms, red,
wrinkled and squalling. What a miracle! Within days she was
the beauty she had remained.

"My," he would say, and his eyes would twinkle. "My, but
you are an ugly little thing."

"Oh, Papa!"

Oh, Papa.

He remembered the first day she talked, and do you know what the first word she said was? It was "Papa." He remembered the first day she walked, and it was he who held his hand out to her and smiled as she stumbled towards him. Then she was tagging after him. He was forever slowing his steps.

"Too fast, Papa."

He believed she had a special understanding of those things that meant much to him, secret places in the mountains where unnamed streams rushed down over the stones, where water beetles walked on the water in quiet places, where freshwater mussels lived that the Indians had used for wampum in days just gone. They knew where the slide-rock was once disturbed by the Indians who buried their dead underneath; they knew sudden openings in the dense timber — some called them parks and some, meadows — where white flowers shimmered before the eye and birds surprised there disappeared like birds who had hoped never to be seen. He and Beth knew where at each season the clouds caught and held the last glow of sunset, where the wind moved over the prairie and chased the tumbleweed before it. He believed that coyotes were not afraid of them and they both knew what gods were delighted with the scolding squirrels.

Only he and she — and she was only a little girl then — had been asked to assist at old Chief Tendoy's funeral, and this is why that was: Only they among the whites could make out in the sagebrush and slide-rock on the side of a certain mountain the imperious face and head of an Indian chief dressed in a warbonnet, the nose haughty and keen, the cheekbones high; there it seemed to float towards the west, protector of that valley and all those in it — those who had seen it. Good medicine for those who had seen it. None of the other children had seen it, nor Emma. Emma thought he was joking.

It was Beth this and Papa that. But Emma was a powerful

woman, as events showed. He would have been content with the old log house and the acres as they were, but that was not enough for Emma, God knew exactly why, and of course she was right, a house with a sod roof is no right house for children if you can manage otherwise, and Emma could manage anything. It beat all.

He knew what he did not know. She knew what she knew, and that was that aristocracy is a local affair and that they were aristocrats thanks to George Sweringen's being the first white man in the valley, his discovery of gold, the acres and the extended acres, all those sheep and cattle and Emma's ancestors who had fought in the Revolution. He didn't know who his ancestors were — Pennsylvania Dutch people yes, but not who they were.

He was inarticulate and could not well have expressed his grief when at fourteen Beth was sent off to St. Margaret's down in Boise to be educated as a young lady must be in ways he did not understand. Why must she learn a foreign language? Where would she talk it? There was nothing they could teach her down there about how to walk across a room, or ride like an Indian.

From that school she wrote regularly always to both of them, Dear Mama and Papa, Mama first because Mama was Mama and Beth must know that a letter directed to him alone required him to answer and he had never written a personal letter in all his thirty-nine years. If he did write, he would write, Dear Beth, I wish you were here. Food didn't taste good anymore.

Only Beth almost got herself expelled from that school.

It came about like this: a young woman teacher at that school had been seen by other teachers probably not so pretty talking to a young man in the town right on the street, flirting, they said, so the headmistress fired the young teacher.

He was glad Beth protested. Why wouldn't a young woman

talk to an attractive young man on the street? You see, Beth was fair. She led friends of hers up and down the halls of that old school, they all in their nightgowns and wouldn't go to bed and they did what they were not supposed to do after lights were off. They made fudge in their rooms in chafing dishes and talked loud. Some of the young teachers joined them. It looked like the Bishop was going to have to get called in to handle a situation that must not have crossed his mind at his ordination. Emma knew him.

Beth, brave as could be, stood up as ringleader, and she was expelled, but not really.

The headmistress knew a thing or two. She called Emma on the telephone; Emma got into her traveling clothes.

Emma and the headmistress palavered awhile and he imagined that by the time Emma was through the headmistress felt a bit smaller, for Emma would have said, he could almost hear her, "What kind of a school have you here that you can't handle girls of fifteen?" Emma had a way. She knew that everybody has weaknesses and that you can get at people through them.

To him, Emma said, "You can't allow a daughter to break rules, Thomas."

He went for a walk. He hadn't much patience with many rules.

He looked with dismay on the young dudes who came as surveyors for the railroad, out there for a lark, and he objected to Beth's being a part of a lark, but only in his heart, for the world would have said, These are the young men a beautiful girl marries and goes away with. But maybe back there in the East their families might think Beth no more than the daughter of a woman with a few sheep. And if one thing made him sick, it was thinking anybody could hurt little Beth. She was still Little Beth to him.

Sometimes he wished she were ugly.

The young man had a sandy mustache and an answer to everything. One time when somebody said something about crows, the young man stopped short and said, "What do you want to know about crows?" He was cocky and walked with a springy bounce. You could imagine him laying down the law. But Emma and Beth had accepted him, and the parties around the valley began. It was not much to hope that, from now on, he would see Beth only at Christmastime, the past all forgotten and all those clouds that rose up from behind Gunsight Peak promising one thing or another.

"Beth," he asked, "do you love this fellow?"

"I —" she looked at him, and then away. "I don't know, Papa."

"Then you don't. They say you know if you do."

"Well, he's well-off, and he comes of good people."

"So do you come of good people, and you don't need his money. If you needed *him* it'd be different."

Her eyes were gentle on him. "You know I'll never love another man as I love you."

"Sure, but that's different, too. It's like your mother and Tom-Dick."

"Well, I'll never *like* a man as I like you."

So she didn't love this fellow. But Emma's will and Emma's influence and Emma's way of being right — why, Emma was like a brushfire. When you checked her in one place, she flared up over there.

But then, by golly, something happened. And a good thing Emma was in Salt Lake.

The original train schedule was possibly drawn up by an Easterner who did not consider such imponderables as cows wandering along the tracks, and blizzards. It called for the train to make the round trip from Salmon over the Divide into Montana and back in a single day. That would have been a sight to see. But in the wintertime it often took twenty-four hours to make it one way, and it was not unpleasant to be stuck all night on the top of the hill waiting for the second locomotive to come with a rotary snowplow, so long as you had your lunch, and enough kerosene in the lamps and coal for the stove down the car. You got to know strangers well, knew their nicknames, exchanged pictures of wives and children, saw them react in a pinch. Many who had shared sandwiches and confidences while the wind howled and leaned against the windows vowed to keep in touch over the years, and they did.

A more practical schedule called for the train to leave Salmon at seven in the morning on even days, lay over the night in Beech, Montana, and leave there at seven in the morning on odd days. The train did not run on Sunday. Because of the perverse nature of the days of the week, this meant one Sunday in Salmon and the next in Beech. Ideally, this called for either two wives or two homes. It was a situation disruptive to domestic life. The engineer was unmarried and assumed to be celibate, for surely a man with his responsibility would make no shabby arrangements. But the rest of the crew — the conductor, the brakeman and the fireman — were normally carnal. Tempering their lust with convention, they married. It followed that on odd Sundays the wives in Salmon and the husbands in Beech imagined what was going on over the hill in the other place and by the time the G&P had failed in 1939 and the track sold as scrap to Japan, they had all been divorced and remarried and divorced.

Whenever Emma Sweringen went on a trip, those left behind fell into the mood of holiday. The camp tenders whistled as they led their packhorses from the barn; the barking of the dogs was like laughter. The cook in the cookhouse took little nips of lemon extract.

When Emma left for Salt Lake to see Old White, the younger girls, Polly, Maude and Roberta, were all home from school in Salmon on Easter vacation. They began to make their plans. Roberta, just sixteen, wrote in her diary:

"Mama says you are only supposed to write your diary after supper when everything is over but now it is ten o'clock in the morning and Mama left for Salt Lake City just a little while ago and I'm writing in it. She says diaries are a good thing because later on you can read it and find out what you did and learn from it. Well for one thing Polly isn't going to wear hair ribbons all the time Mama is gone and Maude is going to do dance steps she learned from an awful girl who used to live in Denver. She's going to put Everybody's Doing It Now on the Edison. It's crazy.

"It rained night before last and we all caught rainwater off the roof in the boiler so after we all wash our hair we are going to make fudge and then Papa will let us drink coffee because he always does.

"Beth promised when she gets married to that fellow back East I can go back there and she and I will go to New York City and up in the Statue of Liberty. You can go clear up into the head I read in a book and when I get up there I am going to throw pennies down to the poor people. Won't they be surprised, though!

"Tom-Dick went off fishing this morning and I saw out the window Mama kissed him. He's pretty big to be kissed, for a boy. She thinks he doesn't do anything wrong. Ha-ha. He and some of the boys go swimming naked in the river. He probably smokes, too. I'm glad I'm not ten years old. I don't see why people like to fish because they are so slimy.

"Mama promised to bring me back a chocolate pot from

ZCMI. That means Zion Commercial Mercantile Institute. When I go back to Salmon I am going to give a party and not ask a lot of people. Some of them are snots."

Thomas Sweringen liked to see what was going on in the distance. He kept a pair of field glasses on top of the gunrack in the dining room and another tied to his saddlestrings. His eyes were as keen as a timber wolf's, and with field glasses he could judge conditions on the range forty miles away; not much closer he could give a man a name by how he sat in the saddle. If you know what's going on in the distance, you can get ready for what is to come.

As the train from Salmon approached the bridge where it stopped for Sweringens, he noted that it had already started to slow down. He picked up his glasses and looked across the field. It was just after nine in the morning; the train was almost an hour late. Something interesting must have happened.

He saw a man get down from the train with a sample case. A tall young man who made a wide gesture to Andy as the train pulled away. Walking across the field towards the house with that big case, the young man smiled as if he knew eyes were fixed on him, and Thomas, who did not intrude into another man's business unless asked, lowered his glasses and set them back on the gunrack. The girls were giggling upstairs.

Then the young man was at the front door and the spring sun behind him cast his shadow on the carpet in the hall. Thomas opened the door just as the young man raised his fist to knock.

"I saw you coming," Thomas said.

"I'm Ben Burton," the young man said. "And you're Mr. Sweringen and I'm blamed happy to make your acquaintance." He shot out his hand that was at the end of his long arm and Thomas took it.

Now, how do you treat a young man who thinks you like him and would be hurt if he thought you didn't? You are good to him. All you can judge a man by is the way he treats you. It is not easy to be a salesman, you know, because you have what they want — your money — and if you wanted what they have, you would already have it.

He now shook the young man's hand. "You might as well get right down to it," he said to young Burton. "What have you got in that case? The Rawleigh man was here time past so we've got plenty of medicine and vanilla and lemon extract and spices. You see we've got lightning rods."

Ben Burton grinned. "It's myself I have to sell," he said. "I want you to have something absolutely free."

"Now, what would that be?"

Burton explained that he was with Everfresh Products and that he was prepared to hand over a year's supply of any two vegetables and fruits that instantly came fresh simply with the addition of water, in exchange for advertising space and the Sweringen good will. "You Sweringens are held in high regard in this valley."

Well, on the face of it that sounded reasonable. Dried fruits and vegetables could be easily packed on the horses, and would be lighter for them to carry. Canned stuff weighs a lot, all that water. As for advertising space, Thomas assumed Burton had metal signs in the sample case he hoped to tack to fence posts.

"Sounds reasonable," Thomas said.

Thus, Ben Burton entered the Sweringen ranch house. He followed Thomas into the dining room, a big high-ceilinged room whose windows, beyond the flourishing tangle of geraniums, looked out on Gunsight Peak. The dining room was not used for eating because everybody ate in the cookhouse below except for holidays when the whole family gathered, all the cousins and everybody.

"Open your case right there on the table," Thomas said.

It was after Burton opened the case that Thomas realized

what was up. No metal signs in there. Aside from the small sample bags of something or other, there were neat folded sheets of paper of the sort that fit together and are for covering a lot of space.

"Just a minute, young man," Thomas said. "Just hold your horses."

"Yes, Mr. Sweringen?"

"By any chance do you have the barn in mind?"

Burton's eyes looked innocent enough. He made a little motion with his head. "Why, yes, Mr. Sweringen. When I came into this country not ten days ago I noticed the barn — the prominence of that fine, big barn. I believe I have never seen so fine a barn, and so well situated, not even back in Iowa where barns are looked on as works of art. Your barn gives a grand aspect to the whole valley."

"Young man," Thomas said, "I don't know what you heard about the Sweringens around Salmon. Not much, if you didn't hear that my wife would skin any man alive who put a poster on that barn."

Burton made that little ducking motion of his head, "Oh, now, Mr. Sweringen," he said, "I don't think she'd do that. We had a fine talk on the train, she and I. Just a capital talk."

"You talked to her on the train?"

"Yes sir. Oh, we talked and talked. Your wife and that daughter of yours, and I. We talked about the whole wide world and we talked about people's hands. Let me tell you, I was impressed. She said what I believe, that you can make anything you want of yourself. A truly fine philosophy."

"That sounds like her."

"And don't you think she meant by that you have also to sell yourself, what you think you are? Oh, a fine conversation. And let me tell you, Mr. Sweringen, I have never seen a lovelier girl than that daughter of yours in all my life, and Mr. Sweringen, I may be young, I was twenty-two years of age last March, but I have traveled a great deal, due to circumstances I hope to tell you about."

"Mr. Burton," Thomas said and spoke as gently as he could, but he called him Mr. Burton now to prepare him for the blow, "I was once a young man myself, and if I remember, young men rush in where angels fear to tread. I'm sorry, but you might just as well close up that case . . ."

"Papa?"

And there she stood. Thomas Sweringen never, in all his later years and there were a great, great many of them, ever forgot her standing in that room for the first time with the two men she loved, and her beauty, the love in her gray eyes was enough to make a man cry.

"Papa. He told me about many of the circumstances and where he's been. Please let him put the poster on the barn."

Thomas Sweringen had never once refused her anything, even if he got skinned alive. And anyway, it was his barn, too.

10

THE UNION PACIFIC out of Salt Lake pulled into Beech, Montana, at six in the morning; the dining car had not yet opened and Emma Sweringen looked forward to a good cup of coffee which she knew she would not get at the hotel in Beech because the water there smelled of sulfur and so did Beech. Alkali seeped up through the ground there and hardened to a white crust. Nothing grew. The town was nothing. A combination grocery and dry-goods store: canned goods, overalls, house-dresses, gingham stuff. Two saloons did a good business, she imagined, when the ranchers drove in their cattle in the fall; the stockyards huddled down by the stinking creek that ran through them so the cattle could drink. The hills around the place were steep and bare; wild horses wandered up the sides, half-starved. The wind was never still and whined like some living thing.

Nothing of interest in the town except a polished granite slab like a tombstone informing strangers that here Lewis and Clark had passed on their way to the Pacific Coast, guided by the Indian woman Sacajawea who, at this point, recognized the country she had left as a child. Rather touching. Emma Sweringen knew what a pleasure it was to recognize one's own land.

It was not yet quite light; an electric light glowed upstairs in the yellow-painted Union Pacific depot. When she stepped down off the train with several others she heard the putt-putt-putt of the gasoline electric light plant, a strangely lonely sound. The paler light of a kerosene lamp was upstairs in the store. The hotel was dark, but now the train was in, it would light up.

The wind still blew. The G&P waited across the town, the headlight of the locomotive a bright path through the dawn. Switch lights blinked. She felt a sudden affection for the little train, couldn't help but think of it as hers, part of her life anyway, a sense that it played a part in her life, always would.

Yes, now the lamps in the hotel were lighted. Over the entrance, Mrs. Forest had had somebody tack a bleached set of elk antlers. Emma made it a point to be kind to Mrs. Forest who lived there with her little son. God knew what had become of Forest. Mrs. Forest was an apologetic woman with a habit of placing the palm of her right hand against her cheek where there was a frightful scar all the way down to her throat as if somehow she had spilled acid there.

Several well-dressed drummers were sitting at the tables in the small dining room. On each table was a jelly glass of paper flowers to spruce things up. One drummer was so sleepy he held his cup in both his hands. She would know them all before the day was out; they'd be her companions on the G&P.

Mrs. Forest came through from the kitchen and asked how she was.

"Now that's kind of you, Mrs. Forest," she said. "I'm first-rate and trust you are. So now tell me about that boy of yours."

Mrs. Forest went right ahead and did. "And he's back in

school now and doing so much better. He was sick so much last winter, Mrs. Sweringen. That wind goes right through you."

"Indeed it does."

"And so much more active now. Mr. Bradley over at the store, he's so kind to children now his own boys have gone away, Mr. Bradley has taught him how to fish. I think it's good for a boy to fish, don't you, Mrs. Sweringen?"

"Best thing a young man can do. Teaches 'em how to be alone, what it's worth to be alone. You can do a powerful lot of thinking when you're alone, Mrs. Forest."

Her own thoughts were on the awesome accident of birth. Mrs. Forest's boy, to succeed, must escape his background, a vanished father, some tragedy that had resulted in that ugly scar on Mrs. Forest's throat. He must escape the hotel — what would you call it, a poor little boardinghouse for transients? — and he must show the town of Beech, Montana, a clean pair of heels. With all her heart she hoped that his struggle and adversities would make such a man of him he would be heard of, one day.

Tom-Dick, on the other hand, had only to accept his background, stay right where he was and improve and expand what he already had. Seemed so blamed unfair! Well, she for one was going to keep an eye on young Forest; the time might well come when she could be of service. She would be of service simply because his mother and she had something in common.

Sons.

Simply something in common? If having sons in common wasn't something, she didn't know what was!

"Mrs. Forest," she said, "you just hang on right here while I open this bag of mine." She knelt before all those sleepy drummers, opened the bag and began to rummage through it. She was no good at packing bags. At last she brought out the package of Royal Coachmen. "I picked these up for my own little boy. I know he'd be happy to share them with your little boy."

"Oh, Mrs. Sweringen!" Mrs. Forest cried, and placed the palm of her right hand against that scar. Mrs. Forest refused to accept payment for the coffee, and Emma Sweringen did not press the matter.

A few minutes before seven she walked in the everlasting wind over to the little train, followed by the drummers with their sample cases.

The little train chugged on up towards the Divide where the tunnel was. It slowed and paused at Brewer on the Montana side to take on water; nothing but a wooden water tank like a huge teakettle on stilts and a spout that swung around. The station was a dark-green boxcar relieved of its wheels. The sun was high now and bright on the big log house of the Brewer ranch maybe a quarter of a mile across the valley. The house looked deceptively like a story-and-a-half bungalow until you got close to it. It was said to have sixteen rooms. The Brewers were looked on as special people in that valley; they had come out with a great deal of money from Boston at about the same time she had come out with little more than her sturdy luggage. It was said that Mr. Brewer dressed always in suits, never rode a horse but inspected his holdings from the seat of a buggy behind Orloff trotters. Some said Mrs. Brewer dressed for dinner which everbody else called supper. They were said to use finger bowls. Their barn was quite different from hers, long, low, and constructed of logs whose chinks and bumps would discourage anyone's painting signs there.

However, Mr. Brewer was not the Cattle King of Montana as she was Sheep Queen of Idaho. There were many of him; one of her. She looked with detachment on the house of sixteen rooms and possible finger bowls.

There were three Brewer sons. Only one of them was married.

Now the train passed through the tunnel, not a tunnel long enough for the conductor to bother lighting the lamps overhead, but voices fell silent and mouths did not speak again until you were out the other side into a new state. That brief darkness, like going out of a stuffy house out into the night under the stars, had long been a time of reflection for her when she returned to her valley. Closed in that tunnel perched high between Montana and Idaho, she felt humble, and thanked her stars things had worked out as they had.

And here now in the full light was the state of Idaho, the Land of the Shining Mountains.

She liked talking with men; she was glad of a political discussion with two of the drummers, both unusually well-spoken and both comfortably Republican. She could not discuss politics with Thomas; he remained a stubborn Democrat, States' rights and all that when anyone with any gumption knew power had to be centralized. He favored wild legislation that would help them who would not help themselves — his politics were of the heart, not the head. He favored a low tariff and the first thing you knew you'd be competing with Argentine beef and Australian wool. He favored silver and first thing you knew you'd be off the gold standard and there'd be a panic, the country in ruins, the rabble in the streets. Three times he had voted for William Jennings Bryan, and so had Nora; three times when Bryan had been defeated the two of them had walked around, sad as orphans. Bryan was a charlatan who used that voice of his to move those who wanted to be moved.

Thou shalt not crucify mankind upon a cross of gold!

The man must have thought he was God. Beware of such.

"Did you ever think of running for the Legislature?" one of the drummers asked.

"I doubt if the world's quite ready for anything so radical as that," she said.

"Don't forget there's Jeanette Rankin right over there in Montana and there's that Wyoming woman. Let me tell you, Ma'am, the day is coming when women will be considered almost the equals of men."

"Now, you certainly don't believe that," she said, smiling.

"Indeed I do. Mark my words."

That got her to thinking a little about the Legislature. And after the Legislature?

The train was now running through a right-of-way on her own land. She would wager she was the only woman in the United States who rode on a train that paid only slightly more than she in taxes, a train that ran through her own land for a good twenty minutes. Believe me, it was a good feeling, and old White was a sound man.

And there across the field was her solid sandstone house; they would be watching for her. She wondered what they'd been up to.

And there was her great white barn.

"Is something wrong, Mrs. Sweringen?" the drummer asked.

Not surprising that Tom-Dick and not Thomas met her at the tracks with the buggy. Thomas avoided a situation until the last minute, as if time would alter it and, altered, he could handle it.

Her eyes were still narrow but her anger had begun to subside. The letters that spelled out EVERFRESH PRODUCTS loomed a foot high; the windows of her barn had been cleverly included in the bars of the letter E and every letter was black, black, black. The legend, black against the pure white of the barn was as garish as a circus poster, shocking as a funeral announcement. Well, it would be somebody's funeral.

Tom-Dick took her bag and set it carefully in the rear of the buggy. "I'm glad you're back, Mama."

"I missed you, Tom-Dick. Where are Beth and your father?"

"They rode up the creek early about some cattle."

"I'll bet they did," she said.

She saw it all. With Beth, young Burton had used his looks. With Thomas, young Burton had used his youth. Thomas had a soft spot for the young; it was irritating how he continued to think like a young man and even to look like one. And Thomas would be moved by Burton's wandering to Siberia and joining the circus, seeing in those perversities an appealing rootlessness, a suggestion that Burton had no home, needed friends. Thomas was a great one for taking in strangers, opening his wallet, extending his hand. A wonder it was not more often bitten.

Tom-Dick drove her to the front steps and carried in her bag. No sign of the girls, but she knew small sounds in that house, the careful footfall, creaking floorboard, opening door; they were upstairs, waiting.

She sat at the dining room table piled high with the newspapers that marked her days away — among them the *Salt Lake Tribune*. The sight of it was depressing, like old letters one has written and never addressed and sent.

After a few minutes Roberta appeared in the hall, having come down on tiptoe. "Oh, Mama!" she cried in a rather small voice. "You're back!" Roberta laughed uneasily, and then she and Maude and Polly — instead of gathering around her for their presents like bum lambs at feeding time — fled before her like quail. She knew they took up positions in the grove of tall trees beside the house where they could be on hand to see or hear what happened next, as interpreted by Roberta, who was old enough to begin to understand situations still mysterious to the younger girls.

She drew one of the newspapers to her and prepared to wait. When at last Thomas and Beth found the courage to face her, there she would be, ready to be faced.

Within the hour the shrill triangle down at the cookhouse sang out for the hired men to come to dinner. Dogs barked; she heard the splash of water tossed out from basins through the bunkhouse door; the men talked and whistled. Knowing she had returned, they would seat themselves at the table and then wait a few minutes for her to join them before they leaned to their food: mutton, boiled beans, boiled beet greens, canned fruit and cake. Hired men are as suspicious as children of altered diets.

Young Burton would be staying at the Shenon House in Salmon; there was no other place for him. Mrs. Cook at the Irvinton Rooms no longer took salesmen because they stole soap and towels and sometimes moved furniture. It was up to Thomas to telephone Burton, for it was Thomas who had allowed the desecration of her barn. It must be Thomas who saw that the sign was torn down and Burton himself who did the tearing, whether or not in his fine summer suit. No reason on earth why Thomas or a hired man should repair damage caused by Burton. In years to come Burton might look back and thank her for a lesson taught — that you do not alter other people's property; surely it had occurred to him why her barn was spotless in a valley where every other barn was a crazy quilt of announcements and appeals. She could not believe that Thomas had not warned Burton of her views. For whatever else Burton was, he was not stupid, and meeting him she had made the force of her personality felt.

When Beth and Thomas got back, they would take as long as possible to unsaddle their horses. They would walk slowly to the house, stopping as they often did to look back at their magic mountains — they were both pagans at heart. She had not seen Thomas in church since she married him; how uneasy he looked in his new and only suit; at any sudden noise he would have bolted . . .

. . . and when at last there was no earthly reason for them not to come into the house and face her — she who had had no dinner because of them, was tired from her trip, had been left waiting some hours at a table reading stale newspapers —- when they walked up the steps to the back porch and in through the kitchen and pantry past the water bucket and dipper into the dining room, there they would find her with her eyes on the paper before her, and she would look up and order Beth upstairs *and she would have it out with Thomas then and there!*

Time passed.

The younger girls, tired of hiding in the trees, had gone on down to the cookhouse to eat and now chased each other like wild young things through the tall grass in the front yard; Roberta who now fancied herself a young lady, flung herself about like a filly. By and by they wandered in for their presents, accepted them and, without opening them, went upstairs; they knew this was no time for exclamations. The giving of the foolish robe to Beth had been ruined. It would be days, weeks, before the time was ripe even to speak of it. She put it away in the library.

Nor did she like having to speak to Thomas. Usually she did not have to speak. He seldom opposed her so things ran smoothly; after twenty years he understood she was usually right. When she was not, he didn't twit her with the fact. Only when the lightning rod man came around had he adamantly opposed rods on the house in the belief that they attracted rather than tamed lightning.

"Set them up on the barn, if you will," he told her. "When it storms you can go out there." So when the electric storms crashed down from Hayden Creek and like monstrous spiders the lightning stalked the valley and the air was sharp with the smell of ozone, she sat it out in the barn — some circumstance for the Sheep Queen of Idaho, but by and by she could even laugh about it.

"How was it out there?" he would ask later on. "Damp?"

Now the dogs were barking. She got up, walked over and looked out through the geraniums on the windowsill. The plants had grown so tall and thick it was hard to see around them. One of them she had nursed for almost twenty years; its growth and the moist green shade it cast were so closely woven into her satisfactory life with Thomas and her children she had begun to look on it as a talisman just as Thomas looked on a small, smooth agate he had picked up and dropped into his pants pocket the first time they had walked together.

There halfway between house and barn Beth and Thomas made over the dogs who leapt, chased their tails and fawned. Beth and Thomas were putting things off. And then their feet were on the steps of the back porch; she sat down quickly and put her eyes to the newspaper; it is wiser to be seen gainfully occupied. Then you have the advantage. He who approaches you is unoccupied and feels not only an intruder but inferior.

"Emma!" Thomas said, as if she were unexpected.

"Mama!" Beth cried.

She looked up. "Beth. Run on upstairs."

But what was this? For Beth hesitated.

Thomas said, "It's all right Beth. Go on up." Their eyes met. Beth left the room.

She waited long enough for Beth to go upstairs, into her room, to close her door and to sit on the edge of her bed with one foot tucked under her. They all did it. Thomas, the girls, even Tom-Dick. When they sat, they tucked one leg and foot under them.

But Thomas spoke first. "Emma. You're wrong in taking a high hand. She's a grown woman."

"I won't discuss how I rear my daughter. After supper you will telephone young Burton to come tear down that poster."

Thomas turned to the gunrack. On the top one of the many

124

clocks he attended ticked away. It was five o'clock, four hours too early to wind it but wind it he did. When he had finished he closed the little glass door firmly. "I'll do no such thing, Emma."

"Won't, won't you? Yes, I can understand why you wouldn't want to. You have never liked to discipline anyone and you have never been able to say no."

"I am saying no, now."

"It seems to me that putting up that poster is as much your doing as his. If you won't call him, I'll call him. I can tell you I'll be a good deal harder on him than you would."

"Why would you want to be hard on him?"

"Because he's an opportunist."

"Why shouldn't a young man make use of an opportunity?"

"You don't understand the word opportunist. Nothing wrong in a young man's making use of opportunity. But an opportunist makes use of *you*. Let me tell you, Thomas, I can smell an opportunist. He operates at another's expense."

"Expense? That sign cost us nothing. And we get something. He's giving us two cases of Everfresh Products."

"He's doing no such thing. I will not be obligated to him. Will you call him or shall I?" She fanned her broad hands before her as if to rise and move to the telephone in the library.

Thomas spoke quietly. "If I were you, I wouldn't call him. Not until I'd talked to Beth."

"What does that mean, sir?"

"Beth can tell you better than I."

She lived to be eighty-five and in all those years maybe a dozen moments in her life stood apart like signposts where the road forked or turned, or stopped, and that trip upstairs was one of them; upstairs past the elk head on the first landing — it struck you if you didn't remember to duck. She recalled her foot on the fourteenth stair that always creaked; she never forgot the wan north light through the window at the top of the stairs; in any season, it prompted thoughts of winter. It was cold upstairs; it was seldom anything else, for even in midsummer, something of winter lingered. She paused beside the window, leaned a moment against the sill for the stairs had tired her. She looked across the valley to Gunsight Peak. Through the deep notch at the summit from which it took its name, God himself might have trained His eye on the wild behavior of human beings. Yes, cold. The stairs and the walls and the floors had absorbed so much of fall and winter and early spring there was little room for the brief summer; the stoves up there were never used because of Thomas's fear of fire. Upstairs had a climate all its own.

An atmosphere of its own, not exactly secrecy. Privacy? When the children were little, she had each evening stepped into each room and sat a few minutes on each bed and said goodnight and kissed them. As they grew older, she respected their closed doors; they might as well have been locked. All the keys, except that to the door of Roberta's room, had disappeared. Roberta locked her door when she wrote in her diary. The diary, too, had a key. It had occurred to Emma that if she truly wanted to know her children, she should look in that diary. More than once she was about to demand to see it but she knew she would be met with such an outburst of temper, with such flashing eyes and an outrage so like her own, before she had learned to control it, that she hesitated. When, a few years before she had sat on the edge of Roberta's bed and had remarked that it was now time to start thinking about St. Margaret's School, Roberta had hurled herself out of bed. "No! I'll throw myself out the window! I won't go there. I'm not as pretty as Beth!" So Roberta went to high school in Salmon and stayed with Nora.

Now it was in Tom-Dick's room alone that she felt welcome. When at night she stepped into his room, he would move over in bed. After she had sat, the first thing she did was lay the palm of her hand on his forehead as if feeling for fever, but really for love. Then Tom-Dick would smile.

"Hello, Mama," he would say, and then she would hum him a little tune.

"My boy." Oh, but her heart would swell, and she would thank God for him. She saw him at twenty and thirty and forty, sitting straight in the saddle, lord of all he surveyed. In him, she lived. Because of him she did not regret the passing years — she rejoiced in them. It was he who would stand last at her deathbed, he who would comfort and support the others.

"Want to see my birds' eggs, Mama?" He kept them in a wooden salt-cod box filled with sawdust. He would recite, like a poem:

> "Bluebird, robin, snipe.
> Blackbird, sage hen, crow.
> Magpie, sparrow, *grouse*."

And she would finish:

> "And that's about all
> The eggs in this *house!*"

What a crazy pair they were!

Against one wall was his old toy box filled with the fancies of his first eight years, never opened now, but one day he would lift its cover to the wondering eyes of his own little boy. Leaning against the wall in the corner was his BB gun. With it he had learned to shoot, as a man must. As a man must learn that death is present in the Pattern. One of the milestones was that moment she gave him his first rifle, that .22 leaning against the wall, oiled, polished, ready.

Yes, it was cold up there. The younger girls were in Roberta's room, the door closed. Beyond that closed door was a lively silence; they had heard the warning of the fourteenth step of the stairs. Roberta would be leaning forward with a finger vertical against her lips, her eyes bright with mischief.

She passed on down the hall and stood before Beth's door.

And hesitated. The door had become a wall and Beth, on the other side, a stranger. Whether that was because of what she — Emma — had been at twenty-one or because of what Beth had become at twenty-one, she did not know. Anyway.

She knocked.

"Come."

Beth stood beside the window, looking off down the valley, her profile in the cool, pale light of that awful afternoon as perfect as Liberty's on a silver dollar.

"Beth — your father suggested I speak to you."

"Yes. He said I would know when it happened. I told him."

"Told him what?"

"That I'm in love."

"With that young man?"

"With Ben Burton."

Love — that emotion stronger than greed. In the name of love a man deserts wife and child. In the name of love a woman goes hungry, will beg in the streets, will walk the streets. Oh, yes. Love. Excuse for violence, selfishness, cruelty. In the name of love, men murder. She spoke carefully, evenly, wishing the words like links in a chain to shackle Beth to her.

"Beth. Do you know what love is?"

"I didn't, until now. All my life I've been told I was beautiful. If I have beauty, I can tell you it's not much to have. It means you can sell me to the highest bidder."

"What an ugly thing to say."

"I had to. I was about to be sold. I would never have known what love is. I would never have been allowed to know. And if sometime later on I met somebody and I did know, I couldn't have done anything about it. Because, Mama, I'm a good person. I think I am. I would not hurt anybody."

"Beth, please."

"I'll tell you what love is. To want to touch. To be able to touch. All my life."

Now the Sheep Queen of Idaho reached into myth, legend and experience as into so many bags and brought out a collection of nouns: honor, respect, friendship, worth, security, future, Family, responsibility, education, duty. As if these were blocks she began to build in her mind an argument against what Beth thought was love.

"Now see here, Beth . . ."

There is a family story, probably Roberta's, that on at least one occasion she locked Beth in her room, but surely she was not so foolish as to have done that.

Three

11

AS I SAID, my name is Tom Burton.

Apart from the beauty of that spring morning on the coast of Maine a few years ago — a beauty just slightly marred, perhaps by that uncharacteristic behavior of a black-backed gull — I recall nothing unusual about the first hours unless it was a reference my wife made to my mother. But she often spoke of my mother. My mother was on hand when each of our three children was born. She wanted to be there to wash dishes and scrub floors and to tell me how lucky I was. She was quite as delighted to be a grandmother as I was to be a father — each time. We are all fools for Family.

My mother looked on my wife as one who had saved me from a Mormon girl who rode in horseshows and wore net stockings and earrings before noon, and from a girl who cooked for us on the ranch in Montana and also rode horses, but not in horseshows. My mother worried because I was a dreamer and left the ranch and security and wanted to write books. She knew no one who wrote books and although her father, my grandfather, was himself something of a dreamer, he certainly never left the ranch in Idaho because his wife, the Sheep Queen, would never have put up with it. She did not put up with much.

My mother knitted suits for our two little boys; anything so homely as knitting is the last thing you'd associate with my mother, but so was her insistence that when she scrubbed a floor it must be done on her hands and knees. And that's how I scrub a floor.

That morning on the coast of Maine the forsythia was waning and the lilacs were waxing. Each year our friends are afraid the lilacs won't be ready for Decoration Day to round out the artificial flowers that strike me as a better argument for eternal life than fresh ones.

The tide was coming in. A tart breeze began to whistle in over the ocean and my wife and I discussed birds, about which I know little, even with Peterson's bird book in my hands. Many birds look alike, except crows and robins and bluebirds and gulls. The others won't stay still long enough to identify, but I was glad to see the birds back and I spoke of the chickadees, which I knew.

My wife was reading. She reads and she reads. She read *War and Peace* during her confinement with our first son when they used to keep them in bed for ten days, and again with my second son by which time hospitals had decided ten days was nonsense. By the time our daughter was born the hospitals had so shortened the period of confinement my wife had time only to get through *Bleak House*. During the Depression she and her parents were poor because her father was a professor of English and for entertainment they made fudge and ate it and read all the novels of Dostoevsky and *Gone with the Wind*.

Scarlet O'Hara was not beautiful . . .

"Chickadees?" my wife said. "They've been here all winter."

"I had catbirds more in mind," I said. "And all those vireos."

"They've been back for some time."

"The catbirds are flirting around the chokecherry tree," I said.

"They nest there. One time your mother and I picked choke-cherries up in the hills where somebody saw a bear — you know, that year we were on the ranch in Montana during the war and people had to color their margarine in those funny plastic bags, it was sort of obscene, except of course we didn't because we had butter on the ranch. Your mother was the most beautiful woman I ever saw, the most beautiful person."

"She knew how to dress."

"And how to walk. For so small a woman she seemed so tall, and all those hats. I never understood how to tie a scarf. We had long talks."

"I remember."

"We talked a lot about you. She was afraid something awful would happen to you."

"Maybe it will."

"So of course she was glad when the movies gave you fifty thousand dollars because they understood that, out there."

"Chokecherries are bitter," I said.

"But not the jelly and not the syrup. Can you imagine eating the way we used to out there on the ranch, and at six o'clock in the morning? Pancakes and fried eggs and ham and potatoes? And when I was pregnant it made me ill when the cook began searing those big roasts."

"Roasts have a basic quality," I said. "Something elemental and cruel. Roasts are a reminder that no cow gets off scot-free."

The mail came into Georgetown, Maine, in a pickup truck at ten o'clock. By ten-fifteen the mail was sorted except during Christmas season when all those cards come bringing a sense of guilt and leaving you to wonder what to do about Jewish friends. Christ is a sore point. However, had there been no Crucifixion, there'd be no Resurrection. I drove the Volvo through the woods to the post office and opened Box 263 with the combination CHF. Inside I found an appeal from the blind who had sent me a necktie for which they expected I would send five dollars. The blind send quite nice neckties, and quite often, but as a novelist I have little use for neckties, but what are you going to do? I seldom go anywhere and when I do it is to lunch at the Ritz in Boston, paid for by my editor at Little, Brown, and I assume Little, Brown reimburses him. Not even successful editors can afford many lunches at the Ritz; martinis and open-faced sandwiches there demand magnificent money. My editor is a capital companion. So few have a sense of humor. His ancestors got here on the *Mayflower* and something of them is reflected in his shoes which are highly polished and never new. I have often wondered who first wears them. It is my understanding that old Emperor Franz Josef hired people to break in his *lederhosen*. The neckties from the blind are not quite good enough sometimes; they have an annoying sheen.

I found an appeal from a priest in Montana who runs a school for Indian children, and who signs himself Your Beggar — most effective. The enclosed literature included a snapshot of a thin little girl with enormous eyes. Did I inherit my mother's concern for the Indians? And she her concern from her father, Thomas Sweringen? Each Christmas she sent the Indians boxes of food; they often visited the ranch where she gave them sides of beef and sacks of flour. The squaws came in and had coffee and cigarettes with her in the living room and they talked Shoshone. *Zant-nea-shewungen* means I love you. She bought their gloves and moccasins at twice the price the stores paid for them, and distributed them among her friends. She once wore a fancy pair of high beaded moccasins to a cocktail party in New

York given by a tony friend who knew Edda Mussolini and later committed suicide on Capri. Money isn't the answer. When I got married, this handsome woman gave me a pair of white silk pajamas, five hundred dollars and a mandolin.

Also in the mail was the proof of the dust jacket for my new novel. It showed a handsome face very like the Arrow Collar Man, *circa* 1912, but not so handsome as my father who much resembled the fellow in my novel. Somewhere around the house I had a few studio photographs he had taken at the time he tried out for the movies. The contrived shadows point out his cheek-bones and Barrymore nose; he casually holds gloves and looks into the middle distance where are perhaps fame and money. Why on earth he didn't make it when Rod La Roque and Richard Barthelmess did, I shall never understand. His presence before the camera of those days could not have been more wooden than theirs. As lookers, he and my mother in their brief years together must have been quite a pair.

He ended up editing trade journals in Los Angeles for the painters' and carpenters' unions. I was disappointed as a boy when at last I knew what a trade journal was.

And here was an ad from the Kozak people urging me to buy a special rag so processed you can wipe mud and grit off your car without scratching it. The remarkable thing was, the rag worked. The company would do well to make their product available in retail stores and not require you to send for it. Life has gotten so complicated nobody has time to sit down and send for things. There is no time to locate, to box, to wrap, to secure and address and stamp and mail the raincoats and hats and eyeglasses and single earrings left behind by departed guests. One friend of mine now dead of alcoholism made it clear to guests that she had no intention of ever mailing anything back to anybody, that she simply couldn't and wouldn't do it. She had a special closet for the leavings of guests: gloves, hats, tennis racquets, Hallowe'en masks, even a set of tails. She was interested in local theater groups and played whoever it was in *The Philadelphia Story.*

Hello, Mother. Hello, Dad. The calla lilies are in bloom again . . . When I knew her in college she didn't drink at all. Alcohol isn't the answer, either, nor is many marriages. I wrote a novel about her that was published in 1970.

The last piece of mail was a surprise, a letter from my youngest aunt, Pauline. The return address was simply, "Polly, Salmon, Idaho." Everybody in Salmon knew who Polly was. She and her husband Bill were still known in the family as "the kids" because her father, my grandfather Thomas, had lived to be a hundred, and his sister, my great-aunt Nora, was still living at a hundred and two. Aunt Nora was working against time finishing up writing "The Early History of Lemhi County." In it she speaks of her father's discovery of gold and the gold chain he made during the winters when the water was frozen and the sluice box was idle. The chain was four feet long. I had last seen Aunt Nora when she was a hundred and one. Her black hair had just begun to gray a little, but she was nicely made up with a bit of rouge; she wore beads and earrings. She took me aside. "You know, Tom," she said, "I am very old."

We all love each other. My aunt Maude, the middle aunt, once told me, "You know, Tom, we've always liked each other better than anybody else." It is not that we think we are better than anybody else but that we are better company, at least for each other. We like to have fun.

I have felt especially close to Polly and her husband Bill because they are scarcely fifteen years older than I. They have treated me as a contemporary. They like picnics in the backyard at night by the light of tonga torches — cans of kerosene on sticks poked into the lawn, wicks smoking away — and music from old seventy-eight records pouring out from the open doors of the garage.

> *I found a million-dollar baby*
> *In a five-and-ten-cent store.*

Fun was a sudden decision to drive to Las Vegas, and to telephone the other relatives to join in and drive south in convoy through the Craters of the Moon country, stopping occasionally to have a drink and let the others catch up, and then into Nevada where all those good hotels are, and the gambling and meeting interesting people.

Polly went to the College of William and Mary in Virginia where she flunked Greek. She came back to Idaho on the Milwaukee out of Chicago wearing a suit whose folds and drapes were inspired by the opening of Tutankhamen's tomb; she carried a long gray swagger stick. A few years later I remember her driving her fiancé's brown Chrysler 60 roadster down the road, sitting up on the folded top, steering with her feet; the sun was just coming up. That's a nice way to remember an aunt. There had been a party the night before that my mother gave at the ranch in Montana, my stepfather's place. A woman had been hired to play "Marcheta" and "Tea for Two" on my mother's Steinway and a guest who people said would have been a professional if she hadn't married sang "The Life of a Rose," a song that like certain sunsets and the smell of sagebrush after rain remains with me. That night they mixed their gin with Silver Spray; I have never since known anyone who has ever heard of Silver Spray. And then the sun came up and there was my aunt steering the Chrysler with her feet — my God, almost fifty years ago.

She had never been much of a one to write. And so? Was Aunt Nora dead? Hardly likely. Had somebody been divorced?

There had been a good many divorces in the family. If anybody felt himself too much of an individual and insisted on standing apart from the family, he was divorced, usually quietly, usually with little ill will. He should have known what he was getting into. One man had to be divorced because, as my mother pointed out, he didn't take his wife out for a steak. He was sullen and jealous, always watching. Some had been divorced because they were no fun, had balked at fishing and camping and horses and hotels; others had disliked what they interpreted as our ancestor worship. Our attitude seemed natural enough to us. We felt that our ancestors were worth worshipping. Their possessions, wooden churns, candlesticks, gold scales, Bibles, firearms, reading glasses, mirrors, coffee pots, dishes, ledgers, valentines and bookmarks were cherished and displayed. My aunt Polly sometimes gathered up the stubs of old candles and recast them in the old candle mold. I myself, one Christmas, stole the only studio portrait of my great-grandfather. It is here in a box at my side. He is wearing the gold chain he made.

We picnicked annually, sometimes as many as fifty of us, on the very spot where George Sweringen had discovered gold and we ate what he had eaten: beans and bacon and trout fried over the fire, and dried apple pies. We felt we could reach out and touch him and his wife Lizzie who had often sung hymns. We were proud of them and felt they would be proud of us. They would have liked us better than anybody else.

My mother divorced my father in 1917 when I was two years old. I had heard it remarked that he was "no good." "No good" was a phrase often on my family's lips. Applied to women, it meant they slept around. Applied to a man, it meant he slept around or drank badly, didn't know the value of a dollar, was a poor provider, was cruel or indifferent or selfish or didn't fit in. Any one of these faults was liable to lead to all the rest. As a child growing up, I did not often dwell on what "no good" meant, for as a son I wished to believe the best of my father, to read what I wished into the studio portraits and the snapshot of him with his fancy car.

Dear Tom:

The stationery my aunt Polly wrote on was long since outmoded. It was headed THE STATE THEATRE. And under that, *Where there's always a good show.* In that theater, long before my aunt and uncle took it over as another one of their numerous projects, I had cheered Tom Mix and Yakima Canute. There in the darkness Dracula had scared the hell out of me. When television brought moving shadows into the house and scuttled the movies, my aunt and uncle had the seats removed, installed dim lights and turned the place into a bar, soon to be called a cocktail lounge. The music on the juke box, whose plastic front was lighted up with a swooning display rather like the aurora borealis, had a strong western flavor, for the Old West and the Cowboy were a lingering presence in Salmon and even gas station attendants wore high-heeled boots as if, but for adverse circumstances, they too would be riding the range instead of looking at it across the Salmon River.

THE STATE THEATRE was now THE STATE LOUNGE. The tilt of the floor towards what had once been the stage gave strangers who drank there the feeling they had drunk more than usual or that they were on board ship.

The town of Salmon, populated by scarcely two thousand, supported eight more bars and lounges for the ranchers and cowboys and sheepherders who came in from up and down the valley with their high heels and Stetsons and their faithful dogs that went on inside, out of the heat or the cold.

But there was the problem of what to do with all that stationery, but really no problem at all. My aunt Polly simply used it, and it was a pleasant reminder that nothing much had changed. She kept the many boxes of paper in the garage along with a professional vacuum cleaner once used to suck up popcorn and chewing gum wrappers from the aisles of THE STATE THEATRE, and a fetus preserved in alcohol. The fetus had belonged — if belonged is the right word — to Polly's father-in-law, the second doctor to come into Lemhi County. The first doctor to come into the county was my great-aunt Nora's husband, Uncle Doctor. Uncle Doctor had died rather young, shortly after he bought a Model T Ford, retired his buggy and turned his team out to pasture, but Aunt Nora continued to prepare with mortar and pestle certain capsules of medicine which she passed on to friends and relatives who had counted on their magic while her husband was living years and years before. It made no sense to her that what she was doing was illegal so she ignored the fact.

Sometimes over drinks my aunt Polly and her husband talked of abolishing the fetus, but there was the question of whether there should be a service of some kind if they buried it, or should they simply take it to the dump, since it had no name to grace a marker. There might be some legal question, some regulation on the books down in Boise.

And there in the garage was the old Victrola and stacks of records and extra rolls for the piano in the house. "That Old Gang of Mine."

"Valencia." Spain got a big hand in the twenties — roses, romance and castanets were on the loose. Some sang that they were determined to marry the belle of Barcelona. In his Hispano-Suiza, Alfonso XIII raced off to Cannes.

Somebody remembered a roll that was certain to retrieve certain nostalgias — must be in the garage — and drinks in hand, host and guests traipsed across the lawn where they came on many wonderful things; a warped ukulele prompted long thoughts of Whispering Smith singing "Gimme a Little Kiss." And here was a hearing aid once used by a long-ago Sweringen who embarrassed the family by asking strangers if they believed in the Lord Jesus Christ, and huddling close to hear their answer. The thing resembled the larger intestine.

Again and again they were brought up short by the fetus in its boozy limbo.

In her letter, my aunt Polly urged me to forgive her scrawl. Her typewriter, she wrote, was broken and the man who fixed them had suddenly moved to Idaho Falls where his daughter was, some kind of trouble, she guessed. Anyway, an attorney in Seattle had called her. They had just got back from Las Vegas and had scarcely got into the house when the telephone rang, this attorney. He had tried, he said several times. He said this woman client of his claimed to be the daughter of Elizabeth Sweringen and Ben Burton. The next day came a letter from the woman herself.

I stood there in the post office in mild shock, and then I surprised the postmistress by laughing. But what an irony, I thought, that the attorney's preposterous call and the letter from this preposterous woman should come almost to the day on the tenth anniversary of my mother's death.

12

WHEN I HAD last seen my mother, not six months before she died, it was not the possibility of her death that concerned me — all of us live to be very old. It was her drinking. I find this hard to say because nobody wants to admit that anybody close is a problem drinker. It is painful — part shame, part concern, part helplessness — to see someone one loves expose herself to the opinions of those whose opinions she would once have dismissed and on whose opinions she is now somehow dependent. Anybody who has an alcoholic parent, spouse or child will know what I mean. We wonder how much we ourselves have to do with their drinking.

Some years before this, my stepfather retired from the ranch in Montana that was just fifty miles over the Divide from my grandmother's ranch in Idaho. He and my mother moved to Missoula, Montana, a small city but big for Montana, one with a certain style because the university is located there. A professor in Harris tweed with patches at the elbows is as likely to be abroad in the sunny streets as a cowboy or sheepherder from the surrounding hills and valleys. Books are read and even written there.

They took an apartment on the top floor of the Wilma Building — the Skyscraper by the Bridge; eight storeys tall, it did not scrape much sky but it was a good address. It housed Mrs. King's Dress Salon where were pretty little chairs and mirrors that reflected the faces of those bent on purchase. Mrs. King herself sometimes served up coffee to those who were in no hurry to make up their minds. A woman need not even leave the building to have her hair or teeth repaired, for Miss Rose was ready and apt with her combs and curlers, and on the floor above, Doctor Murphy waited with his probes and drills. He was so expensive it was fashionable to approach his chair. Movies on the ground floor offered distraction from the real world. Once Barbara Stanwyck came there in person with her husband of the moment. They appeared in a revue called *Tattle Tales*. Miss Stanwyck granted an interview to a reporter from the university paper who found Miss Stanwyck "charming."

I had not realized my mother had a problem. I felt I could not mention it to her, since I had not actually seen her drinking. I saw only the result of it, the vague but calculated guess at the distance from one piece of furniture to another, each of which she touched as if there she found sufficient courage to proceed to the next piece. I recognized almost nothing in the apartment; almost everything was new, and expensive. The old things were left behind at the ranch with my half sister and her husband. I wondered if the old things would have lent her greater courage. I think not.

I doubt if I would have spoken to her even had I seen her pour whiskey from a bottle, for I knew enough of alcoholics to know they simply deny what your eyes have seen — and then what do you say? Do you say they are not only drunks but liars? You do not. You grieve. I believe she knew that I knew, for in the blue-gray eyes was a timid apology where once there had been a pride that matched her superb carriage, a way of moving about a room that had so impressed my wife.

That she had a problem puzzled me. No one else in the family had a problem, and I watched my stepfather watching her with a certain coldness that I was afraid might erupt into anger. Before his anger, she would be quite defenseless. Before his anger she would only shake her head and smile that timid smile she hoped might shield her. My stepfather angry? He seldom was. So far as I knew he had never done anything wrong in his life except make people uneasy. It had been said of his father, who had had an astonishing resemblance to the late Kaiser, that "nobody liked him and everybody respected him." Such a backhanded compliment is not unlike saying someone has "matured" which means he used to be a son of a bitch and is now somewhat less so. Perhaps the same could be said of my stepfather. Certainly everybody, including me, respected him. Who can but respect a man who pays his bills promptly and has the means to, who has never been seen without shoes or shirt, refuses to discuss personalities and will not be drawn into trivial conversation? As a child I never doubted he would be a good President of the United States, would deal easily with disarmament and the Japanese threat in the Pacific. He would lay keels for other carriers than the *Lexington* and the *Saratoga*. He held all the cards as one does who is not known to have sinned or erred like the rest of us, who has never lusted, gambled on the future nor waked to a hangover with frightful apprehensions, a man who has never been known to weep. I had both admired and feared him and — quite without his permission — I had as a child begun to call myself by his last name instead of my father's name. I tried to acquire his swift, precise handwriting. To this day I see something of him in my signature.

I felt I could count on him as I could not count on my father.

I saw my father when I was five, again when I was twelve, and not again until I was thirty and had two sons of my own. By the time I was eighteen I felt ghostly under the cloud of my assumed name, and I thought maybe being with my father might give me an identity, that my presence might even be a pleasure to him.

I telephoned him in California. Long Distance, in those days, was impressive. The words "Long Distance is calling" were as arresting as "This is Western Union."

His voice on Long Distance was pleasant, carefully modulated as if he spoke from a stage, but guarded, and at last he told me gently that "the exchequer," as he put it, would not allow my visit. So I knew he was poor as well as selfish and had so little pride he would admit poverty. On my mother's side of the family, to be poor was to be immoral. It was well known how easily the poor fall into sin.

I know now that my father was then living with a woman who later became one of my several stepmothers.

I now believe that my mother married my stepfather to give me the very security I thought I might find with my father. Why else would she have married a man of such frightening rectitude?

My mother had once drunk very well. As a child I had thought her drinking and smoking quite dashing, thoughts probably prompted by pictures of women so much like her that appeared in *Vogue* and *Harper's Bazaar* and *Country Life*. They are dressed *pour le sport;* airdales strain at the leashes they hold. Those were the days of bottled-in-bond whiskey, orange blossom cocktails and Fatimas — What a Whale of a Difference Just a Few Cents Make. I have a snapshot of my mother taken on a camping trip down the Salmon River — she was the first woman to shoot the rapids on that River of No Return. A bottle

147

of whiskey is beside her. She is lovely even in riding pants and high laced boots. No, I couldn't understand it. And I was afraid that the minute I left the Wilma Building to fly back East, my stepfather would speak to her, and that would be that.

Except for what remained of her beauty, she held no cards at all.

Six months later she had an operation, and then another. Something had gone wrong with the first. She lay back in her hospital bed, her arms bruised with needles. An ugly tube in her exquisite nose fed her oxygen. It's too bad the beautiful can't be spared such indignities. A bubble in a gauge marked from one to ten showed how much oxygen she needed to keep her alive, some days more, some days less. Each evening in the apartment in the Wilma Building my stepfather, one or all of my aunts, sometimes my grandfather who was ninety-two at the time, and I would raise our drinks in a salute and my stepfather would say, "Well, here's to Beth." Beyond his calm I sensed despair. I could imagine him as a stolid, frightened child. For whatever reason my mother had married him, I knew now he had married her because he loved and needed her. I was surprised to find that I liked him. We might have been friends, and I could understand how painful my presence must have been over the years, for I was a constant reminder that he had not been my mother's first husband. The stepson as well as the stepfather is the villain of the piece ...

I said little prayers in the sterile elevator in the hospital as it rose and descended; I said little prayers in the long, clean halls off which doors opened on pain and death. In those days I half believed that God might save a woman whose death at sixty-seven could benefit nobody. I more than half believed. A few years earlier I had written a novel about God and a miracle in a church in Boston where were — and are — gathered together a mixed bag of Harvard professors, blacks, Cabots, reformed alcoholics, paupers, millionaires and jailbirds, artists and writers. A sentimental book, readers wept through it and a thousand wrote me, among them two admirals and a United States senator. It was my worst book and it made the most money because people need to believe in miracles. What but miracles can save them? Is there another answer? Love? You may have seen that book on television, but who now remembers old Studio One? *Où sont les neiges d'antan?*

I was an Episcopalian because the whole family was. They said they liked the dignity, but except for my aunt Roberta and her daughter Janet, who both liked singing in the choir, few in the family ever attended services in the little stone church in Salmon where my mother married my father and where I was baptized. You see, services began at eleven in the morning, and eleven was a little early on a Sunday for those of the family who lived in Salmon; they all enjoyed sleep, all liked to sleep late, never having outgrown their youthful ability to sleep late. They believed that one reason why everybody lived so long was that they got enough sleep — that, and not worrying. Worrying was a waste of time, so they didn't.

But as the daughter of a Civil War captain who went on to become the warden of a penitentiary, my grandmother the Sheep Queen had been taught that the sooner people rise in the morning, the better for everybody: Thomas Edison had required but two hours sleep and look what became of him. Sleep beyond six each morning was shameful except, of course, for Thomas Sweringen who was different from other men.

But the Sheep Queen could not be expected to journey the thirty miles from the ranch to church in Salmon even after the invention of the automobile. Each year, therefore, the rector of the church managed the journey from Salmon to the ranch even *before* the invention of the automobile. There he was invited to say grace over the boiled mutton, boiled navy beans and beet greens to the embarrassment of the hired men who were so out of touch with God that even the mention of His Name was painful and called into question their misspent lives, their boozing and whoring, their estranged fathers and heartbroken mothers. During grace my grandfather looked into the middle distance; he treasured his father's buckskin-bound Bible, not because it was perhaps inspired but because it had belonged to his father who had signed it whose father had signed it and whose father had signed it.

The Bishop of Idaho, too, stopped at the ranch on his yearly visitation to the parish and remembered to bring along old clothes because he was certain to be invited to walk across the frosty fields and look at sheep. He knew that my grandmother paid taxes second only to the railroad, and she did indeed give the church in Salmon a stained-glass window of Christ as the Shepherd of His Flock. The Bishop knew well that my grandmother's philosophy was summed up in Henley's "Invictus":

> *I thank whatever gods may be*
> *For my unconquerable soul.*

She sometimes quoted the entire poem in a quiet, sepulchral voice — she had been trained in elocution. At the words, "My head is bloody but unbowed," she inclined her own head slightly and then snapped it up on her spine. It must have struck the Bishop as an outlandishly unchristian philosophy with its gods and self-determination, but invited by one who believes her soul to be unconquerable, there was nothing for it but go out and look at sheep.

I see now that my belief was not in God or church but in the family and the family's traditions; this belief I hope to pass on to my sons and my daughter because I don't know what there is to believe in except Family.

So I said my little prayers for my mother in the halls of the hospital and watched the bubble in the oxygen gauge, and she died, she who had moved from chair to chair six months before, who in 1908 had been presented at Court in Ottawa. She died at dawn, my beautiful mother. Outside, across from the hospital, a neon sign still flashed EATS EATS EATS.

She was buried from the little stone church in Salmon.

The word *woman* can possess strange overtones. Opposed to the word *man* it simply identifies sex; one imagines a skirt rather than pants, soap operas rather than baseball, jewelry rather than power tools. But the word *woman* taken alone can be threatening. It is not by chance that a witch was thought female. One hears little of wicked stepfathers.

It is the Jones *woman* who allegedly fell and injured her hip at the yard sale and caused the estate to be tied up in the courts. Her attorney sues for a hundred thousand dollars — the entire estate. It is the Smith *woman* who gives the damaging testimony and then vanishes. It is she who got mixed up with Richard Roe and caused him to leave wife and child destitute, and she who waits out there for the right moment to come forward and cause trouble, she who turns up in hat and veil when you thought all was settled and you dared to smile. She knocks on the door and takes up the telephone. She has a stalking patience and may be mad.

And now we had the Nofzinger woman.

"I flatter myself," my wife said, "that I knew your mother well enough and she loved and trusted me enough so that she would have told me if anything like that had happened. That's how close we were, those times we'd walk up on the hill and build a sagebrush fire and sit and talk.

My aunt Polly wrote that she believed the woman should know there was no truth in what she believed or said she believed, and that I ought to write her.

I would indeed, and at once.

Dear Mrs. Nofzinger. Dear, indeed!

I wrote the woman that I couldn't imagine where she had gotten hold of my mother's name, and that as a novelist I was quite equipped to judge character and so knew that nothing in my mother's life or in any of her actions or tendencies could reasonably lead one to believe that she had had a child other than me and my half sister by a second marriage. I wrote that my mother's love for me and my half sister was certainly no greater than it would have been for another child — why should it be? I wrote that she would never have abandoned me in any conceivable circumstances and would never have abandoned an earlier child, let alone a little girl.

"You would be asking me to believe that my mother was unnatural," I wrote. "Loyal is what she was. I think she never — ever — thought first of herself."

And I wrote the woman that so explosive a secret could not have been kept for fifty years, that in fifty years such a secret would have surfaced, that someone who knew would have spoken out in anger, in drunkenness, in spite or in despair. I wrote that my mother was now dead and could no longer be damaged by any disclosure, and therefore if such a secret existed, it would now certainly come out. My mother was dead and out of reach of blackmail.

As I wrote the word "blackmail" it occurred to me that that's what the woman was up to — blackmail. If this woman Amy Nofzinger was innocent, it was a terrible accusation, but I let the word stand. I signed myself Very Sincerely, that coldest of closings, and sealed the envelope with my own spittle. And that was *that.*

"Maybe the woman's crazy," my wife remarked. "Desperate. Anyone who tries to find parents who have abandoned her must know how dangerous it is."

"I'm simply forgetting it," I said. "And I think this would be a good day for a picnic."

So in our wicker picnic hamper we took slices of cold steak, crackers and cheese, fruit and red wine down over the rocks to the sea and listened to what the sea had to say. What the sea had to say is that nothing has ever changed, and that all things pass. That's what they all come down to the sea to hear.

The woman had written my aunt Polly that she had been born in 1912, and her parents, according to the city records in Seattle, were living together in 1912 as man and wife.

Then fancy and romance took over the woman's story; the woman knew the works of the Brothers Grimm; it was absurd: she claimed to have been left on a doorstep. Had it not been so absurd, it would have been pathetic. The doorstep had been arranged by her adoptive mother — so she did not feel herself so abandoned as on a random doorstep or on a bench in Union Station. You see, her own mother had chosen that doorstep.

Yes. An adoptive cousin who worked as a student nurse in the hospital (what a coincidence!) had recognized her as the baby in the hospital who was the child of the beautiful woman who walked the corridors and kept a picture of a handsome man on the table. Since one infant looks very like another I could not credit the adoptive cousin's testimony. Except for name tags, I could not — honestly — have picked out any one of my children from the other babies in the nursery, although at the time I pretended I could. It was all wild romanticism, beautiful woman, handsome man, picture on table, illegitimate child. And if there was anything at all to the woman's story, the woman my father eventually married was not the woman who arranged for her little girl to be left on a doorstep at the age of two weeks.

"It's only a story," my wife said. "And you said you were going to forget it. The world is full of crazy people. Remember, we read about the minister who said he was going to walk on water."

"That was down South," I said.

"But how about the woman who said she was given a thorough physical examination by some people from outer space who flew into New Hampshire?"

"They drink too much in New Hampshire. Highest per capita drinking in the United States, I understand."

"Well then, why don't you write your father and ask him what he knows about it?"

13

AS A BOY, I was fascinated by automobiles and longed one day to own a Rolls-Royce. Eventually I did, secondhand. I bought it in 1950 on Long Island from a fellow who collected all the fabled cars — Rolls, Isotta-Fraschini, Hispano-Suiza, Invicta, Lagonda and Bugatti — and lay in wait for eccentrics like me. My car had been the Rolls exhibited at the New York World's Fair, a jet black *sedanca de ville* with a price tag of thirty-six thousand dollars in 1939. It figured in a novel I wrote about a ruined man's search for perfection.

As a boy I could identify each make far up the road, long before it reached the ranch house where I lived with my mother and stepfather. I knew by heart the boxy outlines of the Essex and the Hudson, the swift profile of the Auburn, the horse-collar shape of the Franklin's radiator, and I knew that radiator was false, since the Franklin was air-cooled. The insignias on the radiator shells of almost every make were as marvelous to me as coats-of-arms. The Packard and the Pierce-Arrow were so obviously grand and expensive that the makers saw no need to place any insignia at all on the cars to identify them; I knew the Packard by the shape of the radiator and the Pierce by the headlights set into the fenders — not very difficult, I admit. I admired a rangy young rancher who drove a Stutz and who went broke some years later in the Depression. I think my sensible stepfather could have foreseen that, and that it was rangy young ranchers who drove Stutzes, so to speak, who had caused the Depression.

I did not expect my grandmother the Sheep Queen to own anything other than that old gray Dodge sedan. Impressive though she might be, she was, after all a woman. A woman did not feel as men did about the internal combustion engine, were not concerned with wheelbase and torque. She cared only to get from one place to the other, and in what she got there was of no moment. But I was puzzled that my stepfather, who could afford anything, drove only a Hudson.

I thought my mother who dressed as she did and walked as she did deserved a more elegant conveyance, for I thought automobiles reflected their drivers, and what a Hudson reflected was not flattering. A Hudson was neither one thing nor the other; the best that could be said of Hudsons was that bootleggers used them to run booze down from Canada. I put my stepfather's owning a Hudson down to his lack of imagination. I know now that he felt himself so aloof from rangy young ranchers that he had no need for their status symbols and thought of them as "boobs," a word he sometimes called those who lurched carelessly through life.

My own father I scarcely knew except through letters and the posed photographs my mother kept a secret in the bottom drawer of her dressing table, a piece of furniture so feminine there was no possibility that my stepfather would approach it. It would never have occurred to him that anybody would hide anything from him.

Late one summer when I was twelve, my father wrote me on heavy paper in that distinguished hand of his that he was coming to visit, that he was driving up from California, and that he was driving a Roamer automobile. At the word "Roamer" I felt a shock of pride, for I knew that the Roamer was an "assembled" car, that the engine was a Duesenberg and that the radiator shell was an exact copy of the Rolls radiator shell. How proud I was of my father — if one can be proud of an abstraction.

What drafts of emotion must have moved through that vast log house as the hour of my father's arrival approached — my stepfather had never met my father and would not wish to. Now my mother was to see once again the man whose pictures she kept in a drawer, once again she would face the man she had married in spite of her mother's objections.

I can see her now, standing before the fireplace in that log house, the fire burning behind her. It had been a cool summer and the wind was whistling down from Black Canyon. She smoked a cigarette. I see my stepfather sitting with his legs crossed, reading the *Saturday Evening Post*, a journal whose opinions were his. He was reading because it was Sunday and he was not required anywhere else. Out in the bunkhouse beside the long, low barn, the hired men washed clothes, shaved, nursed hangovers brought home from town the night before and read *Western Story* magazine and Captain Billy's *Whiz Bang*. They liked jokes about privies; they laughed at the traveling salesman and the farmer's daughter.

I watched for the dust down the road at the top of a rise where any approaching car was first visible, where each morning the stage — at first a Lozier and later on a Cadillac — appeared carrying a passenger or two and the mail for Lemhi County across the hill, for by now the little train ran only once a week.

And then, there it was, there was the dust like smoke at the top of the rise, and out of it appeared my father in his Roamer. A few minutes later the Roamer glided into the driveway and stopped.

My father wore a tweed cap of the sort I'd seen on Englishmen in the movies, and a sleeveless sweater of tomato red, such a color as I'd never before seen on a man. From the car he turned on us a great smile as we stood on the porch. He leaped out of the Roamer without bothering to open the door and bounded up the steps. Douglas Fairbanks couldn't have equaled it. He shot out his hand to my stepfather as if in victory.

And then, "Tom, Tom," he murmured. "It's been so long."

So long? It had been six years since my mother had remarried and I was left with my father's mother in Seattle while my mother went on her honeymoon. There in Seattle my father appeared one morning to astonish me by squatting before me with lather on his upper lip carefully shaped to resemble a mustache. He pronounced "been" "bean" and he said "agane" for "again." Somewhere along the line he had become an anglophile, maybe because of Shakespeare of whom he often spoke in his letters to me in connection with his amateur theatricals. To him, a person did not age, no: "The shadows lengthened." A person, to him, was not happy or unhappy. Rather, a person attained "Olympian heights" or was sunk in "Stygian depths."

Now on the porch he rested his hand on my shoulder. "And Beth, dear Beth." He stepped back to survey my mother as if she were a painting that must be seen from the correct perspective. He slowly shook his head at the wonder of her. "And Charlie, Charlie."

We went on inside after some awkwardness about who would open the door and who would step inside first.

"Won't you sit down, Ben," my mother said as women have said since Eden, not so much to welcome as to relieve a situation. Seated people are easier to manage; they have relinquished a dangerous mobility. Now came tentative dispersals towards chairs and the couch that had a Navajo blanket draped over the back of it, part of a decorating scheme that included similarly patterned rugs on the floor, a harking back to the fundamental West that was catholic enough to include Indian themes of both north and south and the stuffed heads of mild-eyed deer and a stern buffalo, all victims of man's bloodlust and cunning. Since this scene had not been rehearsed, and since seating arrangements tend to be critical, the question of who would sit first and where was prominent: for when, where, and in what people will sit appears to be of atavistic concern and explains the protocol at lodge picnics, on occasions of state and in the parlor car.

My mother solved the problem by sitting down first, and in a chair that appeared to have been fashioned by a maker of snowshoes of bent, varnished wood and rawhide thongs. Then my father, as guest, sat on the couch, first hesitating as if he meant to play host. I sat beside him, grateful that he had not committed the gaffe of sitting in the Morris chair whose back had been adjusted to my stepfather's lineaments and had been shipped all the way from Boston.

Conspicuous in that room was the absence of my stepfather's brother who rudely remained in his bedroom at the back of the first floor, lying (I knew) with his hands laced behind his head, lying on the brass bed whose twin had been abandoned by my stepfather at his marriage to my mother, lying there studying the imperfections in the plaster ceiling.

"Well," my stepfather said from beside the Morris chair. He began many sentences with "Well," as an announcement that he might speak further. "Well, how about a drink?"

My father's smile was warm. "Don't mind if I do, Charles," he said, formal now. "A little libation seems to be in order." He crossed his long legs easily and the gesture drew my attention to his two-toned shoes with wing tips. Like the impossible tomato-red sweater, they were one with the improbable California orange groves and make-believe horizons in movie lots. They were egregious and offensive in this land of sagebrush and reality in southwestern Montana.

The serving up of alcohol, like the carving of the roast, was thought in those days to be a man's prerogative, and both these duties were dispatched by my stepfather with the dedication and dignity of a priest. He now proceeded into the dining room where he removed glasses from the corner china closet. There he kept out of sight the only medicine, to my knowledge, on the ranch — a small bottle of oil of eucalyptus said to cure the common cold. Illness — even the common cold which spared not even my stepfather's family — was frowned upon, looked upon as a weakness, like a dependence on sex or religion which, if practiced, should be practiced in secret. The glasses he placed on a tray on the sideboard. Then he squatted before that huge, crouching mahogany piece; his crouching was somewhat at odds with his dignity. Behind a door was bourbon against the arrival of guests and cattle buyers in big cars who came to dicker for the cattle. It occurred to nobody that anybody but women or foreigners would want anything but bourbon, and anything in it but water.

"Thank you, Charlie," my father said, casual again. He looked with approval at the glass and the liquid.

"Not a bit," my stepfather said, and handed my mother her drink.

"Here's how," my father said, and raised his glass, smiling as if at a memory, and then he raised his chin as if to the future. "Here's to old and new times."

My mother and stepfather raised their glasses but not nearly so high, reasonably hesitant to commit themselves to either past or future. And then my mother glanced around the room. Her eyes, of necessity, rested at last on my father's tomato-red sweater. It shrieked for attention like a coat of mail or a vest of feathers. My mother cleared her throat, a little habit of hers. "What a beautiful color for a sweater, Ben," she said.

My father looked down at the front of the sweater as if puzzled that it should draw attention. "Like it, Beth?"

"Yes," she said. "Very much."

"Charlie?" my father said.

I believe my stepfather was dumbfounded that anyone would require his opinion of any article of clothing, let alone that worn by his wife's divorced husband and a piece of so impudent a color.

"Yes, that's some sweater," he said.

Now my father stood suddenly and tall. In a striking gesture he skinned off the sweater and tossed it to my stepfather who found himself with the thing in his lap, like knitting. It covered his hands. When he freed his hands of it, it moved like a living thing and clung like a leech. I think he had never in his life considered wearing another's clothing — even in an emergency, even after it had been laundered. You might as well have expected him to borrow another man's name, as I had borrowed his. But now, with my father in that room, I felt I had once again my father's name, Burton. My father's great gray car waited outside before the high, sagebrushed hill that shut out the sun long after the rest of the world was awash with light — that great car, that instrument of my pride, that machine whose swift lines suggested instant flight.

My mother glanced away from the sweater that colored and troubled the air around it. "How long can you stay, Ben?"

"Not more than an hour, I'm afraid," my father said.

I felt relief descending upon her. "Only an hour, Ben?"

My father chuckled. "Yes, I thought Tom and I might drive

over the hill and visit his grandparents. How *are* Thomas and Emma, Beth?"

"They're both well, Ben," my mother said. "Are they expecting you?"

My father chuckled again. "I thought it might be a lot of fun to surprise them."

I had caught a note of anxiety in my mother's voice. I knew that the moment we left for Idaho she was going to go to the telephone. This might not be a surprise that would be fun for my grandmother. I had never once heard her mention my father.

"*So*, then," my father said when an hour was up, and he rose slowly as if reluctantly.

My stepfather largely depended on the weather for conversation. He saw change in the shape of clouds, in the shifting winds, in the smell of moisture. He was looked upon as something of a prophet; neighboring ranchers sometimes called him on the telephone to ask what he thought — should they plan a camping trip? Should they start to mow their hay, take a chance on driving into town?

"Looks like rain," he said now, and turned to my father. "I expect you've got your chains with you." I felt he was deliberately avoiding naming my father either Ben or Burton.

"Chains, yes," my father said, and made an easy openhanded gesture towards the car out the window. "But we won't need 'em. That machine out there has four speeds forward. In first gear it gets right down there and digs."

Four forward speeds! My heart leaped. Who but my father would own a car with four forward speeds? And who but he would speak of "first" instead of "low"?

"Chains are a good idea," my mother said, and she hugged herself briefly as if she'd felt a chill. "Charlie's a wonderful driver, just a splendid driver. I hate slick roads. I'd rather get out and walk. It's so easy to slip off." Skillful as she was with

162

horses, she had never come to terms with automobiles; when she drove, she frowned, and seemed to listen for trouble.

"Now, Beth," my father said, "don't you worry your pretty head. So now if you'd get a few things of Tom's together." She rose and my stepfather rose. "I'll deliver Tom back here in a few days after we've made our sentimental journey. I long to see those old mountains over there again, the peaks of my youth, you might say. And then I've got to get back to the land of sunshine. There's always business, you know. Always business, isn't there, Charles?"

"Always, always," my stepfather said, and moved to the barometer on the wall to one side of the skin of a white wolf he himself had shot; the skin was hung head down; the head itself rested on a triangular shelf, built especially; the mouth was open, the teeth intact; a red plaster tongue had been fitted. My stepfather tapped the face of the barometer. "Dropping," he announced.

My father spoke. "We'll be well over the hill before it drops more, won't we, Tom?"

I remember my mother's face as we pulled out of the driveway. She stood on the porch hugging her shoulders as women do who are cold or worried. So you see them standing when husbands are changing tires or are about to kindle fires that may get out of hand and burn everything up. My mother was of course torn between relief at my father's departure and concern for me. Already the thick black clouds were rising fast from behind Black Canyon. Then the lightning began to stalk down over the foothills; thunder bellowed up and down the valley. My stepfather had not only predicted rain; I felt he had caused it. The first fat drops plopped on the dust just ahead, each one a tiny explosion.

My father slowed and stopped the Roamer. "Guess we'd better put the top up, Tom." I had so longed to hear my father speak my name. "You get over on the other side."

He now wore a trench coat with all those flaps and buckles that set apart British officers in the First World War, a dashing, insouciant garment, a costume for those to whom death itself is but a trifle. The wind had risen and the skirts of the thing flapped and snapped. Only with difficulty did my father remove the canvas casing that covered the folded top. As he jerked at the A-shaped structure of the top itself, I realized at once that he had never approached this problem before. His long, thin hands that the kindly might have said resembled a surgeon's fumbled with the simple contraption. His face twisted with pain as he pinched a finger. Aware of my concern, he grinned. "It's nothing," he said.

Under the folded top were the side curtains. These, perforated with metal-encircled eyes like buttonholes, fitted over grommets in the frame of the top. He had trouble twisting the ends of the grommets to secure the curtains, and I knew he had never before either put up the top or fitted the curtains and therefore that he had owned this car a very short time, and since it was at least three years old, that it was second- or maybe even thirdhand. He had never said it was not. Nor had he said that it was. We had been left to believe whatever we wished.

We were soaked in the fifteen minutes it took to get that top up and the curtains on.

I now asked my father the first question I had ever asked him. "Hadn't we better put the chains on?"

I knew what you did with chains. You laid them out in front of the rear wheels, rolled the car just on them, pulled the far length up over the wheel, and fastened them with two mean devices that were the devil if your hands were cold. Somehow they always got bent.

"Good thinking, Tom," said my father, man to man. He went

164

around to the rear of the car, opened the hatch that revealed the rumble seat. In those days that's where the tools and jack were kept, and the Weed chains.

However, there were no chains.

"The devil!" my father said. "Isn't that the devil!" There he stood, the rain running down his handsome face. For a moment his eyes were blank and a second spasm of pain touched his mouth. The wind was in the skirts of his trench coat, the beak of his British cap wilting. "I was certain they were there," he said. "Well, we'll just have to give her a try."

The ranch house was hardly out of sight around the hill when the Roamer slid headlong into the barrow pit. My father bit his lower lip and spun the wheels for a few minutes while the car moved ever deeper into the oily clay that packed itself into what remained of the treads on the tires and rendered them useless.

Then he leaned forward wearily and turned off the ignition and sat looking at his hands. The throbbing silence was pierced by the rain on the canvas top.

I said, "I'll go back and get Charlie."

For the count of ten, I thought he was going to let me do it. My father the protector. "No," he said at last. "That won't do. I'll go."

I remained behind in the now-sloping seat of the disgraced Roamer for more than an hour looking at an early road map of the state of California where the oranges grew and Jackie Coogan acted in pictures and was rich and famous and he was exactly my age. Yes, in those days I, like my father before me, longed to be a movie star. I was stagestruck, but had neither my father's nor my mother's looks. Perhaps I simply longed for a life that was totally different. I didn't know as I sat in that sloping seat, the rain roaring on the canvas top, what I was or who I was or even what name was mine, but with chilling clarity I saw the scene back at the ranch house: my father's approaching the steps quite differently from the first time, when he had leaped at them like a fractious Thoroughbred. Now he would hope not to be seen approaching them.

Then he would be explaining that something had happened to the chains, that they had been stolen in California, some place he had stopped, where he had noticed a suspicious-looking man. He might tell a little story about the place.

Then my stepfather would be taking his battered old Stetson from the top of the bookshelf where he kept it in readiness along with his gloves and field glasses, and he would be reflecting that he had thought he had got rid of my father and me and now here was my father with hat — or rather cap — in hand requesting a team of horses to pull the God-damned car out of the ditch.

And my mother remembering old failures, rented rooms, discontinued utilities, old bad judgments, interested neighbors. A vase of withering flowers.

At last in the rear-view mirror I saw a disturbance, a team of bays that would be Dolly and Molly, hitched to a cart — no more than an axle with wheels and the single seat of an old Deering mowing machine. On that severe and minimal seat sat my stepfather, serene as Caesar in the pouring rain, and beside the cart my father trudged in his wing tips that were far from wings, his silly cap and foolish trench coat.

He stood quickly aside, his feet unsteady in the mud, while my stepfather deftly hooked the log chain to the rear bumper of the helpless Roamer. Roamer, indeed.

I saw, rather than heard, my stepfather speak, and my father nodded at once and got in behind the wheel of the car and rested his long, thin hands on that useless wheel. Dolly and Molly strained and slipped and then the car moved slowly like an awakened beast up and out of the ditch and silently my father and I were dragged backwards to the ranch where my mother waited with the bright bandeau about her forehead and her jewels on her fingers, the sapphires and diamonds.

Next morning after a haunted breakfast and the speech — especially my father's — in single syllables, my father and I took the G&P over the hill to the Sweringen Ranch. There the Sheep Queen — waited.

No. I could not in all conscience write my father about a woman who claimed to be his daughter. At my age I knew well enough what humiliation was, and anyway, I had no reason to believe he would tell the truth. Whatever part he had in the story, he would allow others to guess as he had allowed us to guess about the Roamer and even exactly what he did in "the land of sunshine."

14

I FOUND a letter in our box from the book club who warned that if I did not send a blocking card I would receive a novel written by a policeman. It occurred to me that if policemen patrolled more and wrote less, the cities would be safer. You can no longer walk across Boston Common except with apprehension; only when you have passed on into the Public Gardens can you walk without glancing behind you.

Here was a letter from my elder son; my sons like so many other men's sons have not in the last few years had an easy time of it. My sons like so many other men's sons are gentle, talented liberal arts majors and the business world is alien to them; I'm afraid I taught them a scorn of the business world, of business people as money-grubbers, and of politicians as parasites, like those who inherit wealth. However, these grubbers and parasites are in the majority and scratch each other's backs, and must be manipulated. I did not teach my sons to manipulate because I myself do not know how to manipulate.

My sons sometimes need help and I am happy to help them, since I didn't teach them to be aggressive. I have sometimes needed help.

My neighbor the portrait painter has suggested that I haven't handled things correctly and that he, who regards himself as shrewd and sensible, has handled things better and that it would be good for my sons if from time to time I refused them, and I would refuse them if I were not afraid that if I did they would be going without something they needed. In my view, fathers are supposed to help. I believe that is what fathers are for.

"Very well," my neighbor said.

Then quite by accident I found he had but recently purchased a farm for his daughter and son-in-law because only with a farm could they live as they liked. They wanted to kill their own chickens and make their own bread. Without their own farm it was impossible to be as real as they wished to be.

So, a letter from a son.

And I wasn't surprised to find a letter from the eldest of my aunts, Roberta, for it was she who most often wrote me after my mother's death — took me over.

Dear Tom:

Polly wrote me about the woman this morning and I never heard of anything so crazy in my whole life! I mean I got the letter this morning after I had my coffee. I'm not much good until I've had it. They bring it in at Holiday Inns. In Phoenix, anyway.

Whoever this Nofzinger woman is or whatever she calls herself you can bet your boots it's got something to do with money. That's what they do, these people!

I'll tell you one thing, she's not Beth's daughter! You know perfectly well your mother would never do a thing like that, be with a man before she married him because none of us would and Beth especially because of how she was. I was always closer to her than anybody else because of our age. Anyway Mama would have told me if anything like that had happened and she never did. You can imagine Mama!

I don't think Polly was taken in but if she was it's because she's liable to think the best of people like when the cooks used to steal Papa's field glasses off the gunrack. I think maybe the woman got wind that Mama was Sheep Queen and thought she'd cash in on it. But a good lawyer would fix her! Ours in Salmon is a good one. They're old people — he was in the Legislature and a lot of fun. Beth liked him.

If the woman is anybody, she's Ben's. You're old enough now to know I think the reason Beth divorced your father is that she knew there was another woman and went down and found some of his clothes hanging in the woman's closet.

I've always been happy that we're such a close family.

Oh, by the way. Mary Hester Collins had a nice little party for me right after I got here, you remember Mary Hester — don't you, Tom? She played the piano so well but not like Beth. They have a lovely home here, on two levels, just outside Phoenix, with a pool. She says the filter is the worst part. We sat around it for drinks and then went on inside. They had an animal floating on it for a grandchild.

Then her husband Gene came in with some men and they sat around and joked and talked. They'd been out in the desert doing something for several days in a jeep because they'll go anywhere. He's a good shot, I guess. Your mother liked him but I never much cared how he played jokes on people.

Well, Mary Hester has an aqua-suede couch from Altman's where your mother got her chaise longue with the roses on it, and wall-to-wall lemon shag carpeting. I asked her what she did and she said you can get a little rake thing for the end of the vacuum cleaner and it does it. Yellow's so impractical and the men with their shoes. She has a pretty little Mexican girl and it's a good thing because the room's about the size of our old horse-pasture. Old Billy died more than aged thirty-six and they finally had to file his teeth but Mama loved him.

Mary Hester was tickled because Gene gave her a Cadillac for her birthday but she says the hood is so long she can't see much of the road. You remember how tiny she is and her father was always so tall. I wish I thought I could afford a new one. I hated to see them leave Salmon but he got that lung condition.

Want to do a little shopping tomorrow, but it's so blamed hot. Of course, Mexicans just everywhere and even colored people. They don't mind the heat so much, they say. Guess that's why they're down there. When I go shopping I think of your mother because of her taste. I want a raspberry linen suit to wear with my grandfather's gold chain he made when he was discovering gold during the winter when he couldn't. This is my year for it. Next is Maude's.

Poor dear Beth — gone now from us ten years the 4th. Funny it's now the woman wrote. Sometimes I could just cry. Remember when we left the church and we heard the wild geese fly over with that lonesome sound of theirs, and then in the cemetery how surprised the bees were at all those flowers so early? I love you, Tom. Roberta.

"Your aunts are happy in their little arrangements," my wife said. "It's funny the woman would make up such a story out of whole cloth, and hire an attorney. They don't come cheap these days."

"Maybe the woman borrowed the money because she thought the end would be worth it," I said. "Or maybe the lawyer does. Maybe he's in on it, too."

15

I WENT to Grayling High School in Grayling, Montana, forty-five miles north of the ranch. GRAYLING was picked out in whitewashed rocks on the lawn to one side of the Union Pacific depot so the footloose passengers would know where they were.

I roomed and boarded with a family named Moon. Both Mr. and Mrs. Moon were active, small people; their appeal was like that of certain deliberately dwarfed trees. Mr. Moon was thin and had learned, by leaning into the horizon and taking long strides, to keep abreast of ordinary men.

Mrs. Moon was plump. One could imagine her as a girl. Mr. Moon did something about buildings and loans; on slow afternoons when buildings were not contemplated or loans required, he played rummy with his standard-sized cronies in Jerry's Bar where liquor was available if Jerry knew you. There was often laughter.

Mrs. Moon once very nearly married a man who became famous as a movie producer. She often said she wished she had been able to see into the future; she never dreamed anything like that would become of him, but it did.

The Moon premises, which changed each year as they moved into ever larger rented houses because there were never enough closets, were often redolent of Listerine antiseptic. Mr. Moon was never happier than when, with the use of a twenty-five-cent piece, he could persuade his younger daughter whom he called Bug, to put a towel about his small neck and to apply that liquid, neat, to his balding pate and scrape it with a fine-toothed comb.

Mrs. Moon stuffed and decorated sofa pillows of a curious fabric that was one color when you looked at it one way, and another when you looked at it in another. These and homemade divinity candy she offered up as gifts at Christmastime; she molded aspics of tomato shot through with the commoner raw vegetables said to delight the intestines. On Sundays she served roast pork and applesauce, commenting, as the sun dipped around to the other side of the house, on the sadness and frequency of sickness and death; she carried in her head a list of people who might be comforted by a little visit. After the dishes were quarreled over and done — there were two other children older than Bug — she sat at the upright piano and sang the songs of Carrie Jacobs Bond. "At Dawning" and "The End of a Perfect Day" come to mind. With Jesus Christ she had an almost incestuous relationship that Mr. Moon could not hope to share. Christ's wan, disappointed countenance was hung on several walls in the Moon rooms; implicit in His gaze was the reminder that even the best of us will at last be found wanting.

Sometimes the Moons entered their tan Chevrolet sedan by separate doors and drove out into the nearby hills for picnics. One time perfect strangers from California joined them. They exchanged names, but that was the end of it.

The Moons did not question my misappropriation of my

stepfather's name. I'd never heard them speak of it from behind closed doors. They were deferential, if not to me, to my mother who was, after all, the wife of a rich rancher of good family back East. Brewers had fought in the Revolution. They numbered among their kin the man on whose property was located the dam that broke and caused the Johnstown Flood, a disaster that drowned hundreds and left hundreds of others homeless and thoughtful. Brewers were comfortable in the rooms of a man who had founded Campbell Soup.

It was in the rooms and halls of the high school that I was afraid I would one day be unmasked and revealed for who I was, a Burton — my cover blown. Because I knew the insensitivity of the young and their loathing of impostors, I walked carefully.

> *Go get a rat trap*
> *Bigger than a cat trap!*
> *Cannibal, cannibal, siss boom bah!*
> *Grayling High School, rah, rah rah!*

I learned to type on the third floor up under the eaves and under the tutelege of Miss Metlen, a kind woman who pressed close to inspect my fingering. Up there I learned that the best typewriter was the Underwood Standard and that if you hoped to use one you'd better get up there early or you'd be stuck with a Woodstock or a Remington. I typed "fur, jug, rug," and then later on, *Habits are at first cobwebs; at last, cables.*

From Miss Schoenborn I learned that there exist two forms for the past subjunctive in Spanish, the one used in Spain, the other in South America: *ara* and *ase.* I read *El Sombrero de Tres Picos.* I recall Miss Schoenborn's shoes of a type called "dress ties," and quite different from my mother's shoes. I got extra credit for memorizing the fables of La Fontaine.

La cigale, ayant chanté tout l'été . . .

I learned that the gerund takes the possessive and that the subject of the infinitive is in the objective case. Miss Kirk-patrick.

Mr. Ogren wore brown suits and carried in his breast pocket a black comb with which, in distracted moments, he raked his spiky hair. From him I learned that aqua regia will attack gold and that nitric acid, carefully applied, will remove warts. I look back with wonder at the excellence of those teachers in that small town in that small school under a high hill on whose slope you could sometimes see wild horses grazing. I want here to express my appreciation for what they did for me.

My lab partner was a boy named Bobby Kerwin. His aunt was a busy little creature who gave the impression of having a humped back and who rented a cubicle in the hotel where she typed up letters for traveling salesmen. Bobby was thin and pale, had no interest in athletics and in pauses would pop aspirin into his mouth. Surely he had been a sickly child and it was feared he would perish. Like many of the sickly, who appear to have been granted perceptions denied the hale, Bobby sniffed out faults and weaknesses more easily than he breathed. He knew who had released rotten egg gas in Study Hall. He knew who among the football team carried condoms in their wallets and which girls lay with them. Bobby's wide knowledge of petty thefts and indiscretions was said to be put to use by the principal; he was often seen entering and leaving that official's office where Old Glory, drooping from a staff in the corner, and a bust of Washington proclaimed a national preference, and a bust of Caesar, a literary.

There was no way to punish Bobby Kerwin. Who among the apprehended culprits would dare lay a hand on a boy who looked and walked like a ghost? One could only hope for nature to take its course.

I had done nothing to offend Bobby. Far from it. I let him copy the answers from my notebook, for his gifts were neither mathematical nor scientific, but musical. He had not the breath for horns or even the shriller woodwinds, but his prowess with the fiddle was precocious, as is often true of the doomed.

The laboratory reeked of formaldehyde. At an earlier hour the place was the scene of the selective dismembering of cats and dogfish by those who could stomach it, and it was in that haunting solution that poor bodies were preserved and marketed. Mr. Ogren, professional in a rumpled gray smock that he hoped would protect him from random corrosive acids, moved up and down the aisles between slate-topped benches fitted with sinks and faucets. His eyes, sharpened by thick glasses, were on the lookout for procrastinators and cheats.

My notebook was open; I proceeded with the experiment of the day, the introduction of divers metals, one by one, into the pale flame of the Bunsen burner. Some metals (I forget which) turned the flame green, some orange, some yellow or red or blue. These colors I set down opposite a given metal. Where such knowledge might lead the average student in Grayling High School was murky.

Bobby's notebook was open, too. Now and then he flicked back the pages of my notebook, memorized what he saw there, and wrote it down. It could have been his frustration, his inability to calculate the expansion of gases and to reduce equations that caused him to speak. It may have been no more than the usual human need to hurt whoever has helped you. Bobby's words pressed against my ear like a small, icy draft.

"Your name isn't Brewer," he whispered.

The world as I wished it slid from under my feet. I stood staring into the pale, practical flame of the Bunsen burner. Beyond it I saw my father in his flapping trench coat trudging and slipping in the mud beside Charlie Brewer who sat on a high seat.

The letter I wrote the Nofzinger woman, denying that my mother could be her mother, crossed with the first she wrote directly to me. She said she believed herself to be my sister, told me something about her life, and enclosed pictures. To have heard *of* her was one thing; to have heard *from* her was another. For here was her handwriting, a distinctive, even handsome handwriting. It was obvious that at some time, probably when she was fourteen or so, she had set about to make herself singular through her pen — Parker? Waterman? — a creative effort not surprising for one who did not otherwise know Who She Was. I wondered what arts or hobbies she had later cultivated to further identify herself — music, painting? Or was she simply known as a good cook, or as simply kind?

Scarcely two weeks before, the woman had been only a threatening idea. Now with her signature and photographs beside me, she was a fact. She had become something of a person, and not so disturbing, just as the object that casts a shadow is less ominous than the shadow itself.

Four pictures. One was a formal studio portrait taken at the time of her graduation from the University of Washington; her hair is carefully, artfully parted in the middle; she is well groomed and wears a silk scarf stylishly knotted. She has allowed the photographer (or gifted assistant) to touch her overblouse, scarf and face with just enough color to suggest reality. Whether or not the photograph revealed her true complexion it was hard to say for it had somewhat faded. Whoever had tinted it may only have reached over for that pot of paint labeled FLESH, a hue available in the larger boxes of crayons that grandchildren love, a tint more a mortician's conception of the skin than God's. There was no doubt about the color of the eyes; the artist had touched them with brown. The innocence in her eyes and her untroubled mouth led me to believe that her courses in botany, biology and chemistry had neither broken her spirit nor rendered her cynical. I had a curious conviction that she could be trusted.

Three other pictures were informal. One was a snapshot taken on the day of the marriage that would be so brief and childless — those words she had used in her letter. She wears a pretty dress, fussy with ribbons, and a small hat troubled by false flowers and a rudimentary veil: to such a hat my mother would have given short shrift. I felt that she was playing "dress up" and that the moment she laid those clothes aside she would be quite a different person. The clothes told me it had not been a formal wedding but one before an indifferent official impatient to return to more productive duties. It seemed to me that her bright smile was forced.

Written on the back of a third snapshot are the words "My Love," and it shows the Pacific Ocean; at her feet is driftwood; the black shadow of a tree falls across the foreground. She wears trousers and a worn plaid jacket. Here she appears more at home than beside the pushy hollyhocks in the wedding picture. This snapshot beside the sea is a grown-up version of a snapshot taken when she was seven. She wears new high boots and as she sits on that rock, her eyes are on them and not on the sea. I remember that such boots had a pocket on the side for storing away a pocketknife for cleaning fish and making whistles from a willow branch. I hoped it was not at seven years old that she discovered she was a stray. Even ordinary children, flanked by parents and smothered by grandparents, have troubles and fears enough at seven, punitive teachers, bullying classmates and patient monsters that wait just beyond the dark.

Maybe not at seven, but at some moment she too, if not into a

178

Bunsen burner, had looked at or into something, and the world as she had imagined it had fallen away beneath her narrow feet. But she, unlike me, could not look beyond to real — if separate — parents, could not summon up the awesome presence of the Sheep Queen of Idaho and her gentle husband who would not say no to a grandchild. What had she stared at when she found she was adrift — a chair? A stove? What was the symbol of the nightmare common to many children, that their parents are not their own, this nightmare become a reality?

The knowledge that she was nobody, had no more substance than a shadow (shadow of what?) — that knowledge must have colored every aspect of her days from that moment on. She would wonder if the other children *knew*. If they had been told by their parents who, quite naturally, enjoy revealing information in the name of compassion.

"You see, darling, Amy is adopted."

"What does that mean, Mummy?"

"It means that she doesn't have real parents like you have, your daddy and me. So you must remember to be extra nice to her."

Pity. But children do not know pity, do not know compassion. It is not a childish emotion. It translates in children's minds to persecution.

Amy would wonder if that was why she was the last on the playground to be chosen, if the children feared that her poverty of kinship might rub off on them. Later on, she would wonder if her friends would think the less of her because she dared not show her birth certificate. They might wonder at her silence when they spoke of family reunions, of Christmas and New Year's that leave everybody exhausted and yet nobody would have it any other way; when they spoke of amiably daft aunts who were loved and included because they were aunts, of eccentric cousins who had been drawn into strange religions or had become nudists.

She would forever wonder if she had measured up to the little boy who had been killed, whom she had replaced, more or less, not because she required the McKinneys but because they required her, because with her they would be less lonely and would have something to do with the rest of their lives.

So she had opened the envelope. It was better to know your parents though they be thieves, drunks or bastards.

My father's eyes were brown.

It was difficult writing her. How to begin. Writing her was like writing to those who know they are terminally ill. Like them, she was on a different plane, had a different frame of reference; for them, the sun shed a peculiar light; the closed door said something else.

At that very moment she might be constructing a family background on the belief that I was her brother. Oh yes. "My aunt Maude. My aunt Roberta. Polly — that's Pauline. They write often. You see, we're a very large, close family. I have a brother and his name is Tom."

And there was a chance that she was my father's daughter, but I was troubled by her mulish insistence that my mother was her mother. She must know that my mother would never have abandoned a child, but *how* she must know I did not know.

Blood, however, is thicker than water — even if diluted by half, and I could not help but feel for her a real if reluctant kinship — and for yet another whom nobody had wanted: the poor lady who had walked the corridors in the hospital. How often she must have thought of her daughter. How often she must have wished that somebody cared enough to search for her as Amy searched for me.

"Well, what are you going to do about it?" my wife asked.

I stood beside my desk keenly aware of the days in the not

distant past when I had to do *nothing* about it. There had been nothing to do anything about. My perspective had been altered, too. I might have a half sister in this Amy. I might have to define my duties to her.

"I'll write her again. If it makes her happier, there's no reason she shouldn't believe my father is her father. It may be true. I wouldn't put it past him. My aunts don't put it past him, and they knew him better than I know him."

"Suppose she wants to meet you?"

"Well, why not?"

"You know, Tom," my wife began. When she calls me Tom instead of You or Dear, I know she has had something on her mind and is now about to reveal it. "You know, Tom, she *does* look something like you. I wish the pictures showed her in full profile. Your nose isn't like other people's noses."

"Thanks a bunch." When my half sister Belle Brewer wanted to punish me when she was a little girl of six and I was eleven, she used to call me Old Square Nose. I told her her hair looked like broomstraw.

Having no real family, Amy Nofzinger would not have cluttered up her house with family objects and junk, for such, inherited from a family not yours, could be but a painful reminder and have only commercial value.

This desk with Amy's letter lying beside my typewriter, beside which I had stood in the calm, orderly days before I had even heard of Amy Nofzinger — it was at this desk that I wrote my last six novels. It was once a square piano belonging to my great-aunt Nora. My great-grandmother had it hauled all the way out West and I had it hauled all the way back East. I also have Aunt Nora's Washburn guitar on which she once plucked out lively fandangos. I later sang to the guitar songs of love and death and loss and despair that I'd learned off the records the cowboys and hired hands played in the bunkhouse, songs that pretty well sum up what some lives are about and are now called Country Western.

Before me on this desk is a lacquered leather Chinese box covered with wraithlike Chinese ladies crossing arched bridges and glancing back at the willow trees. It belonged to my mother, who liked Chinese things, and holds hundreds of photographs and snapshots of every member of the family. It holds the only existing photograph of George Sweringen, my great-grandfather. I stole it out of the family album one Christmas. I had convinced myself that I had a right to it because I was the eldest grandchild, but I was afraid of the aunts, who have since forgiven me. One of these days I'm going to straighten out all the pictures and put dates on them. So many of the baby pictures look alike it's hard to know which is which.

On either side of this desk are two bronze statuettes a foot high, one of a little boy in breeches, holding a slate and one of a little girl reading a book. They were wedding presents to Thomas Sweringen and the Sheep Queen, in 1889. To my left, hanging on the wall, is an oriental rug that was a present to Thomas Sweringen from Alexander Pantages, who was to the West Coast what Keith-Orpheum was to the East Coast.

The pewter duck set with jade and carnelian was a present to my mother from the second husband of a Hershey woman who inherited chocolate money. My son-in-law has his eye on it because he likes Chinese things too. However, it was he who gave me the crystal decanter, the brass mortar and pestle I use to grind up the cumin seed I like in mashed potatoes; he gave me the small brass Lion of India studded with turquoise.

Paintings by my elder son are on one wall and over the mantel, and it is he who gave me the two-volume 1870 edition of Zell's *Encyclopaedia and Dictionary*. As it went to press, Napoleon the Third had just declared war on Prussia. I cherish it because my son gave it to me and because it is exactly contemporary with George Sweringen's discovery of gold up Jeff Davis Creek.

The mosaic of colored stones that pick out sprays of larkspur was a gift from my younger son who bought it in Vienna when he was there at the university for his junior year. My daughter gave me the brass ibex overlaid with Assyrian scenes. My first cousin gave me the Toulouse-Lautrec of *Mademoiselle Marcelle Lander Dancing the Bolero*. My daughter's portrait, painted when she was twelve, hangs at my left and to my right is a California landscape, little thin trees under a glowering sky; it was given to my mother by a Swiss artist who was supposed to become famous at his death and never did. He is remembered, if at all, because he sat up all night when Lindbergh flew the Atlantic, making a painting of *The Spirit of Saint Louis* flying dangerously low over the angry waves. He called it *We, at Daybreak*, and it is said to hang in the Smithsonian. Some may remember it on the cover of the old *Literary Digest*.

In the fireplace are andirons I had copied, at a price I couldn't afford, from a set in the Sweringen ranch house. And so it went. Nothing valuable, everything invaluable. This room looks like the Old Curiosity Shop, but the curiosities are dear curiosities and when I sit here in the evening with a drink in my hand and the hi-fi belts out Schumann and Chopin — the very things my mother played so well — I know exactly what we were and exactly what I am. I think a man with such a family is all but invulnerable.

In a hollowed-out book before me, meant possibly for the concealment of liquor or money, I keep certain letters and curios. Since it is leather-bound, entitled *L'Histoire ecclésiastique* and dated MCCCXXII, it is likely to be the first thing pounced upon by a practiced marauder; he will find in it little of value — to him. In it is a snapshot of my grandmother manhandling a sheep. The sheep doesn't have a chance. She is then a young woman and the sun falls so that my grandfather's shadow is quite recognizable in the background. Here is a check from my grandmother in payment for a dozen copies of my first novel, and never cashed because her formal signature on a check was more important to me than the money even back then, when a dentist's bill was a catastrophe. I touch a photograph of my mother taken on her graduation from St. Margaret's School, the profile showing her perfect nose. Father's Day cards. What a sentimental fool I am.

I was going over these things — at it again — while I wondered what to write to Amy Nofzinger, wondered how to tell her without sounding grudging or false that I could accept her as a half sister, and no more.

Now I held a note written to me by my aunt Roberta on my fiftieth birthday. I had read it many times. This time I believe I was drawn to it by one of those forces people say they do not believe in, and do. It was written on notepaper decorated by a pencil drawing of the little stone church, executed by some gifted member of the parish and duplicated over and over again and sold year after year at church bazaars. In that church my mother and father were married; I was baptized there; my mother was buried from there. It meant all that to my aunt and more. She had sung there in the choir and from the windows of her house she could see its gabled roof.

My aunt Roberta's handwriting had always been next to illegible, each word a hurried approximation, often without the vowels, of what she was thinking. The text was rendered breathless by dashes that expressed her irritation that her pen would not keep pace with her ideas. The paper had begun to tear at the fold.

Dear Tom:
I'll never forget that morning fifty years ago or is it fifty one

when I called the hospital in Salt Lake and they said you had arrived and I turned to somebody there and I said, "I'm an uncle instead of an aunt." Here is fifty dollars for you and Betty to go out and have a cocktail and a steak.

There's something wrong with Polly's eye. She won't do anything about it but she's scared. I hate it when anything happens to us because we're not used to it. This is a picture of Saint James Church here in Salmon. The ministers change so often because I guess they get restless here. Years ago one of them went to Williamsburg, Virginia, and that's why Polly went to William and Mary because Mama thought it would be nice to have our own minister there. Here in Salmon in this little stone church your father and mother were married in 1911 and —

My wife's voice interrupted from the dining room. "What was that you said?" And she walked on in.

"Did I say something?"

"Yes. You said something like, 'My God!' and something about 1911."

"They were married in 1911, and not 1912! My father and mother. That makes it absolutely impossible that my mother gave Amy away, because they were married before she was born."

"Did you ever doubt that it was impossible?"

"No. But this makes it *absolutely* impossible."

"Your aunt may be wrong about the date."

"Possible. And possible to know for sure. I'll write the church for a Xerox of the marriage certificate."

"Would they have a Xerox machine in Salmon?"

"At the bank, certainly."

"Why not just call the church and have the minister call back?"

"Because I want the document in my hands." Call it irrational, but I feel that gods and fates must be propitiated or all hell will break loose. In the past it has. I could not have explained why I felt I would find the date to be 1911 and not 1912 if I wrote the church rather than called. The gods and fates would be long-toothed at my casual reaching for the phone, but might look with kindness on a letter as more formal, as they were formal. The date 1911 cleared my mother.

But then the little woman in the corridor walked in an even more tragic light: the man she loved was already married when she gave their child away. She could not hope, having made so appalling a sacrifice, that he would relent, and marry her. The photograph of him she displayed could, like an icon, promise her something only beyond the grave.

I drafted a letter to Amy, meaning to copy it on good bond paper in case she wanted to keep it, as I would have. I would mail it after I'd heard from the church in Salmon. I wrote that it was certainly true my parents were living together as man and wife in 1912, for they had been married in 1911, the year before. I wrote that I understood why she wanted to believe they could not have been married in 1911 because that would mean that a married woman had given away her daughter, and that would have been . . .

I stopped just short of the word monstrous. But however carefully I drafted the letter I could not spare Amy the dismal knowledge that her real mother at the worst had not wanted her, and at the best had been too destitute to keep her.

"If you are my half sister," I wrote down, "you have a right to my support. In a way, I wish all this had been otherwise, that you were my full sister. We could have shared secrets and hurts and bruises. With you, I shouldn't have so often felt like a ghost. We could have had fun, as kids . . ."

I wrote the church, directing the envelope to the Priest-in-Charge for I knew that even the most emancipated of ministers secretly wish to be called priests because that title lends a validity that "minister" does not. The gods and fates must be considered.

The sun was rising up out of the Gulf of Maine an hour earlier; the lilacs close against our house bloomed and faded almost unnoticed. I should have snipped off the dried blossoms, but again I forgot to. Hardly forty days had passed since my aunt Polly had written me about that lawyer in Seattle. I had a curious sensation of suddenly being older and I often looked at my hands. It is the hands that are the first to go.

In the parenthesis of those forty days, I had felt my mother's rectitude and loyalty called into question by a stranger. I had prepared myself to defend my mother and did so in the best way I could. At the same time, I was willing to accept her as a half sister, this stranger, because she did look something like me, and I knew what kind of man my father was. He had betrayed both his mistress and his wife. His prick was more important to him than responsibilities. The result was Amy Nofzinger.

What should I feel for the daughter of a man I felt little for but atavistic duty? My mother had divorced him. I chiefly remembered him because of that awful Roamer automobile and the promise of a pocket watch when I was graduated from high school. The watch had never materialized. It was my stepfather who gave me the watch. I never felt it was mine. I pawned it when I was broke, in Portland, Oregon.

In forty days I had come to be concerned for a lost, pathetic being who herself had lost her love, her child and whatever reputation she had that was honored on her street. Maybe it was now time to send Amy her father's address, let them meet and together search for the woman in the corridor. Not even Ben Burton could be so callous as to forget her who grieved for a little lost girl — especially on birthdays and at Christmas when we all so want to give. If Amy could afford an attorney to sniff out the Sweringens, she could afford to put one on the trail of a tragic mother who simply couldn't have vanished from that hospital into the damp streets of Seattle without a trace. Somewhere was a scrap of paper; somewhere a signature; somewhere a photograph.

The incumbent rector of the stone church in Salmon signed himself Yours in Christ and enclosed the Xerox copy of the marriage certificate. It appeared to be a page cut from a ledger and was headed *MARRIAGES* and signed at the bottom by Zachary Vincent who, for a certain modest sum and free rent at the rectory, had been hired for certain duties: to drive out devils, to forgive sin, to render sex legal, to launch the faithful into the Unknown and, incidentally, to make flesh of bread and blood of wine.

Above the rector's name, the signatures of the principals revealed them as they were. To the written question, "Bachelor or Widower?" Ben Burton had declared himself a bachelor. His signature — I suspected he had often practiced it in secret — displayed a spurious confidence. The upsweep of the final *n* in Burton took up a quarter of the page.

To the question, "Maiden or Widow?" my mother Elizabeth Sweringen had declared herself a maiden. Her signature was that of one who had been taught to write in italics but had made it personal by softening the angles and accentuating the downstrokes so that they anchored each word to a common idea — consistency. It was a declaration of private schooling and a will of her own.

Then came the signatures of the witnesses. First among them was her father's, Thomas H. Sweringen. I could not recall ever before having seen his formal signature and was surprised that it had such ease and authority. He had had only a high school education. So far as I knew, he never wrote letters and it was not he but his wife who signed the checks. But there was in that signature the essence of himself — steadfastness. Then came my aunt Roberta's signature, very like her father's, steadfast, but hurried. My aunt Maude's signature was indecisive, that of a girl no longer a child but not yet a woman. On so solemn a document a signature must make a statement; she made a statement in underlining "Sweringen."

The Sheep Queen's signature, as I remembered it, swept to the right with the force of a locomotive. Emma Russell Sweringen. The *m*'s in Emma rolled on like waves. The *S* in Sweringen flew up and back like a whiplash, and the report that followed it fled along the remaining letters.

I was not surprised that the document was dated 1911 and not 1912. I had had my aunt's word for it, and I had kept the gods and fates in mind. What did surprise me is that my grandmother's signature was not there.

Had she been sick? Of course not. She boasted that she had never had a sick day. She looked on sickness as a weakness forgivable in others but not in herself. Had she been required in Salt Lake? Then the wedding would have been postponed, for nothing like that could go on without Mama.

But it *had* gone on. Without Mama.

16

AS EMMA and Thomas Sweringen grew older they found it harder to keep their eye on things; harder to get on and off a horse. When they walked it seemed the hills were steeper and even the stairs. Emma had grown even heavier, couldn't refuse sugars and fats and starches; as one of a generation who took it for granted that most women grow stout, it didn't matter, but it did matter that it was harder to keep an eye on things, so the time came when she hired first one and then another foreman to take charge — not completely — but, well, you know.

There were even certain small advantages to being semi-retired. Call it that. Now she could regularly attend Eastern Star meetings in Salmon, should she wish; she had time for books that had gone unread for a long, long time. Each year, as she grew older, she slipped yet another year into the past, into the time of her children's youth, then into her own youth when she saw Thomas at those dances and had despaired of ever having him.

Why, back then she had even done a little fancy work because she thought a young woman ought to, but her hands were
no longer up to that, nor her eyes, which had begun to trouble.
It was a different world, then. Of course it was, because everything was all ahead. The trees around the house had grown tall,
tall, and cast so much more shade.

And Thomas? Well, *Thomas*. He had time for his Masonic
meetings now, but didn't do much about them. So many he
knew were gone. And he didn't like to miss the news on the
Atwater Kent but the news was so often bad he turned it off
and then turned it on because maybe the news had got better.
Why, only yesterday he hadn't given Europe a thought. And he
had time for the seven clocks upstairs and downstairs and in my
lady's chamber; he tensed up as the hour approached and they
were about to strike, and she found she had begun tensing up,
too, because it meant so much to him that they all struck at the
same time. What was he looking for — perfection? And wasn't
it funny that it used to be she who looked for perfection. Striking clocks! Curious that when we age it is the small things and
not the big things that matter.

Let the young people take care of the big things.

"Oh Thomas, for the Lord's sake! It doesn't matter if they
don't strike all at once."

He'd begin his tinkering with them.

The years had taught her that nothing, nothing, nothing can
be perfect; the years had taught him that maybe if you tinker,
tinker, tinker . . .

He had taken to himself the homely task of gathering the
eggs each evening just before supper; there was a game about it
because so many of the hens were as wild as pheasants and hid
their nests. Thomas liked to have the grandchildren and then
the great-grandchildren with him because then it was like hunting Easter eggs. He gave whichever child found the most eggs a

two-bit piece. Later on he gave the same to the ones who hadn't found so many, to make up. That was no way to teach children the reward of success, but that's what he did.

He put the drops in her eyes; he was the only one who did it right. She couldn't sit quietly enough for the others. They might hit her eye with the thing and Thomas had the steadiest hands in the family.

Of course there was no question of being lonely in the big house; the girls were back and forth with their husbands and children, all the birthdays and holidays and more every year. There wasn't a month now when somebody hadn't been born. And the cook would come up from the cookhouse with her tales of what she thought was going on in the bunkhouse, and visitors and old friends, and of course Maude.

Maude. When the dust settles, it seems to be one child who ends up at home.

Maude was between Roberta and Pauline. She had married a man too quickly named Dunn whose father was a circuit judge who sat twice a year at the courthouse in Salmon. That's where Maude met young Dunn. Judge and Mrs. Dunn were decent people but it turned out as it often does that young Dunn was a different kettle of fish, maybe because they gave him too much, as parents will to an only child. Young Dunn drove up and down the valley in a Mercer Raceabout and jumped ditches with it. It is likely that Maude was as much drawn to the scarlet Mercer as to Dunn. The car would have been a better bargain. After Maude married Dunn they lived for awhile in California where people have no roots and believe in every crazy thing. Maude sent oranges the first year. Then they were divorced down there without a word about it, and Maude came back to the ranch with the little girl. She had had to ask them to send money. That is hard for a young woman who thinks she has burned her bridges.

Then Maude had a few beaux up and down the valley, but most of them didn't have much gumption and of course she had the little girl.

Maude was almost as stylish as Beth; she could take any old thing and look good in it, so she decided to take a position with the department store in Portland, Oregon. She got it through some people. She began by selling hats; they promised her that later she could be a buyer, but most of her salary went for the woman who took care of the little girl and in the end it didn't work out. You might have thought she might meet a young man, say in the lobby of the Benson Hotel, but young men are already married.

She had had to send for money again.

You couldn't help feel sorry for Maude when she came back to the ranch. When you think you have put something behind you and you haven't, it looks different, or maybe *you* are different. She was cheerful most of the time, but Maude was one of these up-and-down people. When she looked at the trees grown so tall beside the house, or knelt before the fireplace to kindle a fire as the afternoons shortened and grew cold, she might think, "These are the things the other girls left, and these are the things I didn't want to return to."

When the cooks down at the cookhouse quit or were fired because they began to drink or grow trashy or cause trouble among the men, Maude filled in and, like Beth earlier, she cooked up at the shearing sheds and was on hand to see to the big dinners on birthdays and holidays. Visitors often spoke of how attractive the living room was.

That was Maude for you.

Believe you me, a foreman had his hands full and was worth his hire. He saw that things went as they should, that in the spring four hundred calves were branded with hot irons with the letter S and ten thousand sheep with the same letter but with red paint instead of irons. A foreman must know obstetrics because in the spring when lambs and calves came, sometimes they came wrong end to from the womb, and got stuck. A foreman saw that the bull calves had their testicles removed with a sharp pocketknife and the human hand, and then they were steers. And then the ram lambs had their testicles removed with a sharp pocketknife and the help of human teeth, and then they were wethers, and a little later you ate them as spring lamb with peas and mint jelly.

And then all that machinery that made ranches look like a used-car lot: sulky rakes and buck rakes and mowing machines — Deerings, McCormicks, John Deere — beaverslide derricks. The sheep wagons resembled prairie schooners, each fitted with a bunk and shelves with doors to keep the food and dishes from falling out when the horses started up, and its own stove, and very comfortable it was for herders even in wild, cold weather. And of course the old red threshing machine.

A foreman hired good men and fired the men who weren't; he gave orders in a way that made men want to work for him, men who didn't quit and kite off to Salmon and get drunk. He was in charge of putting up the hay — five thousand acres of hayland to be mowed and raked and stacked, two thousand tons.

Then there was the shearing of the sheep in June, and dipping them for ticks. Ticks are about the ugliest insects you ever saw! There was vaccinating the calves against blackleg in the spring and dehorning them in the fall, the blood spurting out from where the horn was cut off with a tool like pruning shears, and then it would be winter — oh, that first day of snow, sheets of it sweeping down from Gunsight Peak. Then the feeding of the hay, and the blizzards, the wonder that winter would ever end, and the spring come. But come it did, it always did, and the trees grew taller.

194

One foreman and then another to see that the camptenders with their packhorses supplied the sheepherders in the hills with the exact things they wanted, the Bull Durham instead of the Duke's Mixture, the canned raspberries and not the canned peaches, not this time. Flour, spuds, sugar, eggs, butter, canned milk, canned peas and canned tomatoes, slabs of bacon and hams that Thomas cured himself, or used to — and made the lard too, he did. Yes, all those pigs. It often seemed that the herders up in the mountains ate better than they did down there on the ranch, but herders could afford to be picky, and they were. Good herders were hard to find, the job was a huge responsibility — eighteen hundred head of sheep to a herder. You couldn't really blame them, that after staying up there in those hills all summer with nobody to talk to but themselves and a collie dog, why, you couldn't blame them if they hiked off to Salmon after they'd brought their sheep safely down in the fall, hiked down there and drank and did what some men will until their money was gone and they crept back sick and penitent.

Sometimes she wondered how she and Thomas had done it. She knew how she did it. She knew why she did it. For Tom-Dick.

Yes, a foreman would stay a year or so and then he'd get to thinking about responsibility, why it was they who had the ranch and he the responsibility. Why it wasn't *his* grandfather who had discovered the gold that bought the land. Sooner or later he'd quit or have to be fired — no matter what people said, she'd never liked firing people — because he no longer attended to business or the hired men didn't like him. He saw himself getting old and ending up in the Cabbage Patch down at the end of Salmon.

A foreman had his own house on the place and his own outhouse to set him apart from the hired men, and to give him a sense of self, and it would have been all right if he had married, except that it never works out when somebody who works on a ranch gets married, somehow. As for the hired men and herders, there'd be no room for their women, no place for a wife, and that's why there were nine disorderly houses in Salmon.

John Weston was the last and best foreman she ever had. He was a Mormon, or his folks were, and he had had to work very hard as a child. You saw that in his face; something of the little boy who had worked so hard was in that narrow face. He worked so hard he sometimes went to sleep after supper in his chair. His father had a ranch in the southern part of the state, but he was the youngest son and there wasn't room for him so he struck out. Work, work, work. He didn't run off to town. He didn't drink. Sometimes you'd catch him flipping through the *Saturday Evening Post*, just flipping, looking at the pictures apparently, but never, never, not even when she herself and Thomas were in charge, was the hay so fine, the lambs so fat or the wool so heavy.

You see, an arrangement had to be made, and at once; it was awful to think, to walk through that big old sandstone house thinking that sooner or later John Weston would step into the dining room where she made out checks, and ask for his time.

So he was included in the next round of holidays, and although he may have found it somewhat awkward at first, he relaxed, and in the spirit of the thing he had a drink or two with Thomas. Then Nora handed him her guitar. Ah-ha! It turned out he knew many old cowboy songs. Shortly after, he moved into the Big House where only the family had breakfast, and before long, Maude married him.

You might wonder at all that fuss and concern all those years about a good foreman. You might wonder, Where all this time was Tom-Dick? Mama's darling, who said, "Hello, Mama . . ."

But Tom-Dick died many, many years ago. His room upstairs

was just the same as it had been the winter morning he left it, and all his little things just the same.

As foreman, John Weston rose at one or two in the morning during lambing season and went on down to the sheds. He saved many lambs. He knew little, understood little but work and bolted his food to get back to it. The backs of his hands were raw and chapped. His nails were sometimes bitten to the quick. His palms were thick with callus, and perhaps the lines on them told the same story as the many little scars.

One morning he stood gulping a cup of coffee, before reaching for his hat. He paused, stared out the window, and dropped dead.

The Sheep Queen was dead by then, and Thomas.

The ranch was sold and everybody got a couple of hundred thousand dollars apiece after taxes. It wasn't much in exchange for parting with one's heart, for all the Christmases, the view of Gunsight Peak and the music of the water falling over the stones down Sweringen Creek.

It was painful to drive along the new highway that ran along the right-of-way where the old G&P had run, to see the sandstone ranch house and the big white barn, the property of strangers. You have to work harder at being a family when the land is gone. And you have to write letters.

Maude moved down to Salmon where she would be close to Polly and Roberta and they could talk about how it was.

Here is a letter from Maude.

Dear Tom:

I'm not sure of the date because last Christmas the bank forgot to send me a calendar, but it's May something towards the end.

I guess Roberta was pretty upset when she heard about the

Nofzinger woman, but she gets upset and then she gets over it after she's upset everybody else. When I get upset I stay that way, so I try not to. I worry about her because she does too much for her kids. One of these days she might have to pull in her horns, but maybe De Witt left her more than I think or maybe his family was one of those families that seem to have money even when they don't. Of course she and Beth were so close that the very idea that some stranger should think she knew something about Beth, and she didn't would drive her wild.

Mary Margaret is working for the sheriff just outside Los Angeles and likes it a lot. I don't know just what she does. I guess a mother should know. Maybe one of those jobs it's not worth explaining. She always says you're her favorite cousin. Paul never fitted in with the family, and his people were some kind of Russians. Foreigners always look sort of deaf to me.

Mary Margaret has a little waterfall in her house. I've always hated the sound of water dripping and we were better off at the ranch before we got water in.

We took the jeep to Cougar Point for the first real picnic of the year. Polly made her potato salad again. I read somewhere the other day, probably in Reader's Digest because it's the only thing I've got the patience to read, that sometimes whole families are wiped out with potato salad if it sits. Wouldn't that be awful for us, but Polly's never sits. Frankie did most of the driving because I am almost seventy, and I think sometimes I don't look a day younger. Ha-ha! It's nice to have grandchildren. He wants to go to Europe so I guess I'll let him. When you're young you like to go places. Adele and Cathy plan to be up from California as soon as school closes and I'm bracing myself because of all the boys hanging around, but I guess that's what a grandmother is for. I asked for it!

They're trying to stop the gambling here in Salmon again —

state people or federal — but it doesn't seem to work. I don't see why people should try to stop things people are going to do anyway. All you have to do is go to Nevada. I felt bad when they got rid of the slot machines. I could hardly wait to get downtown and lose money.

Salmon is a lot bigger. The state and the Chamber of Commerce sends out these flyers about the good hunting and fishing and how friendly everybody is, and the people come from all over and some of them settle here, retired people who want to see the mountains before they die. Good enough reason. Two new motels and a swimming pool in one. I don't think much of swimming pools. So now the bridge across the river in Salmon is too narrow with all the cars. Years ago they phoned down from Challis that some tourists had fallen in the river and drowned and at the rate they were floating they were supposed to show up at the bridge in Salmon around three in the afternoon, and everybody in town was on the bridge hoping to be the first to spot them. Some people brought lunches. The bodies never did show up.

Went out the other day to the rest home by the hot springs to see Aunt Nora. Sometimes she's a little vague, but Tom she's over a hundred years old. She dresses well for her age, earrings and everything. I wonder why we all get so old, except your mother.

Would have been nice in a way if the woman turned out to be your sister, so many of us have died off we could always use another one. If we had somebody out there in Seattle we could all go there and a lot cheaper than motels. More fun, too.

But the trouble is, if she had been your sister, all those years Beth would have wondered and grieved. I know she would have, and that's not a good thing to think about . . .

199

My mother the woman in the corridor? No.

But something in the tone of my aunt Maude's letter, her harping on change and the past, maybe that brief reference to my mother's grief, moved me to write to Amy and to send her my father's address. Was it my aunt's reference to a possible descent on Seattle? For in her loneliness, that is precisely what Amy would have wanted. What was the point of my aunt's letter?

I scarcely knew how or what to feel about Amy. She was a ghost but not a ghost. My half sister, Belle, was not a ghost. I had grown up with her, but that wasn't the point. She wasn't a ghost because she was my mother's daughter. It didn't matter who the father was. If my daughter had a child, I wouldn't give a damn who the father was, because I would be its grandfather and my mother its great-grandmother, and the Sheep Queen its great-great-grandmother and so on.

It was a crazy thing — it all seemed to center around whether one was married or not, and what was marriage but a document and a ceremony? Written words, spoken words, the first subject to fire, rot or theft and the second no sooner uttered than vanished. It appears that an exalted idea of marriage can be quite as destructive as divorce, even more so. For without marriage there can be no divorce, and without marriage there can be no adultery.

Why should a little child suffer because its parents weren't married? Given away and forever after clothed in the rags and tatters of illegitimacy that no adoptive parent, however kind and understanding, can mend or cleanse. Small wonder the young people are taking a second look at marriage.

I wondered if I owed Amy love. Can you love one you have never seen? I had often wondered at the injunction that a Christian or a Jew must "love" God. An abstraction sits in the mind

— well, it sits in the mind remote from every single one of the five senses. But Amy had substance, such substance that at least two nouns clung to her like burrs: self-doubt and loneliness — the first because she couldn't answer the question, Who am I? and the second because she had no family, and having no family at least doubles the ordinary human fear of death.

One who has a family has the strength to be an example of detachment or courage even in dying; if you leave a family, you do not really die. You crop up in conversations at the breakfast table. Your name is offered as proof. You appear at picnics because the lunch in the basket and the contents of the thermos bottle are the foods you ate and the liquid you drank. You chose the sites because the cold spring wind couldn't find you there, and the pretty shells were in greater variety for the children. The stick you carried when you walked in the woods or to the garage stands ready for son or grandson — see! it is polished by your sweat and the skin of your palm. They remembered how you laughed. What was weak in you, or selfish, is often forgotten. Time has burned the dross out of you.

But without a family you are gone. Done. You never were. The last hours of a derelict lying abandoned in a room in some cheap hotel can't be lonelier.

There is no one to want your picture.

Amy knew what blood was, what a family meant. A family is the group that has to take you in. But damn it, she had no right, for her own peace of mind, to think my mother was her mother. Let her search for the woman in the corridor. God grant that something good had happened to her.

I began to wonder if Amy had tried to call me. If she had had an extra drink, as people do, and tried to call. Maybe it was a good thing my telephone was unlisted.

But I was not yet ready to hear her voice, the intake of her breath across three thousand miles or so. I didn't want to hear her silence, for even her silence would lend her an added dimension and somehow increase my responsibility. It was quite enough to have those pictures, especially the smiling one taken on the day of her marriage that failed. Especially the snapshot of a little girl seven years old in those God-damned boots.

One day, though, we would meet.

17

WHEN SOME ghastly thing happens to me or to someone I love, familiar objects suddenly look threatening — the pine trees that flank the road through the woods, the moon caught on the last snow — and hint at even further disaster. The whisper of the returning tide, once a comfortable reminder of eternity, becomes sibilant warning that nothing, nothing lasts. I see malice in an open smile.

Now as I drove back through the woods from the post office, the trees had that look.

My wife was asking, "What's wrong?"

The letter was from my aunt Roberta.

Dear Tom:

Yesterday I wrote a letter to Polly and one to Maude. I've been worried about Maude. She tries to do too much for her grandchildren. She's going to absolutely ruin them and somebody ought to tell her that money doesn't grow on trees. I thought awhile and then decided I'd better write you one.

I'm still here at the Holiday Inn because it's easier than the hotel. I hate the traffic now that my hands are so bad for driving. I meant to be home by now but it's still cold up there and how the wind whistles around, but I do miss our mountains and my view. I'm always surprised Phoenix is so big because when I was little and down there once, more like a place with cowboys and Indians, and then I'm always surprised. Certainly a lot of Mexicans, though! Their men are smaller than ours, but I guess colorful. I can't seem to get used to men with small feet.

People here are terribly nice to me. One nice couple has a grandson at West Point. I could never understand how you could live back there. You could do your typewriting out here just as well as back there. Maybe one of these days. Your mother loved the West so.

Several people here know Senator Goldwater. I'm sorry I missed him, but he flew to Washington Sunday. He has the store here. He would have been a grand President and if Mama had lived she would have liked him because his feet seem to be on the ground, and his profile.

Mama was eighty-five, and had just finished the last of her Christmas cards sitting there at the dining room table, and that signature of hers. All the presents for her are still someplace, unopened. I guess they got lost when we sold the ranch to the Mormons. I hate to go by it. I wish we hadn't, but there wasn't anybody to run it after John died. If only he hadn't had that heart attack.

Senator Goldwater has enough money so he wouldn't need to do what so many of them do.

I meant to do some shopping today and then it was Sunday so I got ready for church instead. Janet sings in the choir. She looks just lovely, singing away up there like she sang the *Mes-*

siah in our own little stone church, but down here the minister calls himself Father and they call it Mass, but I guess they do, down here. Must be something about the Mexicans or the early Spaniards. I'm glad we're all Episcopalians because it makes it easier, except Aunt Nora, and I always thought she wasn't, to spite Mama. You know how Mama was about in-laws and how stubborn Aunt Nora is about change. She won't even get any older! I don't think Papa was ever anything. Do you realize Aunt Nora is going to be a hundred years old this Hallowe'en? Sort of a shame Papa couldn't have lived another two months and been a hundred but everybody can't, I guess.

Janet is having a little party for me tonight. The minister Father Ferris will be there. It's a lot nicer when they drink like anybody else. It makes me nervous when people don't drink. You get to thinking they have a problem.

Tom, the reason I bring up Papa is something funny that's been on my mind ever since this Amy Nofzinger thing came up.

It was several Christmases ago, maybe ten. Well, Papa had got in a lovely tree from up Sweringen Creek and a small one for in the hall where the elk was that I think your mother shot. The big tree had all the old decorations on it, some of them from the time I was little and you weren't even born. I always liked the pink swans and the doves with spun glass tails but Mama wouldn't let us touch them. I liked it more when we had real candles in those little things like clothespins, on the tree, and Papa was there with a bucket of water because of the time the orphanage burned down in Boise while Mama was still in the Legislature from Lemhi County. It was in the papers and so awful. Papa was always scared of fire, and how he wouldn't let anybody have fires upstairs and how Polly used to smoke up there and blow the smoke up the drafts when she came back from William and Mary so Mama wouldn't know. We used to say, "Ashes to ashes and dust to dust. If Camels don't get you, Fatimas must." Polly hated Greek! I didn't know until I married De Witt that there was such a thing as a warm bedroom in winter, having to pull the covers up over our heads and breathe out until you got warm. Time goes so fast but I'm glad we don't seem to get much older.

I miss Mama and I miss your mother. I could never dress the way she did, but I sure tried. Whatever she did and whatever she had I always tried to have, too. Part of it was how she walked into a room, and then stood there. When she and Charlie were in Canada up there on the Fraser River camping on their honeymoon you stayed with me and De Witt at the mine in Gilmore. That was before Ralph was born and I said to myself, "Well, I'll never love another child as I love Tom," but then after Ralph was born I loved him just as much but you have always been "special" to me. I guess that's why I let you play with my engagement ring. De Witt was so mad when you lost it, but we found it on the trail going up to the mine. That was lucky, wasn't it.

Well, the day I'm thinking of, that Christmas morning at the ranch ten years or so ago, Beth was alive and she and Charlie were on the way over the hill from the ranch over there for Christmas dinner and everybody was coming, Aunt Nora and all the cousins. Some years before, they had to put Daisy Haines in an institution. She would ask for things that weren't there.

I had my violin with me because Mama liked to hear Beth and me play together, "Allah's Holiday" and "Liebestraum," because that was about all I could manage. I didn't keep it up like Beth did. I always wanted to play the violin because of how Papa played the fiddle when he was young. Beth played so much better. Mama used to keep a little willow switch behind the piano and Beth did her practicing.

The Chickering was sort of out of tune later on because when we all grew up and went away they closed the double doors into the living room when nobody was in there and it got cold. Not many people cared whether their pianos were in tune or not, so when old Mr. Loomis died there wasn't a tuner except when Mama had one from Salt Lake. Mr. Loomis used to bring us little brown paper bags of candy because he didn't have any children.

I don't think Mama ever got over Tom-Dick's death.

So Maude had two big geese in the oven and you could smell them. Tom, I used to be afraid of them when I was little because of how they chased you and hissed!

Papa was standing in, I mean by the grandfather's clock in the living room. He made the case with his own hands. Remember all his clocks and how they'd usually strike on time? He was standing there smiling because everybody was coming, so I asked him if he'd like another drink and he said, Yes, he would. He loved to have everybody around, and Mama, too. He had such a twinkle in his eyes, there are so many of us. So I brought his drink in from the pantry, and I said, joking, Papa, how many grandchildren do you have? Because I knew he liked to talk about them. He thought a minute but of course he knew without thinking. He thought, and then he said, You have two kids, and Maude has one, and he went on counting on his fingers and then he said, I have seven. And then, Tom, he hesitated, and he said, Maybe eight.

I remember now. I think it was 1912 and Mama got a letter. She took it upstairs and read it and left it lying on the bed. I don't know what got into me because you know we never touched anything of Mama's. She used to be around even when she wasn't. She used to say she could see around corners and I was almost a grown woman and married to De Witt before I realized she couldn't. She could do everything else so I didn't see any reason why she couldn't. I sneaked in and I read the letter, but not carefully because I was so scared. I was only sixteen and it wouldn't have made much sense to me. But it said something about a miscarriage. It was from Beth because of her handwriting she learned at St. Margaret's and that's why I read it because I loved her so and she would tell me I was pretty when I wasn't. I don't know whether she said she had had a miscarriage or whether she was afraid she might.

I love you, Tom
Roberta
P.S. What do you think?

What did I think?

I thought my aunt's reporting of facts was wildly casual and always subjective. She altered facts to suit the moment, how she felt from moment to moment. She could believe that what was true once was true now, or what was true now had always been true. But whatever one said of her, no one could question her loyalty to the family.

Her loyalty was now confronted with a hateful equation: A childhood memory of a letter and something her father had said at Christmastime were the Knowns on the lefthand side of the equation — if they could be said to be known. She wasn't sure of the date nor was she sure whether there had been or might have been a miscarriage.

If the Knowns were known, *a member of the family might be lost out there.*

The righthand side of the equation was equally hateful: Her sister who could do no wrong *had let that child be lost.*

My aunt offered no solution to the equation. She simply asked, What do you think?

Think? I thought the light had so changed it might have fled not from the sun but from a more sardonic star. It so altered the little lobby of the post office I might have been standing there for the first time. And it seemed to have sharpened my wits. I believed I saw the solution to the equation, and that that solution would prove both parts of it false. That there was no equation at all, but two impossibilities: One, that Amy was my real sister and Two, that my mother had abandoned her.

I turned to the encyclopedia, A to Aus, and opened it to the lengthy article on Adoption. I wondered why I hadn't turned there before — maybe because to do so would be to admit there was even a slim chance I would be called on to defend my mother, who needed no defense.

In that article I found confirmation of what I had always believed, that an adopted child must first be released by her parent or parents — only by the mother, if illegitimate, by both parents if legitimate, and that there is a document that must be signed by one parent or both parents.

Because he was an attorney, Amy's father would have kept that document close at hand. It was certainly in Amy's hands now.

"My mother's handwriting," I wrote Amy, "was both beautiful and singular. I know she would not have stooped to disguise it. The signature on the document would be in her own handwriting however she signed herself, whether as the Virgin Mary or as Hester Prynne."

Amy had dreamed up a sand castle and now the tide would be lapping at it, for the handwriting on the document she must possess would not be that of my mother.

Of course I felt sorry for her. I began to wonder if, when she walked, she knew the names of the flowers along the way, if she waited until Christmas morning to open the presents, put mustard on chicken sandwiches, if when she wrote a letter or signed checks she preferred to face a door so no one could surprise her. We might have had a lot in common besides a father. My father I was now prepared to grant her.

But she was lucky to have found a half brother who was

neither mad nor criminal — nor was her father, who worked at his trade journals and lived with his fourth wife deep in the hot shade of lemon trees. Would she dare gamble again and search for her mother, that lost little lady? She would be luckiest, alas, if she found her mother dead, and did not examine too closely the preceding years. Maybe the little lady had married, had lied and presented herself as a virgin, and with lies had fashioned a bearable life.

Days passed. The summer people closed in on the coast of Maine; they opened their cottages whose rooms smelled of the stale air of the old winter and of the wooings and couplings of mice that shredded handy paper and cloth and nested in bureau drawers and there gave birth to their naked pink young. Sometimes there was evidence of illegal entry, smashed windows, broken locks, charcoal in a stove that had been left clean, soiled linen and empty beer cans. But rage, when there is no face or shape to rage against, gives way to an acceptance that summer people, in their possession of at least two homes, are fair game for the determined poor.

I began to wonder if Amy would answer at all. Maybe she looked on my request for the document as unkind, even cruel. But the memory of my mother as I knew her was too precious to me to allow doubts in anyone's mind. If Amy wouldn't be accepted as only a half sister — well, too bad.

Once again the post office looked as it had before that first letter from my aunt Polly that told of a strange attorney and a strange proposition. The lobby of the post office scarcely accommodated ten standing people. One wall was a bank of mailboxes with glass doors. Under a window, a wooden bench was seldom sat on. To sit was rude when others stood, or to sit was an admission of failing legs. On it were used magazines abandoned there by readers who had got the good out of them. The *Reader's Digest* was rich with cheerful, instructive articles, and popular because more lengthy articles tried the patience of those who wanted to get on down to the beach. As the summer people moved in, the *New Yorker* appeared, but was seldom touched; those who would read the *New Yorker* had already read it. *Forbes* and *Business Week* declared that a thirst for money is unquenchable.

The ball-point pen on the counter under a second window was attached to a surprisingly stout chain of shiny metal beads; it would not function if not prodded. Beside it, a jelly glass contained mayflowers picked by a local carpenter — exactly where he would not say. He had an eye for beauty and a nose for perfection. The fragile, rose-colored flowers, out from whose trumpetlike lobes perfume floated like music, were in jolting juxtaposition with a fresh batch of mug shots sent out by the FBI and tacked to the near wall. A man addressing a tender letter might look up and remember having seen so desperate, so chinless a profile only days or hours before at the A&P or under a crippled car at the service station. I find the women among the criminals especially troubling.

The window that looked into the mailroom was fitted with vertical brass bars to block any attempts to crawl through and overcome the postmistress who was having a cup of tea. It was she who reminded people what day of the week it was, when dog licenses were required, where taxes could be paid, and when the liquor store would be closed.

I had quite a bit of mail stuffed behind the little glass door. As I opened it, the postmistress remarked that the day was beautiful and the tide in the cove unusually high. The moon had been full the night before. The next low tide would be fine for clamming. Two dogs had met with porcupines. They would never learn.

I talked with her a few moments. She is a natural lady. I think it has something to do with acceptance and a soft voice.

I turned with my mail to leave. The door of the post office opened inward, and it stuck. You might have thought the carpenter who picked mayflowers would have fixed it.

The postmistress was speaking again. I turned.

"A letter fell out back here from your box," she said, and handed it to me through the barred window.

four

18

HERE IS my answer to that letter.

My dear Amy:
I have here your letter and the release signed by "Elizabeth
Owen."
I want to tell you something about my mother, but where
begin? Her spirit is to the right and left of me and before and
behind me. Her face looks out at me in the darknesses of my
childhood and I have seen her profile in the shifting clouds. She
is near me when I hear Chopin's *Nocturnes;* I see her fingers on
the piano keys, and her foot on the pedal. I have only twice in
my life seen women who were as beautiful and both were strangers and so brief in my sight they were little more than ideas. I
suppose they reminded me of her and that's why I'm now reminded of them. Sometimes she sits with me when I drink
coffee; she loved strong coffee in tin cups around a campfire, or

from Wedgwood before the fireplace in the cold, cold living room of her second marriage where, just beyond, a hill shut out the morning light. Her perfume was an essence of jasmine.

I was two when she divorced my father in 1917. She had suspected another woman, and she was right.

She must have been grateful for the money my grandmother the Sheep Queen sent by check for the trip by Pullman from Seattle back to the ranch in Idaho. I imagine she looked long at the money translated from the check, the heavy silver dollars and the smooth, costly paper. For some time now my mother had had little experience even with small silver, let alone paper. When she left him, my father was a salesman for a cigar company, a job that took him into poolhalls and bars; there they would have found him charming with his looks, his stories and comic monologues. His scenes from Shakespeare were impressive.

Europe was at war. In this country men flocked to the factories that turned out the guns and boats and ammunition, cloth for uniforms and leather for shoes and puttees. It was the beginning of the flock to the city, and sheepherders were hard to find.

And so my angel mother, grateful for a chance to be of service to her mother who had rescued her from poverty and humiliation, went off into the hills with a saddle horse, a sheep wagon and a team to pull it, a dog, and me. When she rode she carried me before her on the pommel of the saddle; when she walked she carried me on her back. A two-year-old isn't much of a walker; the sagebrush was taller than I, and I hadn't yet the sense to fear the rattlesnakes that sunned themselves on the slide-rock.

Her father visited her twice a week, leading a packhorse. Under the diamond hitch or the squaw hitch were beans and bacon and flour, canned peas for freighter's mulligan, sugar and dried apples, soda crackers and cheese. He brought her books to read while the sheep grazed in the sudden parks in the timber or high along a ridge where the wind blew. She once mentioned the early mystery novels of Mary Roberts Rinehart, many of them laid in such fashionable places as Bar Harbor or Tuxedo Park which she would have come to know had she married the first man who asked her, had she not met my father. She spoke once of Harold Bell Wright, the first novelist to make a million dollars. Willa Cather's *The Song of the Lark* must have heartened her. It was the story of a woman who made a good life for herself, alone.

"You must get lonely, Beth," her father told her. "It might help if you smoked a cigarette." And my grandfather handed her a red and yellow pack of Fatimas.

No gold tips but finest quality.

My grandmother would have been furious. I wonder exactly what she would have done.

Three summers my mother herded sheep. Three winters she tended to the big house and scrubbed the floors on her hands and knees. Three springs she cooked for the lambing crew and a little later for the sheepshearers. She was the last one in bed at night.

Amy, maybe you have read *Pride and Prejudice,* a strange book to mention on the same page with Fatima cigarettes and freighter's mulligan, but the opening of that book is nearly perfect as the opening of a romantic novel, and that is what the remainder of her life might have been. Jane Austen wrote, "It is a truth universally acknowledged that a man in possession of a large fortune must be in want of a wife."

Across the hill — "over the Divide" — in Montana there lived a man of thirty-five who for some reason had not yet wanted a wife. He was — or his father was — in possession of eleven

217

thousand acres of hay-and-range land and two thousand head of Hereford cattle.

The man not yet in want of a wife was the youngest of three sons.

The eldest son was good natured and apologetic. He had gone to St. Paul's School where he wrestled and played games. A baseball cap sat easier on his head than a Stetson. Recently I was handed a photograph of him clad in wrinkled black tights and a jersey, a costume favored by athletes in a day when even males were careful to cover themselves. He is flexing his muscles and smiling straight into the camera. Smile or not, he had never been trusted with money or responsibility — it was noticed that he stumbled and was accident prone. The truth was that even as he flexed his muscles the crippling disease that was to kill him was already upon him. After his wife left him for another man, his life was a series of sudden disappearances. His was the curious habit of writing his name over and over on whatever scrap of paper was at hand. He died in a private hospital so remote it was inconvenient to visit him.

Charlie, the third son, may not then have been in want of a wife, but his father was in want of a grandson. Charlie was solid, priestlike and remote. Had he been a priest, he would have been a bishop, and parish priests would have dreaded his visitations, but for the life of them wouldn't have been able to tell exactly why. He could be trusted to see that steel was sharpened and bearings oiled, that a gate was closed and a rifle on safety. No crazy thought had ever seduced him, no vicarious affection for Europe, a Mercer Raceabout or the open road. His gaze often strayed out the windows to the distant mountains where he might have been happier far removed from human beings and their unceasing demands and explanations. Had his chunky equestrian statue been set down in a public park, its long shadow would prompt those innocently picnicking below to

consider how shrill and disorganized their lives and to turn
guilty thoughts to their lapsed insurance, unanswered letters and
broken promises.

But across the Divide in Idaho was the beautiful Beth Sweringen — divorced, and encumbered by me, five years old.

I used to think Charlie looked on his marriage as a duty to his
father, a man much concerned with Family — not as my family
was concerned with family, concerned with everybody's being
together as much as possible and assuring everybody else that
what he had done was the only possible thing to have done, in
the circumstances. No. Old Man Brewer's concern for Family,
his family, his name, arose, I believe, from the fact that his
family was not so acceptable as that of his wife, who had been a
Boston socialite. Brewer had been in trade as a young man. As a
merchant, he had sold iron horseshoes to the Boston Traction
Company. In marrying him, his wife broke the rules, and lived
to regret it.

I believe the Sheep Queen looked on the marriage as my
mother's duty to her. My mother had defied her once — and see
what happened. She looked on the Brewers with respect. Their
fingerbowls must have amused her, but she honored their acres.

I believe my mother looked on the marriage as her duty to
me. I think she hoped Charlie would adopt me, and I would be
secure forever.

Then Charlie came calling over the hill in his Hudson Super
Six. The Brewers saw no need to drive expensive cars. I wonder
how that silent man found words to propose, and what he
thought when he was shown trays of engagement rings.

They were married in Butte, Montana, a mining town a mile
high and a mile deep; the countryside was desolate as the moon,
poisoned by the rank smoke from the smelters. The year was
1920. Guests at the reception in the ballroom of the old Thorn-

ton Hotel included the governor of the state and certain relatives of those Copper Kings who had so profitably raped the
public.

A honeymoon up the Fraser River in British Columbia, hunting and fishing and snapping pictures of moose with a Kodak.

While they honeymooned, I was lodged with my father's
mother in Seattle. She was a handsome woman, called in her day
a "beauty." Aware of a nearby camera, she quickly offered her
profile. Her mother had come across the Oregon Trail by ox-
team and had married a judge in the state of Washington who
left some money and a lot of wheat land around Walla Walla.
But my father's mother had an insane fear of the poorhouse.
That must account for why, in their days of want, she did not
help my mother or her son. She was easily moved, was quick to
tears and a sender of sentimental cards. All her life she wrote me
regularly of how she had walked that day in her yard, looking
at what she called her posies and noting the antics of her kitty-
cat. I was embarrassed by her letters, not because they were
sentimental — I believe children take sentimentality for granted
as the other face of cruelty — but because they were addressed
to Master Tom Burton, who was then hiding in Montana under
his stepfather's name.

Amy, she bought me a tricycle at Frederick & Nelson's. She
was ordered by her second husband, who owed me nothing, to
return it. It had a shiny nickel bell. It was not the loss of the
tricycle I minded, but her hopeless attempt to explain. I don't
know but that she knew the man would order her to send it
back.

She used to come close and cry out to me, "Oh, look at your
little hands!"

One morning while I longed for my mother, my father appeared and made a joke of leaving shaving cream on his upper
lip, like a mustache; he squatted before me as one squats before
a dog to diminish one's overwhelming stature. I see a flash of an

incredibly handsome man. I didn't see him again for seven years
— he made a trip up from California by car.

The log house on the ranch in Montana was located, God
knows why, under a sagebrushed hill that obscured the sun until
long after the rest of the country was washed with light. There
were sixteen rooms; that house must have been, after Old Faithful Inn in Yellowstone Park, the biggest log cabin in the country. I suspect that old Brewer, in choosing logs, hoped to identify himself with a pioneer West as he had never been identified
with the Back Bay. Both the living room and the dining room
were thirty feet square. Severed and mounted heads of plains
and forest creatures, pensive in death, looked at the opposite
walls. Deer, elk, antelope. Under the head of a bearded bison
was a Steinway grand piano, a wedding gift from the Sheep
Queen.

The cowboys and hired hands ate in the back dining room
beyond the kitchen. You could hear them laughing when the
kitchen door was opened in answer to the tinkle of a sterling
silver bell in the front dining room. There we ate off Wedgwood and Spode and used napkin rings, after we had dipped our
fingers into the fingerbowls that were used until old Brewer and
his wife went to live in a corner suite of the old Thornton
Hotel a hundred miles away in Butte. There they played mah-
jongg, kept up with the Cabots and the Carvers in the *Boston
Evening Transcript* and dressed for dinner.

I was glad to see old Brewer go. Not only did he look like the
Kaiser but like the Kaiser he was wrong-headed and imperious.
His wife fared no better at his hands than anybody else but her
long-ago threats to divorce him — "to go to Indiana," as they
put it then because of the more lenient divorce laws there —
came to nothing. He paced. Back and forth up and down the
living room, he had worn a path in the carpet.

Five years old and not having heard of his awesome dignity

and mystique — a child in his innocence may see the true man and not be confused by the shadow — I once kicked him in the shin when he raised his voice to my mother. The earth did not shake, neither did the sky fall, but shortly after that the Old Folks removed to Butte.

Now it was my stepfather who each Sunday evening attended to the heavy brass weights of the tall clock beside the door that told a peculiar time of silence and carefully closed doors. He now sat at the head of the mahogany table — so vast that it had its own horizons; he carved the twenty-pound chunks of beef served up one day as roasts on a silver platter and the next as stews or hashes. My stepfather carved as skillfully as a surgeon, with bone-handled English instruments. That family looked on the ability to carve the flesh of birds or breasts as the sure mark of a gentleman. Beyond, out the dining room window twenty miles away, Old Baldy rose to eleven thousand feet, never clear of snow. Many long thoughts found refuge on that remote summit.

Now my mother sat opposite, pouring coffee from a fluted silver pot. Just so, smiling with a little lift of the chin as she offered the filled cup, had she learned to pour at St. Margaret's School.

Now that I have achieved self-confidence, having learned that simplest and most difficult trick — to be myself — I find it hard to believe that meals could be ordeals of such tension and self-doubt. The means were a game: the opening gambit, my stepfather's.

"What'll you have?"

Well done? Medium? Never "rare," for ranchers are personally responsible for the death of the animals they devour; red meat recalls the unappetizing horror of the butcher pen, and consequently they prefer meat gray or brown.

At last, while my pulse knocked at my temples, my stepfather would turn to me, knife poised above the threatened flesh. I would be tongue-tied. In that house I felt I had no right to express a preference for anything, that I should be glad of any morsel suffered me.

But see here — my stepfather was not a bad man. A man of few words? Few indeed. I had once thought he was silent because he thought so deeply he had no time for speech, his brain no room for its formulation. Now I think he simply had nothing to say.

Amy, I told you of the eldest son, the tragic one dismissed as an incompetent, but I have not told you of the middle son, Ed. Ed was a bachelor by profession, a woman-hater. He was brilliant, quick at chess, puzzles and word games. I recall that he knew the meaning of "baobab." He read widely in such top-drawer periodicals as no longer exist — *Asia, Century Magazine, World's Work, Mentor.* He would pick up a magazine, open it, and would be lost in it. Only a most courageous man would, in speaking, attempt to draw Ed's attention from a treatise on the Rosetta Stone, the truth about the Witch of Wall Street or Teapot Dome. *Country Life* he tossed aside as directed at climbers and others who required the crutch of possessions.

He was lean, had a craggy profile under thick black hair he had cut no more than four times a year. He despised towns where hair was cut, where men gathered to engage in silly banter and chewed food in public. His long, sharp nose was an antenna quick to pick up the faintest rumor and to send it on to his brain to be amplified. He seemed proud of his rather small feet; he sometimes crossed his long legs and watched them, as if speculating on what they might be worth to one not having such finials. His laughter was an insulting bray; it crowded and pushed the air ahead of it.

He said many true words about other men. I never heard him say a kind one.

My mother had asked me to call my stepfather Uncle Charlie. What title to alert a stepfather or stepmother must at last be dealt with. You can call them Stepfather or Stepmother behind their backs, but you cannot address them so because legends and fairy tales and facts have damaged those salutations that conjure up death, divorce, displacement and altered wills. A salutation — any salutation — is meant only to draw the attention of the one addressed. Since I would not dare be so impudent as to require my stepfather's attention, I had little use for my mother's suggested courtesy title.

My mother had decided to call Ed "Brother Ed," hoping to please, to establish a close relationship, a reasonable enough hope since the man shared the house.

Her first and only use of the title was disastrous.

"Get this straight," he said, his day-blue eyes reinforcing the message. "I'm not your brother by a long shot." His eyes were like certain glass marbles of childhood.

My mother told me this later, long after the man was deservedly dead under a heavy stone. She told me hesitantly, her eyes apologetic, as if in telling me I might then think the less of her for having been humiliated. We do wear humiliation like a deformity.

"For God's sake," I said, "and what did Charlie have to say to that?"

"He wasn't in the room at the time," she said.

"You didn't tell him?"

"What was the use? Ed was his brother."

So she was afraid to speak to Charlie. If she did, she might find out that his brother was more important to him than his wife.

What a gauntlet she ran in that house. Ed's cruelties were subtle.

Amy, you have perhaps known people who, by the lift of the

224

eyebrows or the ghost of a smile indicate they have secret knowledge they might well use to blackmail, explosive knowledge come upon by accident, maybe deliberately hunted down. Part of Ed's secret knowledge is that he knew that almost everyone is vulnerable, that almost everyone can be destroyed.

I seldom heard Ed speak directly to my mother in the next fifteen years, not even to ask for the salt. If he required salt, he reached across her for it in what he called his "boardinghouse reach." He could be wryly humorous, but never at his own expense. His humor had a down-home quality. So he called the sun "Old Sol"; he called tobacco and cigarette papers "the makin's." He relished jokes about the Irish and referred to the blacks as "coons." Those who bored him he called "boobs" and "scissorbills." He was above playing practical jokes that required reptiles, lengths of rope or buckets of water as props, but it delighted him when others played them. He smiled at others' consternation.

He looked past my mother, through her, as if she were of no more importance than a broodmare he kept in the back pasture. He knew, incidentally, of my mother's love for horses. Riding on the road in front of the house he often abused his saddle horse with quirt or the vicious bit he had fitted to his bridle.

As a broodmare, my mother was expected to produce an heir who would one day ride a proud horse over the eleven thousand acres and sign his name with a flourish.

Each evening she dressed for supper — out there you ate dinner at noon. Whatever she wore was perfect for the hour or occasion; she made the hour or occasion. I used sometimes to stand in the hall and watch through the door of the bedroom; she stood before her dresser and chose this little pin, this clip, those beads of jet or that choker of turquoise and silver. And always around her, like a frame, was the odor of flowers.

As a man, if that's what he was, Ed could not sit opposite his priestlike brother and pour from a silver pot. No. He sat opposite me, his back to the majesty of Old Baldy, and around him, like a frame, was the stench of urine.

The fact is, Amy, he never bathed. His bizarre modesty precluded his using the bathroom between his room and that of his mother and father. I can't recall his ever mounting the eighteen steps that led to the second bathroom; and of course bathing required the exposing of his flesh and skin. His modesty still puzzles me. Did he bathe in the summertime — Huck-like — in the creek in the thick bushes behind the house? Maybe. But certainly not in the wintertime. I presume that when his drawers became loathsome even to him, he buried them. Once a year he appeared in stiff new Levi's. He seldom wore gloves, even when doing rough work. Sometimes he glanced at his capable hands. He was a hacker and a spitter. No meal was done before he blew his long, inquisitive nose into a filthy blue bandana and then examined those strong, hard hands for traces of escaped mucus.

My mother was at first baffled and then fearful of his searching intellect which he nourished by his vast reading; he was often seen squatting as easily as a boy before the *Britannica* that ran along the bottom shelf of the bookcase along with *Living Animals of the World*. He would be boning up on Buddha or the refraction of light. Nothing at St. Margaret's School had prepared her for such intellect — and what might lie behind it. She had only heart and feeling. And style.

When I was old enough to be aware of her — not as my mother but as a woman — I was hard put to reconcile what I knew of her and what she was before I was born: her riding bad horses, her bringing down antelope and mountain goats, her shooting the rapids of the River of No Return. All that was long in the past, subjects of dusty, fading snapshots, a legend of days long gone.

I often wished Ed dead. How I wished I had been older and ready to pit my intellect against his, to find the clue to his own weakness and destroy him. But when I was old enough, sure enough to speak out, he was dead, but too late for my mother's good. By then her drinking was a prison, and I watched as she moved carefully from chair to chair. Her destructive drinking had started earlier and was more serious than I would admit, then, even to myself.

Why didn't Charlie speak out to Ed? Indifference? An abysmal lack of sensitivity? I don't know. Maybe he thought it unfair to ask Ed to find other quarters, to leave a house he himself had largely built with those strong, naked hands, and clearly unreasonable that he himself and his wife should abandon a house of sixteen rooms.

The wanted child was born scarcely a year after my mother's second marriage, a fact wonderful in itself, for it takes a flight of fancy to believe that Charlie would so forget himself as to commit the sexual act. But he managed. The child was not, alas, an heir but an heiress. And that was the end of it. The eastern relatives, noting the event, responded with monogrammed mugs and rattles and tools of sterling silver. The mails carried their congratulatory letters and the wires their calls and cables.

The little girl became for Ed his chief instrument of torture; he began to woo her away from my mother. He did a fine job. The little girl sat straight beside him on the wagon seat when he went down into the fields to irrigate, the bed of the wagon piled high with a stinking mixture of hay soggy with cow manure and urine, a compound ideal for damming streams and ditches to deflect the water off onto the meadows. Their lunch was beside them in a covered lard pail, deviled-ham sandwiches and an apple. Together they ate in several favorite spots.

For her he carved tiny chairs and tables and beds with his clever naked hands. For her he constructed wooden cages and he stocked them with a succession of burrowing rodents, gophers and cottontail rabbits. Blind with fright, too terrified to eat, they died and were replaced. It was nice for a little girl to have cuddly beasties of her very own.

Ed talked to the little girl around my mother. That her daughter found Ed so lovable and so responsive to her will must have made my mother doubt her sanity. Well, blood is thicker than water. It's a wonder my half sister and I ended as friends.

My mother would attempt escape in music. Her moving to the piano under the bison to play Schumann or Schubert was a signal for Ed to rise, pace down the long, dark hall and shut himself in his room. There he would pick up his five-string banjo and pluck out "A Hot Time in the Old Town Tonight" — brass bands, gazebos, lemonade and baseball in the park. "Ta-Ra-Ra-Boom-De-Ay!"

> *I got a gal in Baltimore,*
> *She's got carpets on her floor ...*

He played very well and by ear. He would have succeeded as a professional musician could he have brought himself to recognize the shallow world of entertainment. He could have been many things. Led an Arctic expedition — he admired Peary — been an eccentric and brilliant professor of physics, a grand master at chess.

But, Amy, his purpose was narrower. His purpose was to destroy my mother, and that is what he did.

Evenings she would walk away from the house and sit cross-legged before a little sagebrush fire. God knows what she saw in the flames, what words written in the drifting smoke. She once told me she was "thinking good thoughts." When I walked out with her, we seldom spoke, but once I took her hand and said,

"I love you." It was hard to say because it was so true. She squeezed my hand and looked away.

Almost twenty years of this, Amy. Almost twenty years.

One fall afternoon Ed was making a fence around a haystack down in the field. Upper Field, First Field, Second Field, Dairy Field, Wire Field, Horse Field, Side Field, Big Field. It reads like a litany, and it covered eleven thousand acres. The haystack was in the Big Field, and the poles he worked with were slick with cow manure wet from the fall rains.

He got a splinter in the palm of his naked, horny hand. The little wound bled.

Anthrax is one of the few diseases of animals that a man can catch. Ed was dead within days. Fitting that he died not from human illness but from a beast's. I was back here in the East at the time, in college, but surely even in New England there must have been something high like music in the air that day, an unaccountable ripple like a smile on the Charles River, the sun brighter on the gold dome of the State House.

I wish I had been in Montana to see him put on his hat for the last time.

But it came too late for my mother.

I'll speak but briefly of my mother's death. What to say, except that it was shattering. It began with bowel trouble, an obstruction. They operated. The operation didn't work. They tried again.

She was too weak to fight the pneumonia; she lay back against the pillow, her arms bruised with needles, a tube in her nose, gasping for oxygen.

She died early one morning. The undertaker dressed her in an ugly brown garment somebody had bought, certainly not she. I knelt beside her and kissed her. I never before knew the dead were so cold.

My grandfather stood beside the grave. The undertaker had concealed the telltale mound of earth beside it with a blanket of fake grass too green for April in Salmon, Idaho. My grandfather was ninety-two, and I thought, We're all going to be all right. Because here he was, clothed in all those years, standing so straight I forgot he was not so tall as he was, this old man to whom we now owed everything. I understood why the Chinese revere the old. The old are the repositories of the complete human experience. This old man was the son of the man who had discovered gold, who brought in the Christmas tree and stood aside with a pail of water that the family not go up in flames. The confidant of children, the friend of grandchildren and great-grandchildren, who felt he understood them best. He taught but he did not scold. There he stood who had survived the death of his wife the Sheep Queen and now his daughter. He told us with his posture that all things pass, that endurance is everything, that we must never forget who we are, that each of us must support the other. I remember the thin spring sun on his face.

But then they began to lower the coffin.

My grandfather's face crumpled and looked like a tired old monkey's. He turned away and his shoulders were humped in grief. For no matter what the years said, she was his little girl, and I thought, *My God — is it now up to me?*

But there was an earlier death that accounted for the sadness that never left my mother's face even at the end. That death was even behind her infrequent smile.

She was three months pregnant when she married my father, and the Sheep Queen did not attend the wedding. She would put no approving stamp on any such performance, certainly not in 1911. But since the young couple meant to leave at once for Seattle where she need not lay eyes on them, she might one day have accepted the grandchild and forgiven my mother her sin if sin it was — had the child been a boy. But a month before the unwanted grandchild was born, there was that other death.

Fresh fruit was a rare treat out on the ranch and sparked awareness of a strange, exciting, fruit-rich world beyond, where one had only to reach up and pick. My aunt Maude once said she still couldn't look on a banana or an orange without instant thoughts of Christmas stockings. The Christmas of 1911 was rendered special not only with bananas and oranges but with hothouse grapes brought in on the little train.

These precious grapes, faintly powdered with the sawdust in which they had been packed against the freezing Idaho winter, were not distributed bunch by bunch in the children's stockings that hung from the mantel of the sandstone fireplace, as the oranges were. Not expecting anything so exotic as grapes, the children might crush and destroy them. No. The grapes in their deep, oval basket of woven wood were set in under the tree along with the grown-up presents, the box of good cigars and the pocketknife for Papa. He had many pocketknives, but what else can you give a father who does not wear neckties? A muff for Mama made from the skins of beavers Papa had trapped; a box of Pears' soap because Mama said it smelled so good. You could *see* through it.

There under the tree the grapes were discovered by my grandmother's son, Tom-Dick. He represented the future of the Sweringen Ranch and was the only one who was not in awe of her. So, asked, he did not hesitate to admit he had found and eaten a handful of Concord grapes. Controlling her voice, she asked him if he had swallowed the seeds?

He lied, for a change, and said he had not.

She said, "Good. You could get terribly sick, eating the seeds. A person could die."

She had thought he looked frightened, but decided that was because of what he might have done, rather than what he did.

Was it the grape seeds, or were they but a coincidence? Who was at fault? Tom-Dick had lied, but it was she who had set the basket of grapes under the tree. With her own hands. A few days after Christmas, Tom-Dick got a sharp pain in his stomach.

"Right here, Mama."

She bundled up her boy and my grandfather drove them across the field to the little train bound for Salmon. That was a Saturday.

Nora and Uncle Doctor were just sitting down to supper.

"You're just in time," Nora said. "I'll just — Emma, what's wrong?"

"What have we here?" Uncle Doctor asked.

"My boy is in pain."

Uncle Doctor kept his office in the house beyond glass double doors mercifully covered with a cretonne a man wouldn't have chosen. His examining table was of iron, wood and leather straps; it resembled a vile instrument of the Middle Ages. Nobody but Nora would have put up with it, an office in the house and what went on in there while she bent over her everlasting needlework or pea-shelling, but then Nora was not likely to make much even of the Second Coming. What she heard in there would not have been so terrible had Uncle Doctor not been a surgeon and done more than take out stitches and set broken bones.

"Now young man," Uncle Doctor said, "you just climb up here and we'll have a look. How are things at the ranch, Emma? I trust your hay's holding out well."

He had a kind voice, and she began to feel a little easier. No wonder he had a good practice.

He had good hands; they began to explore.

When Tom-Dick flinched with pain, her face reflected it.

"Right here?" Uncle Doctor spoke gently.

Tom-Dick nodded.

She nodded.

"Well, well," Uncle Doctor said, and turned. "Emma, I think you'd better get this young fellow down to Salt Lake."

She was instantly alert. "What is it?"

He did not speak at once. *He did not speak at once.*

"It's my opinion that it's a lock in the bowels."

"Your *opinion?*" She had no use for opinions. Either he knew or he didn't.

"Emma, human beings can be wrong."

"Then I must have a second 'opinion.' This boy of mine is in pain." Many would have hesitated to question Uncle Doctor's competency, but this was her *boy*.

"Do you want me to call Doctor Hanmer?"

"If you would. Please."

Uncle Doctor turned to the telephone on the wall.

She did not know Doctor Hanmer, only of him. He had not been long in Salmon and now she had, so to speak, become dependent on a stranger. His table, that of a surgeon, was even more frightful, a rack of pain, blood and . . .

Young Doctor Hanmer had thin, narrow hands. He might play the piano. "Bless his hands," she was saying to herself.

Now his hands began to search. She heard Tom-Dick breathing; she heard Doctor Hanmer breathing.

"Right here, son?" She was now prepared to do anything for this doctor for the rest of her life, anything he wanted, anything he asked. But then he stood erect so suddenly she gasped. "It's appendicitis. This young fellow requires immediate surgery."

"Surgery!" she cried. "Doctor Whitwell said nothing of that. He said I should go to Salt Lake."

"I believe that's what he meant."

It may have been what Uncle Doctor meant, but it was not what he said, and it could have meant some special drug down there, they were doing such wonderful things, and here was this young, young man in primitive Salmon recommending surgery.

"No, no, no," she said. She could not bear a knife's touching her boy, not in the hands of so young a man, in the hands of a stranger so young he could have had but little experience. Experience! He was not going to get experience now. She must get to Salt Lake. She would have old White's doctor. There was no finer hospital —

"Mrs. Sweringen, you must, you really must listen!"

"No, no no." She would not hear. Her mind rushed on. Tomorrow was Sunday. The train did not run on Sunday.

"Doctor, may I use your telephone."

Thank God for a friendship, if that's what it was. She called the president of the Gilmore & Pittsburgh railroad.

"Yes. This is Mrs. Sweringen."

The train did not run on Sunday, but it ran for a thousand dollars. It ran for the Sheep Queen and it ran within the hour, the locomotive, tender and a single coach.

Well, Amy, a few minutes after the little train had passed over the Divide into Montana, my grandmother believed she had reason to thank her gods, for Tom-Dick sat up in the red plush seat and he smiled. "It's all gone, Mama." And then he said, "Mama, please don't cry."

It was gone, all right. The appendix had burst. Three days later she passed back over the Divide with her dead boy, her little boy who had made it all worthwhile, who used to say, so nicely, "Hello, Mama."

After she buried him she stood in the middle of her dining room and screamed. And except for a little humming sound, that's the last sound her mouth made for two months. She could not speak but only hum, and that she did night after night. She sat on the edge of Tom-Dick's bed, humming a lullaby she had sung when he was a baby. A frog, it seemed, would a-wooing go. She would allow no one else in the room. When she was done with her humming she sorted out the birds' eggs packed in sawdust — put the robins' eggs here and the snipes' eggs there, and then she would lie on the bed and sleep.

Time passed, and after awhile she found her tongue, and slept in her own bed.

Amy, old people out there still talk of the winter of 1918, but they speak softly, and with respect, should the raised voice or a careless word reawaken that beast of a winter and set it off again on its mindless rampage. That winter followed a summer of dry creek beds, a shrunken river and withering grass; all that summer long the sun had blazed away in a cloudless sky; the leaves of the cottonwood trees crisped around the edges. The heat lay close, like water; sane men reported having seen a mirage of lakes and streams floating high above the sagebrush.

Fall found but one haystack where there should have been two; none where there had been one. Indian summer came on silently, and lingered. Who could remember so warm a Thanksgiving? No snow at all.

That winter struck on New Year's Day, and it left them reeling. It roared in. Snow fell in sheets. The wind howled down from Gunsight Peak; honed on the flinty minus forty cold, it went directly for the heart. Starving stock stumbled into the blizzard, fell and froze. January, February. Wandering horses, all skin and bones, pawed through the snow and swallowed pebbles, their bellies bloated with the gas of hunger, eyes glazing over as death sniffed at their poor, faltering heels.

In the ranch house, doors were shut quietly. Whispers. What would Mama do? The hired men watched her and fell silent when she sat among them at meals. What would become of them? Who else cared about them? The cook watched, too.

What could Mama do?

Some said the winter had broken her. She needed hay shipped in on the little train at sixty dollars a ton — four times the price the winter before. She needed money she didn't have, they said, and couldn't borrow. Too many sheep about to starve, too much winter-worthless land, and when you got right down to it, she was a woman. It looked like the end of the Sheep Queen.

But not to her.

She stood at the window, a cup of strong black coffee in her hand, looking out at the drifting snow that hid the barn not a hundred yards away. They saw her drink from the cup; they saw her look down and pour what remained into an empty flower pot on the sill. She turned.

She got herself into the old maroon coat the family later laughed at. "Mama does love that old coat. Wouldn't you think she'd get rid of it!"

She put on that old coat and her hat and picked up her bag and took the little train out of the valley. In Salt Lake she bearded old White, the banker. They are gone now, those rugged old "personal" bankers. They lent money as much on character as collateral, gone now, for today the government regulates the banks, and character is perceived as of little importance. I remember a picture of old White my grandmother had cut out of the Salt Lake paper and pasted in the scrapbook she kept up most of her life. He resembles the elder Mark Twain, at once fierce and understanding.

She bearded him in his den, sat across from him in her old coat and a hat to which still clung two false plaster cherries. Maybe she had thought them pretty. It is more likely she had never noticed them at all. She had no gift for clothes, seldom seemed to think of them except in terms of warmth or modesty. She knew she was plain, that rings were wasted on her broad, thick hands. She had more than beauty. She had presence. Some women own diamonds. She had four daughters and ten thousand head of sheep. She sat with her naked hands in her lap.

"Mr. White," she said, "I want a hundred thousand dollars."

Few know the question old White asked her, and few know the answer she gave. But I know.

"Mrs. Sweringen," old White asked, "why should I lend you such a considerable sum?"

"Because I believe in myself, Mr. White."

It was not only the Lemhi Valley that was stricken by that heartbreaking winter, nor even the state of Idaho, but the entire Mountain West. Old White knew that when it was over, except for those few like the woman who sat before him, there would be nothing but foreclosures, idle land and stinking carcasses. There would be no bank. There would be no banks anywhere.

"As you wish, Mrs. Sweringen," Old White said, and reached for his pen.

In the Depression that began twelve years later, they remember her coming into Salmon in the rusty old Dodge sedan whose rear doors were secured with bailing wire because something had happened, and were not easily opened, so she sat in front beside my grandfather. She had never learned to drive. She came into Salmon to buy soda crackers and cheese, sacks of flour, gallon cans of peaches for her sheepherders, boxes of dried apples. Sometimes she came to go bail for a sheepherder who had got out of hand in the Smoke House or the Owl Café or in a whorehouse and now waited for her in jail across the river in the courthouse. Her sheepherders promised this would not happen again; she had their word for it. This was the last time. She was tolerant of their escapades; she did not expect others to have her standards and those she expected of the Family.

I drove west one year with my family in my splendid black

Rolls-Royce, which emptied pool halls and beer parlors all the way out. Strangers lined up beside it to have their pictures taken. They had all heard of Rolls-Royces; they had never seen one. I did not explain that the car was secondhand.

Remembering the creeping old Dodge, I thought my grandmother might enjoy riding down to Salmon with me to her Eastern Star meeting. She would have the entire back seat to herself. So there she was, very heavy now, sitting on a seat of fawn-colored suede, surrounded by tulipwood and silver fixtures, at her feet a carpet of Persian lamb. That alone, I thought, might interest her.

"What make of machine did you say this was?" she asked.

I told her.

"I don't think I know that make," she said.

I thought that couldn't be possible, but it was.

"Tom, you remember our old Dodge, it was so good in the mud."

Well, what did the old Dodge matter? It was not the Dodge but who rode in it who was the symbol, she who was above money, above worry, above fear — God knows — of failure, and of death. She had served in the Legislature, represented the state at wool growers' conventions. San Francisco, Omaha, Chicago.

IDAHO'S SHEEP QUEEN TO SPEAK HERE TODAY.

She was generous to charities, never forgot a friend nor some battered old creature who had once worked for her.

She got her little wish to travel. She lunched in Germany with Ambassador Dawes and bought a clock with a bird that chirped the hours for my grandfather. She visited a great house in Scotland and inspected Lincoln, Hampshire and Cotswold sheep on their own turf. She had an audience with the Pope. From Switzerland she brought back a little music box that played the Triumphal March from *Aida*.

But long, long before that, the time did come when she could be of service to young Forest, whose mother bore that scar on mouth and throat, such a scar as some bear on heart or conscience. From the beginning, her peculiar stars ensured that one day she would come to know politicians and congressmen. It is congressmen who nominate certain young men as candidates for West Point. It came about that Senator Borah — who so strongly opposed this country's getting mixed up with a League of Nations — was a friend of hers. So what she did was really not much; it had all been prefigured in the stars, the everlasting stars. So when the proper time came, she had only to pick up her pen and moisten a postage stamp. Senator Borah had only to pass word along to his Montana counterpart.

Oh, but young Scott Forest looked stern in his graduation picture! So this was the spindle-shanked lad who could not answer questions about his mother and ghostly father! How determined, now, the set of his chin and the shape of his mouth, how level his eyes, and certain. You could almost feel his eyes sweeping the parade ground, and his mouth speaking with unconscious authority. You wouldn't say he would entertain — let alone express — certain emotions that render some of us vulnerable, that he would wear his heart on his sleeve. And yet, across the bottom of the photograph in handwriting she had come to know well, he had written, "To Mrs. Sweringen, with love."

One day before Christmas, when she was eighty-five, the sun bounced like an echo against the frosty peaks. Down in the little town of Salmon, strangers who had come there armed against wild animals or bristling with skis were puzzled: all the stores were closed. They couldn't get their hands on cigarettes or groceries or whiskey. Some found even the whorehouses shut against them.

The town had closed for the Sheep Queen's funeral.

Last words are often remembered, especially those of the loved or powerful. We hang onto last words and repeat them as having been spoken by someone to whom approaching death had brought a peculiar gift of wisdom denied those not yet doomed, some arcane insight — otherwise, what is the point of death? I think the family expected my grandmother to leave some verbal legacy they could dip into in time of trouble, sorrow, need, sickness or any other adversity. She might have made an observation pertinent to suffering, some terse observation of what her long, rich life had been. She might have said, "It was all worth it." She might have said, "Take care of each other," or "Face the truth."

Instead, her last words troubled her image. Her last words were uncharacteristic, trivial and possibly even mad — uncharacteristic because they dealt with a subject quite alien to her, trivial because they illuminated nothing, and mad because they stood quite apart from the context of her life. It appeared that approaching death had brought only derangement.

My aunt Roberta was with her when she died. For days the family had been taking turns. It was unthinkable that Mama die alone, so it was Roberta who heard the words, but as they said, "Well, you know Roberta," which meant, "Roberta often gets things wrong because she doesn't really listen," and "Roberta hears only what she wants to hear." But certainly what she heard couldn't have been construed to mean anything else. My grandmother's last words were, "Yes, cut the cards. I want to play bezique."

She had looked on cards as a waste of time.

Bezique!

Amy, she was also mad — with grief for her dead son — when you were born. Your birth followed his death by only a few weeks, and our mother was certainly mad with grief when she gave you away. Perhaps she felt a need to make a sacrifice to show her mother a woman could survive a loss greater than her own, greater because it was voluntary. Of course she knew how Papa would have felt if it had been he riding out on the little train, she dying in his arms. But our mother was a broken woman the moment she signed in her boarding-school handwriting the fictitious name Elizabeth Owen. She had almost fifty years to see herself in the mirror and to wonder where you were, if you resembled her, and if you could forgive her.

Because she was not an Eastern Star, our mother could not be buried in the same plot with her mother the Sheep Queen. An ornamental wrought iron fence stands between them.

With this release before me, Amy, signed by our mother in her true hand to a false name, I understand a once-puzzling, lost, vacant expression that like a mask often lay across her face. She then seemed to become a stranger afraid of being touched or spoken to — and of course she was a stranger. She had become Elizabeth Owen who had given up her baby. I would see her try to lift her chin. "To face what?" I used to wonder. "To do what?"

Now I know: To face memory. To have done otherwise.

But the instant you moved to find her, Elizabeth Owen was forgiven, and you alone had that power. You made it possible that Elizabeth Owen never was, so now our mother could lift up her chin, and smile.

There's my letter to Amy about the Sheep Queen's pride and of the little boy who walked for a few years at her side. There they were for Amy to judge, caught up in their years and as plain as day in the pale mountain sun — my angel mother and my handsome, helpless father with his used Roamer and some kind of dream. I hope he has it still. My grandfather was looking far up the road for a cloud of dust that meant his children or grandchildren were on their way; his clocks ticked a special time. My aunts made little plans. My silent stepfather sat reading the *Saturday Evening Post* and across the shadowy room his vicious brother hacked and spat.

There they all were, an entity. The life of every one of them had been shaped and altered by every other one. Together they were my mother's life and death. Our mother's.

I sealed up the pages in an envelope. It wasn't a letter for the mails, of course. The gods and the fates, you see, required that I play the messenger myself, and I dialed the airport.

The telephone was still warm in my hand when I called Amy; and it rang only once. She must have been sitting right there. I heard my sister speak my name.

It isn't true that grown men don't cry.